LOUISE WALTERS

Mrs Sinclair's Suitcase

HODDER

First published in Great Britain in 2014 by Hodder & Stoughton
An Hachette UK company

First published in paperback in 2014

2

A CIP catalogue record for this title is
available from the British Library

Paperback ISBN 978 1 444 77745 1
eBook ISBN 978 1 444 77744 4

Printed and bound by Clays Ltd, St Ives plc

Hodder & Stoughton policy is to use papers that are natural, renewable and
recyclable products and made from wood grown in sustainable forests. The
logging and manufacturing processes are expected to conform to the
environmental regulations of the country of origin.

Hodder & Stoughton Ltd
338 Euston Road
London NW1 3BH

www.hodder.co.uk

For Ian, Oliver, Emily, Jude, Finn and Stanley, with love

I

My dear Dorothea,

In wartime, people become desperate. We step outside ourselves. The truth is, I love you and I am sorry that only now do I own it. You love me. I will not forget the touch of your hand on my head and on my neck when you thought I slept. The touch of love, no longer imagined. Nobody will touch me like that again. This I know. This is my loss.

Forgive me, Dorothea, for I cannot forgive you. What you do, to this child, to this child's mother, it is wrong. It is misplaced, like me, forced out of my homeland, perhaps never to return. You too will never return, if you persist in this scheme. You will persist. Yet even now it can be undone. But I know you will not undo. Your soul will not return from this that you do. Please believe me. In welcoming the one into your arms, you must lose another. I cannot withstand. You know why.

I do not enjoy writing these words to you. Actually, I cry. Once this war is finished – and it must finish – we could have made a life together. To spend my life with you has become my only great dream and desire. After our first meeting, as I rode away on my bicycle, I knew you were as important to me as water. I knew you were for all time, even as there is no time. I thought of marriage within minutes of meeting you. But it cannot be. You are an honourable woman, but this thing that you do is beyond honour. You do so much to be good, yet you go back on yourself, you invite dishonour. I cannot write clearly, but you will understand. My truly beautiful Dorothea, despite everything, our friendship must here end. I wish you all joy of this world.

Yours,

Jan Pietrykowski

(I found this letter in a 1910 edition of *The Infant's Progress: From the Valley of Destruction to Everlasting Glory*. I placed the book on Philip's desk for pricing, and it went into the antiquarian books cabinet, priced at a modest £15.)

I clean books. I dust their spines, their pages, sometimes one at a time; painstaking, throat-catching work. I find things hidden in books: dried flowers, locks of hair, tickets, labels, receipts, invoices, photographs, postcards, all manner of cards. I find letters, unpublished works by the ordinary, the anguished, the illiterate. Clumsily written or eloquent, they are love letters, everyday letters, secret letters and mundane letters talking about fruit and babies and tennis matches, from people signing themselves as Marjorie or Jean. My boss, Philip, long used to such finds, is blasé and whatever he finds, he places aside for me to look at. You can't keep everything, he reminds me. And, of course, he is right. But I can't bring myself to dispose of these snippets and snapshots of lives that once meant (or still do mean) so much.

I walked into the Old and New Bookshop as a customer eleven years ago, and returned the following day as its first employee. Quietly impetuous, owner-manager Philip asked me to work with him. As he said, we were soon to enter a new millennium, so it was time to change; time to take stock, literally. He appreciated my way of loving books and my ability to get on with others. He claimed he found people 'difficult'.

'They're generally pretty rotten, aren't they?' he said, and I half agreed.

He also once declared, 'Books tell many stories besides those printed on the pages.'

Did I know that? I did. Books smell, they creak, they talk. You hold in your hand now a living, breathing, whispering thing, a book.

Philip told me, on the day I started work in his bookshop, 'Study books, smell them, hear them. You will be rewarded.'

I tidy shelves. I make sure they are not too tightly packed. I take stock each year, in May, with the blossom trees discarding their petals, the sun shining through the French windows in the large room at the back of the shop, where we keep the second-hand non-fiction and hardback fiction, the sun's vernal warmth thrown over my back like a huge comforting arm and the swallows swooping over the garden, shrieking and feasting on flies. I make coffee in the mornings, tea in the afternoons. I help interview new staff: eighteen-year-old gap year student Sophie, who is still with us, enjoying a gap of indeterminate length; and more recently Jenna, who became Philip's lover within two weeks of starting her job. Jenna was never exactly interviewed. Like me, she walked into the Old and New as a customer; like me, she was engaged in conversation, and offered a job.

There is nobody more passionate about books, the printed word, than my boss, Philip Old. He is driven by his love of books, of the book for its own sake, its smell, feel, age, its provenance. His shop is large, with high ceilings, tip-tappy flagstone floors and a warren of rooms – six in total, plus storage on the first floor. All is spacious and light. We sell new books, old books, antiquarian books, children's books, shelf upon shelf upon shelf of books, lining the numerous walls of this large, luminous cathedral. The building is set back from the busy Market Square, with a neat, pretty garden, lavender and rosemary bordering the stone path that leads to the large oak door at the front of the shop. In the summer we have strings of bunting along the wrought-iron fence, kindly made for us by a customer, and a small hand-painted sign that reads:

Welcome to
The Old and New Bookshop
Open today from 9 until 5
You are warmly invited to browse

As a business, the Old and New cannot be making a profit. We have a band of loyal customers, of course – such establishments always do – but a small band. So there must be money somewhere, keeping this business afloat, kitting out Philip's flat on the second floor so tastefully. I have not enquired. Philip never talks about money, as he never talks about his private life.

I have had my share of romance, if I can call it that. At least, offers of romance. One young man, younger than me, part of the regular geeky Saturday afternoon crowd (and seemingly living in a world at least a decade behind everybody else – he always wears a black and purple shell suit) has proffered me his fax number on more than one occasion. Another, recently (red-faced, not entirely unattractive) told me I was the 'best-looking' woman he had seen 'in months'.

Patently untrue, and the genuinely beautiful Jenna nearby, pretending to tidy shelves, giggling. I threw her a look. She threw it back. And a year ago, a head teacher at a local primary school (our town has three), a regular customer with a habit of putting all and sundry on the school account. Hovering after I had served him, after I had handed him his stylish Old and New paper carrier bag, lingering. Clearing his throat, asking me out for dinner on Thursday night, if I could make it. If I was available. He had a charming smile, and thick black hair I suspected was dyed.

My father brought in some books this morning, old books belonging to my babunia; my grandmother. She has been in a care home for two years now, but it's taken us a long time to sort through her belongings. There aren't even that many things. Babunia, thank goodness, is not a great hoarder. But my father cannot work quickly these days. I have already been through her books, of course, keeping back a few for myself that I recall from my childhood. When she agreed to live in the home, she said I must keep whatever of hers I wanted. She had no use for reading now, she said, no use for sewing. It was an inexpressibly sad moment. Yet there was no option for any of us. Dad just could not take care of her any more. I offered to cut my hours at the Old and New, but neither of them would hear of it.

I saw my father wandering along the path and I waved, but he didn't spot me. I ran to the heavy front door and pulled it open for him.

He explained he had around twenty books. He had packed them into a battered old suitcase.

'This was hers too,' said Dad. 'Keep it if you like, Roberta.'

I would keep it. I love old suitcases. And already I could think of a use for it.

'How are you feeling today?' I asked, searching his face for clues.

He had been, for some time, habitually pale, a ghastly creamy-grey colour. But he never let on how he was feeling. So he shrugged, his catch-all gesture, meaning, 'Well . . . you know.' He had been in remission a few weeks ago. Now, he wasn't. Quite a sudden change this time, and frightening for both of us.

Philip came through from his office and shook my father's hand. They had met before – twice – and both had confided in me that they found the other to be a 'gentleman'. Philip insisted on paying my father for the books; my father wanted to give them to him. In the end, Dad accepted twenty quid, a compromise sum. He stayed for a cup of tea, sitting out in the back garden in the pale spring sunshine. Then he shuffled away, his bold, rangy walk vanquished. I tried not to notice.

I emptied the suitcase. There was a tatty old label on the inside that read 'Mrs D. Sinclair'. Idly, as I sorted and cleaned the books, I wondered who she was. Dad said this was Babunia's suitcase, but it must have belonged to this Mrs Sinclair first. My grandmother has always had a thrifty, make-do-and-mend mentality, happy to utilise the second-hand, the new-to-you. Dad says she learned the habit during and after the war, 'because everyone did'. It wasn't just a fashionable notion in those days.

I cleaned the dust from *The Infant's Progress: From the Valley of Destruction to Everlasting Glory* (a book I didn't recall ever seeing in my grandmother's house) and two neatly folded sheets of paper fluttered out. A letter! There was no envelope, always a pity. I unfolded the sheets. The letter, addressed to Dorothea, my grandmother, was written in anaemic blue ink, the writing small and neat; the paper was an even paler blue, brittle and dry as a long-dead insect's wing, yellowing around the edges, with little holes creeping along the fold. Of course, I wondered if I should read it. But my curiosity got the better of me. I couldn't not.

I have since read this letter again and again, and I still can't make sense of it. At first I experienced the strange sensation of needing to sit down. So I did, on the squeaky footstool, and my hand trembled as I read slowly, trying to take in every word.

Dorothea Pietrykowski is my grandmother. Jan Pietrykowski was my grandfather, never known to me, never even known to my father. These are incontrovertible facts.

But this letter makes no sense.

Firstly, my grandparents were happily, if briefly, married, but in this letter he seems to declare that he cannot marry her. Secondly, it is dated 1941. Polish Squadron Leader Jan Pietrykowski, my grandfather, died defending London in the Blitz, in November 1940.

2

Dorothy Sinclair sweated in her wash house, where the air was clammy with steam. Moisture clung to her face as she wiped her forehead repeatedly with the back of her hand. Her headscarf had long ago slipped off and she hadn't bothered stopping her work to re-knot it, so her hair stuck to her face like the predatory tentacles of some lurking, living creature. It was important to keep busy on this day.

The copper in the dark, far corner hissed and bubbled like a cauldron, boiling Aggie and Nina's clothes. Their uniforms, on a meagre ration, were muddied and stained almost daily. But Dorothy knew that presenting her girls with a pile of clean, starched and ironed laundry once a week was the least she could do. And despite the discomforts, she loved the work, in her own way. Washing frocks, stockings, undies, cardigans, the girls' breeches and shirts and knickers, and all the laundry from up at the house, was more than just a household chore: it was now her living. Scrubbing, dipping, sweating, stirring, all of these had a rhythm of their own and gave meaning to her day. Turning the mangle over and over, as she did now, wringing the life out of clothes and sheets and tablecloths. And the ultimate pleasure, Dorothy's favourite part of the day: pegging the clothes and linens out on the lines, and watching the sheets and cloths and pillowcases billowing and flapping like triumphant angel wings.

It was important to keep busy on this day. On . . . this . . . day.

She mustn't think. About anything. Since *that* day, she had become adept at not thinking. Oftentimes now she thought in images. Language was partisan, ambiguous. She no longer trusted words. Yet she could not turn her back on them completely. She liked to write, so she tried to write. She wrote furtively, alone, in her notebook. She could not draw, so it had to be words. She hoped she was fashioning her ramblings into something like poetry. But it was hard to make sense, hard to sound pleasing.

She looked up from her laundry. She listened, and stared at the open door through which so little steam seemed to escape. Something was wrong. Since losing . . . since Sidney . . . she had developed a sixth sense, almost akin to smell. She 'sniffed' the air now. Letting Nina's breeches hang loose and bedraggled either side of the mangle, she wiped her hands on her pinny and went to the door of her wash house. She looked up, but was dazzled by the sun, by the rows of white sheets and pillowcases and glittering tablecloths. She squinted up into the innocent blue sky. Small clouds sprinted across it, forgetful children racing home for tea.

Then she heard a drone, a low hum mixed with splutters and growls, like those of a threatened dog. Almost immediately she saw it, a Hurricane, weaving through the air. Surely descending too fast? She had never seen one coming in to land this quickly. Her heart began to thump, the blood thickened in her head, a tightness grabbed her around the throat. Was the pilot playing a game? Dorothy stared. No. This was not a game. The pilot was in trouble, and he was not the only one.

'Please no,' she said aloud, as she ran along the red-brick path. Hens scattered before her, cross and fussing and stupidly unaware of the new catastrophe looming above them.

Dorothy reached her back gate, opened it and stepped out into the Long Acre, a field she liked to imagine was as immense as an Arabian desert. She had feared something like this would happen. She had seen the pilots, such young men and so reckless, looping the loop, showing off. It was only a matter of time, she always thought, and now that time had surely arrived. Why didn't he bail out? The stricken Hurricane lurched towards her, listing wildly, like a broken pendulum. Dorothy looked back at her cottage in horror. She turned once more to the Hurricane and, with relief, she saw it veer away from her and her home, heading instead for the emptiness of the huge field. She walked mesmerised through the swaying ears of barley, scratchy-soft and clinging to her bare legs. It was a sensation she loved, usually, and felt herself in tune with.

The aeroplane was close now, close to its inevitable, barely controlled landing, close to the earth and to her and the swaying barley. It swooped over her head like a giant bird, its shadow providing her with momentary relief from the sun.

'Dorothy!'

It was Aggie calling, from a long way away, Dorothy thought. She saw two fawn shirts quivering far across the Long Acre. The girls were running. Dorothy ignored Aggie's shrill calls.

It was good. It was fitting, one year to the day since Sidney. Her poor lost Sidney. She should join him, really she should, and she could, and for a moment she marvelled that she had not thought of this before. She waded through the barley, determined. She marched towards the Hurricane as it gave itself up to the earth. A noise like thunder, a billow of choking black smoke, a sickening thud and the sound of all things smashing.

'Dorothy? Pass the teacup to Mrs Lane, please. Dorothy, pass this one to Mrs Hubbard. And Dorothy? Hand round the plate of Genoa cake. Dorothy, do stand up straight. Goodness gracious, child.'

Dorothy hated the feel of her new white frock, stiffly starched and rubbing at her neck. Her mother, Mrs Ruth Honour, looked at her with her usual mixture of pride and disgust while Dorothy dutifully did as she was told and handed round the cake. Mrs Lane and Mrs Hubbard smiled kindly at her but Dorothy refused to look at them, knowing she would meet pity in their eyes. Pity she did not want, ever. She wondered, why did they pity her? It must have something to do with Mummy. Or, most probably, the death of her father. Mourning was over now, and mother and daughter were no longer in black. But Mummy was supposed to be lonely, wasn't she?

Dorothy stood still, watching her mother and her mother's gossiping friends nibble at their cake and sip their tea. The day was hot and her frock so uncomfortable; she longed to be outside, at the far end of the garden, under the gnarled apple tree, barefoot in the grass, singing songs to herself or writing in her head her great poetry, and dreaming about the past, the present and the future. In her imagination she had six siblings named Alice, Sarah, Peter, Gilbert, Henry and Victoria. She knew her brothers and sisters would be waiting for her now, in the cool grass, sitting in the tree, idly talking, teasing one another.

Watching the cake disappear into the garrulous mouths of the three women, Dorothy began to sway. Her throat tightened, her heart raced. She became aware of falling, falling, letting go and landing with a thud on the tea tray, rosebud cups and saucers smashing, tea spilling all over her new, stiff, white frock and all over the rug.

'Dorothy? Dorothy? Oh, you clumsy girl!'

*

She felt something hot and sharp hit her in her stomach. Something else, hot and soft and wet, slapped her face. All around was choking smoke, black and thunderous.

'Dorothy! Get back!' Aggie's voice was closer now.

Dorothy saw the girls floating on the other side of the burning wreckage, bright beacons in treacherous fog. 'I want to join him,' said Dorothy, but nobody heard her. She rubbed her neck. The new, white frock was too stiff, too rough.

Her mother stared at her.

Dorothy swayed. She fell, slowly, her white frock splattered with blood, her head spinning in a vortex of shame, and the sea of barley cushioning her fall.

It would always be said that Dorothy Sinclair was a heroine, trying to rescue the young Hurricane pilot who came down to meet his death in the Long Acre field on that hot afternoon in late May, 1940. A brave and courageous woman, never sparing a thought for her own safety. A woman to be held up as an example to others, the kind of woman Britain needed in those bleak and fearful times.

Dorothy knew better.

Still, she let people believe it of her, as it did no harm.

Mrs Compton came to visit her later that afternoon, after Dr Soames had been and dressed Dorothy's wounds, which were sore but superficial: a cut across her stomach, and burns to her face. Fainting and falling down into the barley had doubtlessly saved her from worse injuries. She was a plucky lady, the doctor pronounced.

Mrs Compton had the unnerving ability to make Dorothy feel ashamed of herself. Did she somehow *know*? Dorothy thought that she might. Mrs Compton was a witch, Dorothy understood. She smiled weakly at the older woman and noticed a fine white hair protruding from a mole on her left cheek. Or thought she noticed. Perhaps there wasn't even a mole? It was difficult for Dorothy to see people clearly, to see solidity, reality.

'I don't know,' said Mrs Compton, 'what a state to get in!'

'I just thought . . .'

'I know, love. I know. Such a shame.'

'They've been cleaning up out there all afternoon.' Dorothy indicated the Long Acre and its swaying barley with a nod of her head.

'They're nearly finished now, though, I think. Don't you worry about it. You did what you could. You did more than you should, perhaps.'

'It was nothing.'

They sat in silence, sipping tea. The clock ticked on the range mantelpiece. Distant male voices drifted in through the open window, the voices of men clearing up the flesh and metal in the Long Acre. Had Mrs Compton remembered the part she played in the drama of a year ago? Was she aware of this saddest of anniversaries? Dorothy suspected not. Even more reason to distrust the woman. Even more reason to imagine her prone, with her head on a bloodied block, her ugly face contorted in fear, pleading for her life as Dorothy raised a huge axe, told her to—

'He was Polish,' said Mrs Compton.

'I heard they had arrived. A couple of weeks ago, wasn't it?'

'It was. They do say the Poles hate the Nazis more than we do.' Mrs Compton finished her tea with a small slurp. She put the cup and saucer on the table carefully and, folding her hands in her lap, she gazed at Dorothy. Dorothy shifted her own gaze to the window, watching male heads bob up and down, the hawthorn hedge obscuring their bodies.

Dorothy thought about the Polish pilot, dead, burned and disembodied. Part of him had hit her in the face. She touched her cheek, and felt the dressing. She must look frightful.

'And how are you keeping, nowadays?' asked Mrs Compton, leaning forward.

'I'm well,' said Dorothy, standing to look out of the kitchen window, watching a hen scratch at the earth and pluck a worm from it. Dorothy, rational, contemplated the worm's futile struggle.

'Good. That's good.'

Mrs Compton sounded doubtful. She glanced at the clock. She must go, she said. A young woman down at the next village was expecting her first baby and had been labouring since half past four that morning. Mrs Compton's services may be needed by now.

Dorothy stared at her.

Mrs Compton moved towards the door and lifted the latch. She turned back to Dorothy, who remained motionless, her back to the window.

'I'm sorry, Dorothy. I should have remembered. It takes time, you know. It *was* around this time last year, wasn't it? If I remember rightly? Anytime you need to talk about it, I'll be happy to listen. You don't have to ignore it. I know we soldier on with life, but things can haunt us, Dorothy.'

Mrs Compton left then, closing the door, and Dorothy stared after her.

How dare that woman!

She picked up the teacup Mrs Compton had drained so unceremoniously and threw it at the door, hard and fast, before she even knew what she was doing, so that the noise of it shattering surprised her. In pain where the hot metal had ripped through her skin, she swept up the mess.

★

Alice, Sarah, Peter, Gilbert, Henry and Victoria lived and moved and breathed in Dorothy's lonesome imaginings. The trouble was, she never really knew where she, Dorothy, belonged in this family of girls with flowing fair hair, strong sturdy boys playing with catapults and hoops, all six children with bright blue eyes and long lashes. They were blessed, she fantasised, with perfectly perfect childhoods. Was she the eldest sister? Austere, serious, strong, bossy? Or was she somewhere in the middle, forgotten, ignored and unimportant? Perhaps she was the baby, the odd one out among the girls with her long straggling brown hair, her green eyes. A cherub with thick little legs. Oh no, that would never do. Little Victoria was the youngest – she was the angel, with pink cheeks and fair curls and big blue eyes. Perhaps Dorothy was the second youngest? She was allowed to play with Victoria's dolls, and the tiny black perambulator. Yes, that was where she fitted, with two big sisters to hug her when she fell, to pick her up and dust her down. Her brothers were of indeterminate age, but all were tall and raucous. They took no notice of Dorothy.

The first male who did take notice of her – many years after her imaginary brothers and sisters had slipped off the slope of her longing – married her. It was a short courtship; her disapproving mother had proclaimed, 'If you marry that . . . man . . . I shall never speak to you again.'

Dorothy met him at a funeral in 1934. Her aunt Jane, an impressive eighty-two, had died during the summer. Dorothy had rarely met Aunt Jane, and not at all since childhood, knowing her only as her mother's rebellious elder sister who had married beneath her and moved away from home, in Oxford, to the distant north which was Lincolnshire. Dorothy's mother, on receiving the news of her sister's death, had puckered her lips and frowned.

'We must visit that fearful county. Please be sure to pack my fur, Dorothy. I do not intend catching my death in a Lincolnshire churchyard, for the sake of my sister or anybody else.'

'Mother, it is August, and it is quite warm. Even in Lincolnshire.'

Of course, Dorothy did pack the fur – along with many other items – and together they travelled by train, Dorothy gazing out of the window for much of the journey, trying to ignore her mother's constant demands. The fields were golden, this glowing August, and she saw men working in them; she saw tractors and wagons and horses and harvesting. It looked like an enviable life, out in the open air, working on the land, in golden fields, in golden sun, with golden skin.

When she met Albert Sinclair, handsome and bucolic, and he told her all about his life on the farm, she was an attentive listener. Why was he at the funeral?

'My sister was Miss Jane's charlady, and I did odd jobs for her, cleaning the gutters or raking leaves. Very nice lady, was Miss Jane. A gentlewoman. Not liked by her family, they say. But goodness knows why, because you couldn't hope to find a nicer person.'

'"Her family" was my mother and I.'

'I'm sorry. I didn't—'

'Don't be sorry. My mother did disown her. She disowns everybody sooner or later.'

Two weeks later, back in Oxford, Ruth disowned her only daughter upon hearing that she was intending to marry this Albert – '*Bert?*' – Sinclair. Dorothy was glad. And if it meant she would end up just like her Aunt Jane – that is to say, forsaken and forgotten – she was even gladder. She left Oxford by train, alone this time, with a carpet bag of 'belongings' and her mother's final admonitions ringing in her ears:

'You will regret this! It will come to nothing! He's not good enough for you!' In this way, Dorothy burst free of her extended and regretful childhood.

Dorothy remained a virgin until her wedding night, on 12th November 1934. It was her thirty-fourth birthday. Albert, still very much a stranger to her, tried to be gentle and kind, but he was so very eager, and so virile, that he did hurt her a little. Dorothy tried not to show it, but he knew, because he wasn't entirely stupid. He apologised. She accepted his apology. It got better, of course. He was a big man, strong and muscular and leathery-skinned, and Dorothy grew to love the feel of his arms around her, his warmth and strength. Pregnancy followed within four months of their wedding, but it was doomed to early failure.

Then another, and yet another.

Eventually, after nearly four years of marriage and five miscarriages, Dorothy gave up, her longing for a child replaced by impossible, unbearable dreams and a sad resignation. She became a farmhand's wife, adept at baking and washing and sewing and tending a small vegetable patch, looking after a small brood of hens. She heard nothing from her mother, and after a few stilted letters in which Dorothy talked of her husband, her new life, her pregnancies, she gave up on the relationship. It may as well have been her mother, and not Aunt Jane, lying dead in the ground in Lodderston churchyard.

In August 1938, Dorothy fell pregnant for the sixth time, and it was at this point that she began to write poetry 'properly'. Falteringly, at first, unsure of how to put down any words that could mean something. But she tried, and she wrote, alone during the day, while eating her dinner or sipping her afternoon tea. She hid her notebook behind the pots and pans, at the back of the cabinet. She hid it in the table drawer, or under the bed. She hid it in places where Albert would not find it.

This pregnancy lasted beyond the first two months. She felt sick, and was sick, indiscriminately, at any time of day. Her breasts were sore and she burst into tears without warning. Mrs Compton, layer-out of corpses and local midwife, visited when Dorothy was four months pregnant, and looked quizzically at her burgeoning belly.

'Is it a boy, do you think?' she asked.

'I have no idea,' said Dorothy.

Already, the woman was insufferable.

'And how are you feeling?'

'Better, thank you. Now that I'm not vomiting any more.'

Mrs Compton nodded in what she must have imagined to be a sage manner. Dorothy looked away from the older woman. She hated her. She could not stand the gaze that seemed to mock even while it cared. Mrs Compton, somewhere in her late fifties, perhaps sixty, had given birth to six children of her own, five of whom had made it to adulthood. Her eldest grown son had died in the Great War. Her three daughters, fat and fecund, and her younger son all lived in the village, had all married other villagers, and all of them contributed at regular intervals to Mrs Compton's growing army of grandchildren.

Dorothy did, in fact, think her baby might be a boy. She had a name for him already: Sidney. But she did not share this with Mrs Compton. Albert – hard-working and, by now, hard-drinking, losing his looks – had already said she could call the child anything she liked so long as it wasn't 'daft'. Sidney he approved of. Sidney it was to be. Albert was relieved that his wife was to bear him a child at last. Men on the farm, in the village, in the pub, had made barbed remarks about his childless marriage. He couldn't be doing it right. Did he know where to put it? The taunts had got under his skin, and made him turn against his wife; a hard face, a solid back, a shrug, a look of scorn. But at last Albert was proud of his wife's round, hard belly, her wide smile. To him she became beautiful; she became the wife he wanted her to be.

When she was five months pregnant, Dorothy caught the bus into Lincoln to buy things for the baby, feeling like a prodigal daughter returning home. She bought a suitcase, for storing all the things she was planning to sew and knit. The suitcase was compact, eighteen inches wide, eight inches deep, a mere thirteen inches from front to back. It was a rusty brown colour, with a dark brown Bakelite handle, two small catches and a toylike key. Inside, the suitcase was lined with paper in a pale tartan print, and there was a small gummed label upon which she could write her name, so she wrote

Mrs D. Sinclair

in her large, looping hand. She licked the label and stuck it to the inside of the suitcase.

While in town she also bought fabric and wool, and refreshed her stocks of threads and needles. Now was the time to make. The talk of impending war was, to her, as insubstantial as the first wash a watercolour artist applies to the naked canvas. War was obscure, it was obscured, and perhaps it was happening a long way off, and perhaps it was not even happening at all. She was pregnant, she no longer felt sick, and she had her energy back. This was all she knew. The baby would need cardigans, gowns, jackets, bootees, blankets, shawls. The baby would need a happy glowing mother, a capable and creative and provident mother.

The suitcase slid perfectly under the bed, and Dorothy set to work on filling it straight away. Within a few delirious weeks she had made two gowns in a soft cotton lawn, three knitted matinee jackets with hats and bootees to match, a knitted blanket in soft pale lamb's wool, and a white christening robe. She showed nobody the fruits of her labours, not even Albert, who was aware of her industriously clicking knitting needles, her frowns and sighs and occasional exasperations, her satisfied smiles when the work was going well. She sewed and knitted in near silence each evening by the light of the oil lamp, while he read the newspaper and told her about the war that he said was certainly coming. She barely listened, so involved was she in the approaching birth, the motherhood that was within her grasp at last. Each stitch brought her closer to that moment, that new and mysterious state of being. Each stitch confirmed the reality of the baby in her womb. Each stitch brought her closer to the day when she would leave behind, at last and forever, irrevocably, her girlhood. Every hope she had ever had was invested in each click of the needles, in each pinprick to her fingers. The mother-to-be was satiated with life and vigour.

Upon completion, each garment was laundered and, if necessary, starched and pressed. One by one, she laid her handmade treasures in the suitcase, with great care, as though each item were the baby himself. She retrieved her notebook from the cabinet in the kitchen, and hid it under the baby clothes at the bottom of the suitcase. This was her new hiding place, her domain – secret, private, inviolable. She sprinkled in dried lavender she had saved from her garden, ostensibly to keep the moths from feasting on the wool, but really because she loved the no-nonsense, vinegary-sweet scent of lavender, the safest scent in the world. By the time she was ready to give birth, the layette was complete, and generosity had entered her marriage. Albert saved for and bought a perambulator, huge and black. He fashioned a crib, working in his shed after his long days on the farm. He insisted his wife put her feet up in the evenings and he brought her tea, which he prepared himself.

And the suitcase sat under the bed, waiting to be emptied of its treasures, waiting for its lid to be thrown open and its contents grasped by eager, trembling hands. If she reached out, she could touch it, this dream which was no longer a dream. This time, it was solid and large and inexhaustible. If any apprehension entered her heart, Dorothy could not recall it afterwards. She could only remember the anticipation, the exasperating, cloying, heavy desire for the mystery of motherhood to begin.

For surely now it would begin.

3

(Handwritten receipt from the now defunct second-hand baby supplies shop Bibs 'n' Blankets, found inside a Dean edition of *Little Women* by Louisa M. Alcott, with an intact dust jacket depicting Jo March as a beauty. But a nice enough copy, to be found on the second-hand shelves in the children's book room, priced at £2.50.)

Philip lives in the flat above the Old and New, and today is my third foray into his home in eleven years of employment. The first time had been to help prepare a small party we threw when launching the large new books room. Philip had bought ready-made food from Waitrose: canapés, dips, cheese, biscuits, grapes, wine. He needed help taking it downstairs into the shop, where we laid it all out on the large round oak display table in the foyer. On that day, we threw open the French windows and invited customers to sit outside in the garden. That was my idea, and although Philip was doubtful at first, he was prepared to give it a try. It is now something of a tradition that our customers enjoy.

The second time I entered his flat was to check that Philip was well after being struck down by flu, last winter. He was perfectly well, really, but feeling 'shitty'. Coughing, red-faced, curled up on his cherry-red leather sofa under a blanket and clutching a hot whisky, watching Judge Judy. He said he was too ill to be bored by daytime television, too ill to change channels. And – the worst thing – he couldn't read because his eyes were 'melting in their sockets'. Anyway, he quite liked Judge Judy. A guilty pleasure, he said. Tell nobody. And then he said something quite odd.

'Do you know, Roberta, I only took you on here because you genuinely agreed with me when I said most people were utter and complete rotters. Do you remember?'

Despite the hyperbole, I did remember. I remembered thinking, here was a person I could work with. But when he was crashed out on the sofa, clutching his hot whisky, obviously feeling hellish, I was surprised that he remembered our 'interview' as clearly as I did.

Jenna. She is . . . unexpected. Sophie and I watch the lovers with a mixture of amusement and amazement. Philip? Jenna? Philip and Jenna? Customers join us in our bafflement. It will never last, some whisper. She's not his type. He's not in her league. She's not in *his* league. Some say.

Philip is not just a bespectacled, bookish type of man, you must understand. He's scruffy, fond of jeans and loose shirt tails, mousy brown hair curling around his neck. He's surprisingly handsome, when you look close enough. And Jenna is sweet, and very pretty, undeniably. I can certainly see the attraction, on both sides. Six months on from their first meeting and they are still together, against all expectations, holed up in Philip's tasteful flat.

Jenna has stylishly blonde wavy curls, blue eyes. She is the type of woman all heterosexual males between the ages of twelve and a hundred and twelve would stare at in the street, anywhere, everywhere. And here she is, hiding away from the world in the Old and New Bookshop, the girlfriend of its sardonic, forty-something owner. Sophie and I suspect they hold little trysts in the shop. Working together, perhaps hiding away in the back room among the second-hand fiction, the two seem to whirl away from each other if I enter, causing me to stammer an apology, my cheeks burning with consternation. Jenna gives me one of her looks – half amused, half reproachful. I retreat, not daring to look at Philip. I'm never entirely sure which one of the three of us should feel the most embarrassed.

Jenna reads more now, at least. I can't imagine that she read a great deal before commencing her employment at the Old and New. She is just not the bookish type, whatever that is. She unpacks our daily deliveries, biting her bottom lip, ticking off books on the delivery note, making sure they are all there, placing them carefully on the shelves, stacking books ordered for customers under the counter. She concentrates like a little girl learning a new trick on her skipping rope. She asks for help quite often, and Sophie and I go to her aid, patiently. We all have to learn, and we're forming a good team. I know Philip is proud of us all.

Today, Philip's flat is dark and silent. And it is Jenna who ushers me in, not quite touching me, but propelling me nonetheless. She switches on a large Tiffany lamp next to the cherry-red leather sofa. She asks me if I want a drink. I don't. She pours herself a gin and tonic. She has not been at work today: she is unwell. I notice the familiar manner in which she moves around the flat, handling Philip's things, pouring his gin. In these placid surroundings, Jenna is as jumpy as a wren, and I am sorry for her, without understanding why.

There's something amiss.

I feel like a trespasser in Philip's domain. He is at a book fair – he's been away all day – and he warned Jenna not to expect him back until around half past eight that evening. The curtains are still tightly drawn at two o'clock, an empty coffee cup and a plate littered with crumbs still malingering on the coffee table. There's an air of the slovenly, which Philip normally does not tolerate.

'Bottoms up,' Jenna says, and she drinks, quickly. I smile at her, not knowing what to say, not knowing what this is about.

'Roberta, I'm in trouble,' she announces.

'What kind of trouble?'

'Of the old-fashioned kind. You know. "In trouble".'

And now she cries, shielding her face with her hand and her empty glass. I move to stand next to her, and I rub her arm, making noises of consolation. I'm not sure what to say.

In the end, her tears subside. A box of tissues is extracted from the shelf under the large, round smoky-glass coffee table.

'What do you make of me now?' Jenna asks, pouring another drink and sipping more sedately. Her white hands shake, just a little.

'I'm not going to judge you, Jenna,' I say. 'For heaven's sake, you're a grown woman, and Philip's a grown man. It's not unheard of, is it? It might be . . . unexpected, maybe . . . but you'll work it out. How does Philip feel about it?'

She looks at me, aghast.

'Oh,' I say, looking at the floor, at the curtained window, at the large gilt mirror above the fireplace.

'I found out a week ago. I felt tired. My period was late. I did a test. It's been hell, Roberta, it really has. I don't want children, you see. I never have wanted children. I never will want children. I've always been so careful, but now this . . . catastrophe.'

'I think you should be having this conversation with Philip,' I say, and I curse myself for sounding so prim.

'What the bloody hell for?'

'Because . . . it's nothing to do with me. It's Philip's baby.'

'No. I don't think so . . . I mean, I'm not sure.'

Instantly, guiltily, confusedly, I feel a rush of relief. It's not his baby. It might not be his baby. *It's all right.* It's somebody else's baby. But then, whose baby is it? Has she . . .?

I am not a courageous person. I shun conflict of any kind. So I sit in silence, not knowing what to say to the trembling woman before me. I cannot think about Philip – the last person in the world, by my reckoning, who would deal in duplicity. Oh, poor Jenna. I can't imagine how she must be feeling . . . what a mess.

She is incredibly pretty, really. A beauty. And like every-body else, including Philip, I'm a sucker for beauty. So you get drawn in, you don't see. And I can't blame Philip for . . . it's understandable. He's not a monk, and he shouldn't have to live like one. And none of it is any of my business, of course. I'm just an employee, nothing more, though I like to think Philip might loosely describe me as a 'friend'.

Jenna sighs, and puts down her empty glass. 'What are you thinking?' she says.

'Oh, nothing much,' I say. I'm so useless, especially at wobbly moments, and this is one of those.

This is a crisis.

Jenna falls back into the sofa, and she cries, for perhaps a minute, then blows her nose dramatically. I sidle along the cherry-red cushions to sit alongside her, and she leans on my shoulder.

I tap her knee, rub her back. 'It'll be all right, Jenna,' I say.

There's a clinic. A friend of hers . . . anyway, there's a clinic. She has an appointment tomorrow morning and will get it all seen to. She'll clear up this mess. Philip will never know. Thank God he's at the book fair again tomorrow. He must never know anything about this, ever. She loves him. She truly does. She made a mistake. Don't we all, Roberta? An old boyfriend, he wants her back, she broke his heart . . . she felt sorry for him, momentarily. Stupid.

'Have you ever had a termination?' she asks me.

'No,' I say, after the briefest of pauses.

'I don't want to go alone. To the clinic, I mean.'

'I understand.'

'Will you come with me? Please.'

'Yes. Of course I will.'

'Because I can't ask anybody else. There is nobody else.'

'I'll go with you,' I say.

'I don't want to ask Sophie.'

'I know.'

Similar ages, twenty-something, both are straight-up, no arguments, nine-and-a-half-out-of-ten women, at least. Sophie has chestnut-brown hair, with chocolate-dream eyes, she is toned and tanned and quite beautiful. There's competition, whispered jealousies – nothing overt, nothing nasty, but it's there. I enjoy watching their rivalry from the sidelines, safely out of the fray, me, a good ten years older, and a solid seven. On a good day. On a very good day. No competition at all, no need for these girls to feel threatened by me as well as each other, and I can just enjoy the disinterest of the casual observer. Well, not quite. Both of these women are my friends now. And one of them needs me.

'It has to be somebody I can totally trust,' says Jenna. 'I'm not going to tell anybody else and Philip must never, ever know. I can't do this on my own. Please. You're so sensible and discreet.'

'I'll go with you, I mean it. Don't fret. But what about the father?'

Jenna laughs a desperate, queer laugh.

'Oh my God,' she says. 'Roberta, you really are hopelessly naive at times.'

She will tell Philip she is meeting a friend for the day – shopping and lunch – and I will phone in sick. Headache, period pains, whatever comes to mind, whatever sounds plausible. It will be a nuisance for Sophie to be on her own all day. But never mind, says Jenna. She'll cope. We're not busy at the moment, anyway.

I listen in silence as she makes her plans. I recall my last birthday, my thirty-fourth. I brought in cakes, split doughnuts oozing with soft artificial cream, with sweet red syrup described as 'jam', fresh from the bakery next door to the shop. Jenna declined my offer of a cake, stating weight-watching as a reason. I shrugged and told her I would take it home for my cat, who likes cakes – especially on birthdays. I recall Jenna's face, her crushed expression, the redness. She muttered an embarrassed 'sorry', and took a cake. Of course, I felt dreadful; I didn't mean to humiliate her. I later found the doughnut in the kitchen bin, a token nibble missing. I realised then that Jenna is used to being disliked. I don't believe her circle of friends is particularly wide. I resolved to try harder. I'm not the jealous type. And we have become friends, a slow trust growing between us.

So now I must agree to help her. What else am I to do?

'You're a good person,' says Jenna. She blows her nose, and smiles at me bleakly.

And my thoughts wander, as they are apt to do at stressful

times, moments of drama. I want to talk to Babunia. I want to ask her about the letter that is even now whispering its strange words, tucked away in my handbag, calling to me. I can almost remember the letter by heart now. I shall visit her soon; I'm due for a visit, anyway. But can I ask her anything about this letter? I can't bear the thought of upsetting her, of trying to uncover secrets she does not want uncovered.

And Jenna is here now, white-faced and scared. I must deal with her first.

4

Agatha Mabel Fisher and Nina Margaret Mullens descended upon Dorothy in March 1940. They were both London girls, fresh from their six weeks of training with the Women's Land Army. They were employed by those up at the hall as farmhands; they were in need of a billet, and Dorothy lived alone in the cottage. She was fortunate, she knew, to be allowed to continue living in the cottage at all. Albert had left to join up, to do his bit, he said, everybody said, but Dorothy knew, as they all knew, that Albert had left to get away from her, to leave behind his disappointment and grief. He wanted other women too, because Dorothy would no longer sleep with him, and she was wise enough to know this, even to understand it. He was only thirty-three. Let him go, she told herself. She did not miss him.

She had started to hear that some at the hall, and in the village, were questioning her right to stay. Albert should not have left, they said. He was a skilled and experienced farmhand, and could have waited for his call-up, which may never have come. It left his wife in a difficult position. Eventually, they put it to her: stay, and be useful. No rent and a small stipend in return for taking in laundry – all the hall laundry. They installed the latest model of boiler and a mangle in the wash house. There was even talk of one of the new washing machines. They strung up yards and yards of washing lines, criss-crossing the garden. And now she was glad she hadn't taken on goats, as much as she had wanted them, when Mrs Twoomey had offered her a pair of kids in the spring. They were such little darlings, but too fond of chewing on fresh laundry.

Then the girls, Aggie and Nina. They were always laughing at goodness knows what, they were cheerful and chaotic. Dorothy took pride in working hard for her girls, even in boiling Aggie's bloodied undies, and the sanitary pads that Dorothy had hastily sewn when the young women first arrived at the farm. The pads were made from a peach-coloured damask tablecloth she had damaged by catching it irretrievably in the mangle. Poor Aggie, she was so slight and fragile-looking, with her blonde curls, her perfect skin, her silvery laugh, and such a pretty little thing, yet she suffered such heavy blood loss, cruel, regular and punctual. In contrast, Nina, who was taller than Aggie, and plump, with a deep smoker's voice, had scant bleeds, irregular and short-lived. She was a girl who sailed gaily through life with all the finesse of an ocean liner. The girls had not been with Dorothy for long – a matter of weeks, really – but already she felt she knew them, she felt she had the measure of them. She would almost say that she loved them.

Dorothy put them in her own room. It was the room she had vacated after Sidney, leaving Albert alone and bewildered in the large brass bed. Dorothy had set up house in the tiny bedroom, overlooking the back garden, the Long Acre field and, beyond, the distant elm trees and Lodderston aerodrome. The small bed, narrow and in need of a new mattress, suited her perfectly. She liked to lie on it with her notebook, writing. Rarely did she recognise the words on the page, when she read them back, as her own.

She made up a new quilt for her little bed, using anything she could find – large patches, small patches, squares, triangles, indescribable shapes – a crazy quilt. She hung her few clothes in the tiny wardrobe, arranged her undies in the top drawer of the dressing table and put a vase of wild flowers on the table next to her bed. Every night, when she retired, she shut the door firmly behind her. Albert didn't knock, not once, and Dorothy was grateful for that. Then he was gone. In August 1939, he simply fled. She didn't know exactly where he was or what he was doing. She heard nothing from him at all. He sent no money. This is divorce, she thought, and her solitary life began in earnest. She became self-sufficient, baking her own bread, keeping back a few eggs each week from her hens; she made new clothes from old clothes, became a truly accomplished seamstress, and learned to use the old Singer sewing machine that Albert said had been his mother's. This year, she had cultivated all her own fruit and vegetables, with varying success, but she ate so little that it barely mattered. Eating became something she did to survive; there was no pleasure in it. Food tasted vile to her, and the act of chewing and swallowing made her feel sick. She began to hate her body, its thinness, its strange and disgusting needs, its inability to be a normal woman's body, the fact that it could not do that which it was designed to do. Whether that design fault came from God, or Nature, she no longer knew or cared.

Then, the billeting of these girls: loud cockneys, their laughter and energy and bad language filling the house, Dorothy cooking for them, cleaning their clothes and bedlinen, mending for them, tending to their comforts after a long and hard day's work. And there were many of those; she had never known anyone to work so hard. Albert had found it easy, with his strength. But these girls fought hard to get the work done, they sweated and cried and kept going, kept going, they blistered, they chafed, they sustained bruises and cuts and calluses. But they never gave up. They inspired Dorothy; they refreshed her life with a new flood of hope and purpose.

Three days after the Hurricane crashed in the Long Acre, Dorothy – in some pain, still wearing her dressings, but still trying to be useful, still managing to cook for the girls, managing a fraction of the growing mountain of laundry she was tasked with – had a visitor.

She heard the front gate latch being lifted and the gate being shut, and quickly hid her notebook in the cutlery drawer. She was working on a new poem. It felt like a break-through, at last, a couple of sentences with direction. A novelty. Annoyed, she steeled herself for a visit from Mrs Compton. To appear calm, she hummed a tune. She did not want Mrs Compton to get even an inkling of how she was feeling; there was no need. In fact, there was danger in the older woman knowing anything.

But the knock was not Mrs Compton's. It was brisk. Unmistakeably, it was a man's knock. Wiping her hands on her pinny, Dorothy approached the door and opened it.

'Mrs Sinclair?' said the man standing there, in an inde-terminate foreign accent that Dorothy guessed was Polish. He held behind his legs a large bunch of hedgerow flowers, trying to hide it.

'Yes?' said Dorothy. She sounded stiff and formal – like her mother, she realised with horror.

'I am Squadron Leader Jan Pietrykowski,' he said, as though Dorothy should recognise his name. Then, in a deft series of movements, he took her hand, kissed it, released it and, with a flourish, he offered her the flowers.

She blushed. 'Oh! Thank you,' said Dorothy, recovering herself, no longer impersonating her mother. She took the flowers and smelled them, as a matter of politeness rather than curiosity. She could think of nothing further to say. Like all men in uniform, this man looked handsome and smart. Her first impression was of dark hair, slicked across from a side parting, and clear tanned skin. He was clean-shaven, his eyes bright blue. A very bright blue. He had a direct and unflustered gaze that both alarmed and intrigued her. He seemed to be two or three inches taller than Dorothy. Not a tall man, not a short man. But younger – perhaps four, five, six years younger. Too young. Like Albert. It was impossible. And all of this shot through her like a sudden onset of fever.

'I have come to thank you for your brave efforts to save my compatriot on Tuesday,' the squadron leader announced. Dorothy thought him grandiose, but she was prepared to overlook it.

'Save?' she said.

'My pilot. On Tuesday. We have heard of your courage. I am here to thank you,' and Squadron Leader Jan Pietrykowski bowed.

Dorothy stared at him in shock, amusement. Something else. Something she did not care to pinpoint.

'I see you have a bandage,' he said. 'I hope your face is not too sore?'

And damn that woman, damn her to hell. The tittle-tattling—! Dorothy, essentially kind, could not bring herself to even think the word 'cow', let alone 'bitch'. Too cruel, these words, too impolite. And, she was generous enough to enter-tain, possibly not even true.

'I see,' said Dorothy. 'I didn't exactly try to save him. Everybody seems to think . . . never mind. But thank you. My face is not too sore. It will be better soon, I'm sure. Won't you come in?'

The squadron leader stepped over the threshold into Dorothy's kitchen and immediately it struck her that this man's presence was a comfort, even a sudden joy. This house had been empty of menfolk for nine months; it had become a feminine enclave, and even more so since the arrival of the girls. She indicated a seat at the table, and he sat. He looked around, and Dorothy noticed he took a long time looking at the mantelpiece with its candlesticks, its clock, its thin layer of coal dust.

'This reminds me of my mother's kitchen,' he said, sweeping his arm around as if sharing with her a vast panorama, 'back at home where I come from.'

'Where is that?' asked Dorothy, preparing teacups, milk, sugar. Her hands shook.

'*Polska.*'

'Poland?'

'Yes. Poland.'

Jan Pietrykowski smiled at her, a wide grin that Dorothy found herself staring at despite all her decorous intentions. She had to stop being so . . . silly. She lost herself in tea preparations. Her hands shook even more. She bit her lip. She repressed an urge to giggle. Had her knees been *punched*? Surely, they had been.

'I know, I know,' she said, trying to steady her voice, which was becoming high-pitched. 'We are all so damned imperialistic. Aren't we?' She cleared her throat. What exactly was the matter with her? Surely, she should know.

If he was taken aback by the coarse language, Squadron Leader Jan Pietrykowski failed to show it. Perhaps he didn't know the word? But his English was pretty good. Dorothy couldn't believe he hadn't heard such words and understood their meaning. Still, she sensed that here was a man she could swear around without incurring judgement.

'My girls taught me that word,' she said. It sounded to her like a boast.

'"Imperialistic"?' he said.

'"Damned". They taught me "bloody" too.'

'Your girls . . .?'

'Two young ladies from London. They work here on the farm. Since so many of the men have . . .' She tried not to sound bitter as she thought of her husband's abandonment of her. 'Since so many of them have gone away.'

'You are an angry woman, Mrs Sinclair.'

She chose to ignore the remark. She made tea, busying herself with the strainer, then pouring in milk – but no milk for him, thank you. Stirring in sugar, one for him, one for her. She was on guard, warned off by this man's perception. Angry? Yes, she was angry. Of course. But was it so obvious?

And she was listening to this man, this strange man – who did not take milk in his tea (extraordinary!) – an unexpected guest in her home, a guest in her country, telling her about his life. He was an only child, he said, brought up by his mother alone, his father not known to him. His mother had been strong, independent, left to fend for herself in a small Polish village near a town he called 'Krakoof'. Dorothy didn't know where 'Krakoof' was, let alone its surrounding villages. The squadron leader's mother was an intelligent woman, he said, and loved to learn languages, and she taught him English from an early age. Thank God for that, he said, because it was making a terrific difference now that he found himself in England, helping, at least, hoping, to set up a Polish squadron. One day soon, he hoped, he would return to his home, perhaps his mother's home, perhaps not, but he would resume his life, go back to a reinstated Polish Air Force, be normal again. Damn the Nazis. Damn the Russians.

He does know those kinds of words, Dorothy thought. 'Yes,' she said. How old was he?

'I am thirty years old,' he said.

Did she actually ask *aloud*? Voices then – hers, her voice, hers aloud, in her head – all were blurring, converging in a confusing mix of anger, revelation and, above all, she realised with horror, titillation. Nine years. *Nine* years? Oh! Oh no.

'And you are a . . . pilot?'

'Yes. A squadron leader.'

'Ah yes, you said. I'm sorry. You must think me terribly stupid. It's just that I am tired, rather.'

'Of course,' he said, and he stood, gulping back his tea.

'I didn't mean that you had to leave. I'm sorry. Please tell me more . . . are there many Polish pilots at Lodderston now?'

'Many, enough to form a squadron. But we are not believed in, our talents it seems are not obvious. We are told to do exercises. But all of us have already fought the Germans, in our own country and in France. We are not novices. We are forced to have English lessons! But I explain I can translate, teach my men myself. We are frustrated. So some of my men play the fool in the air, and now one of them dies without need. But I can see that you must rest. Thank you for what you did. I will myself inform the pilot's family of your brave actions,' and the squadron leader made for the door, opening it.

'Oh no, please don't. Please. It was not . . . it was nothing. It was stupid, in fact.'

Please don't, oh, no, no, please don't go. He was such an *interesting* person.

'Brave,' the man repeated, firmly.

'I'm an only child too,' blurted Dorothy.

'I thought that was so,' he said, stepping through the door, out into the bright afternoon sunshine, obviously determined to escape.

She knew she was being ridiculous. But she liked the way the sun shone on his black hair. Again, he took her hand and kissed it. He nodded to her, and said goodbye. He left. She crept through to the lounge and watched him through the lace curtains, the lace curtains that had become yellowed by the girls' cigarette smoke, and needed laundering. The man had climbed on to a bicycle, and he rode off in the direction of Lodderston and was gone, swallowed by the May blossom, the blue sky, the thick green hedges, the heat haze rising from the road.

Dorothy wandered back into the kitchen. She picked up the wild flowers, she smelled them again, she filled her best enamel jug with water and arranged the flowers, lingering over the task. She placed the jug artfully on the mantelpiece. She stood a while, looking at the flowers. She took out her notebook and wrote feverishly for minutes, perhaps half an hour. She felt she had something to write about. Finally. She smelled the back of her hand where he had twice kissed it. She breathed in, long and deep. Nothing. She picked up the teacup that he had drunk from, and held it to her nose. She smelled the rim, the handle, examined it closely. Impetuously, without any thought of guilt or disgust, she ran her tongue around the rim of the cup, but it tasted only of tea.

He cycled away. He'd wanted to stay longer, of course. He wanted to look back at this Englishwoman, who he knew was watching him through the lace curtains. He wanted to wave. But he thought he had better not. He couldn't explain, even to himself, how he had felt, sitting in the woman's kitchen, drinking her sweet strong tea, listening to her gentle voice. He could have listened to her for the rest of his days.

It was odd how a person of significance could just appear in your life, unexpectedly. He had not known what to expect, knocking on her door. He was there to thank her, as he thought he ought to do. He was carrying out just another of his many duties. And when the door opened, there she stood, instant, charming.

He would see her again. He knew this. He had to see her again. He knew. He would return as soon as he could. And he felt – he was certain – she would want that, and there would be no need for a pretext.

5

A photograph: black and white, a man, perhaps in his late thirties, handsome, with a moustache, his arm around a woman. She is short, with obviously blonde hair, a little younger than him, and she smiles broadly into the camera. On the back of the photo it reads: Harry and Nora, Minehead, August 1958. And under that, in a round teenage hand, it says: Nanna and Grandpa Lomax.

(Found inside a paperback edition of *A Bouquet of Barbed Wire* by Andrea Newman. It's an old copy, but in good condition, so I placed it on the general fiction shelves priced at £1.00.)

I drive to the clinic. Jenna sits resolute alongside me, staring at the people and buildings and trees and vehicles that we pass on our journey. Apart from giving me terse directions, she says nothing. I try to make conversation, but now is not the time, and so I silence myself. We listen to Radio 4 until the building looms before us. A small ignominious brass plaque on the stone gatepost announces that this is the Evergreen Clinic. Evergreen is, I think, a strange choice of name for such a place. I know how Jenna must feel, sitting so still alongside me; yet she appears to be unmoved. I swing the car up the gravelled drive, and park in a marked space.

As if on cue, heavy drops of rain falling on to the roof of the car break the silence.

'Will you come in with me? Please,' says Jenna.

'Yes. I thought that was the plan.'

'Oh, thank you. I'm grateful. But I'm scared.'

Of course she is.

'You don't have to go in,' I offer.

'Yes, I do.'

And I know she does. There is no point in prolonging the inevitable, no point in trying to dissuade Jenna. It's a one-woman show.

We walk across a neat lawn where a single magnolia stands alone in the centre – white, pretty, hopeful. We slowly ascend the imperious steps leading to the door marked 'Entrance'. Inside is dark, oaky, leathery. A lady with long, long blonde hair and a name badge stating 'Rita' sits primly at a tacky, veneered desk. I don't believe that Rita is her actual name. She invites us to take a seat in the waiting room, which was obviously once the large sitting room of a grand house. Daytime television blasts out from what appears to be a 1980s set. There are many women here, nervous, waiting, like Jenna, waiting to do something hellishly profound. Right or wrong. It isn't my place to judge. Of course. Yet I feel vaguely nauseous, clammy. Some of the women are young, just girls, with mothers chaperoning them, mothers as nervous as their daughters. But, like Jenna, they look resolute. There are one or two couples, the men holding the women's hands, stroking their arms. Why are they here? What events have led up to this day, this place, this decision? I shall never know. It isn't my destiny to know.

After an interminable half-hour, Jenna is called and she disappears like a ghost into an unseen room, the door closing quietly behind her. I watch the television and learn how to make triple-glazed chicken in honey, or some such concoction. I clamp my mind off from where I am, what I am doing, what is going on behind the door, the conversation that will be taking place.

Jenna emerges after fifteen minutes or so, white-faced. She beckons me and I follow her outside, where the sun is shining and the birds are busying themselves in the trees, in defiance of this place. Jenna sits on the bottom step and lights a cigarette, which shocks me greatly. Her hand is trembling, cigarette smoke curling around her slender beringed fingers. I didn't know she was a smoker.

'I can have a tablet,' Jenna says. 'Today, once I've seen a doctor.'

'A tablet?'

'It will make the pregnancy come away and I'll bleed. Like a period.'

'You're definitely pregnant, then?' I say, disappointed. How lovely if she had been mistaken, there had been no baby to . . . deal with.

'Oh yes. I could see it. A little flake. On the screen. It was like watching a film, but there wasn't much to see. Just shadows and . . . pulses. Five and a half weeks gone. It's a good job I'm on the ball, eh?'

'Do you still want to do this?' I ask, my voice high-pitched and laboured. 'Are you going to go ahead?'

'I am. Absolutely. This is just a mistake, a great big one. It's not a baby, not yet. It's just a blob of cells and matter. No eyes yet, no mouth or even a proper brain. No skin. There's no crime here, Roberta. Don't go all holier than thou on me. I'm within my rights to do this. It's all perfectly legal.'

'I know that. I wasn't trying to . . . it's okay.' I have nothing else to say.

Jenna obviously does not have a working knowledge of

regret. Not yet, anyway. I don't want to cry, so I think hard about triple-glazed chicken in honey, about driving home, being there, safe and alone. I have a sudden yearning to eat hot buttered crumpets dripping with gooseberry jam, the delicious jam Babunia made each year until she was too old to manage it. I recall the bottles lined up on the highest shelf in her pantry.

Jenna drags heavily on her cigarette. This secret between us is already forcing an intimacy that feels too intense. I wish she hadn't asked me to help. And I wish I hadn't agreed to. Sophie would have done a better job; she has common sense and compassion in bucketfuls. I hold back too much. It's something of a problem in my life.

What is it my grandfather said to my grandmother, apparently from beyond the grave? *Your soul will not return from this that you do.*

And as Jenna prepares to return to the trammelled darkness of the Evergreen Clinic to be 'seen' by a doctor, she suggests I wait for her in the car. She'll be all right now. The worst is over, she says. I sit cocooned in the magnified silence of a car when the engine isn't running and I think of Philip, about him never knowing of the events of this day. And thank God for that, because I understand my boss enough by now to know that he would be appalled and hurt, ashamed of this young woman, ashamed of me. And it wouldn't be the abortion itself, nor even the fact that the . . . baby may not be his. It would be the lies and the deceit. Oh, how I want Jenna to cry and deliberate and to change her mind, run out of this building. I want the door to open and Jenna to charge out, clutching her belly, protecting her baby, embracing the instincts that she must be working so hard to suppress. I want to greet her with a huge smile of relief, strap her in the car myself and speed out of the gate, never to return.

But I know it won't happen.

I have a vision of Philip at the book fair, being charming, being affable – his great skill, considering his indifference to just about everybody – and I wonder what is going on at the bookshop, with poor Sophie, alone all day, stacking shelves, serving customers, probably harassed. I cannot wait to get out of here and back into the world I love so much.

My grandfather's letter is still in my handbag so I can read it whenever I need to. I read it now, while I wait for Jenna. I wish I could ask my father about it, but I can't bear the thought of upsetting him. He has so much to deal with already. Does Dad know that his father was, in fact, alive and probably well – at least, well enough to write a Dear John letter to his mother – in February 1941? And that it looks like his parents may not have been married after all? And that his mother did something unforgivable – at least, as far as my grandfather was concerned – to a child.

Did she have a termination? I wonder.

Was abortion legal in 1941? I think not.

What did my grandmother do to 'this child's mother'? Did he actually mean my grandmother? English was not his first language. Perhaps something was lost in the translation of his Polish thoughts into his written English? I wish I could ask my own mother about it; but that's out of the question. That leaves my grandmother, my beloved babunia.

She's 109 years old.

I look up from the letter to see Jenna emerging from the building. I watch her trip lightly down the steps and across the lawn – past the 'Keep off the grass' sign – to my car. We can go home. She has taken the tablet, she tells me, and she smiles like she has just bagged a bargain in the sales. It's a smile I recognise.

6

'To Marcus, 4eva, luv 'n' stuff, Natalie': The card consists of a pink felt heart on a red card background. Handmade, I think. The dot of the 'i' is fashioned into a heart shape. I think at first how frivolous it is, but it's not at all frivolous. It's simple and eloquent and heartbreaking, so I keep it. I believe it was 'Marcus' who brought in the boxes of paperbacks; I watched as he came staggering up the path with his girlfriend, both of them struggling with two boxes each. He addressed her as 'Kim'.

(Card found in the Harper Perennial edition of *The God of Small Things* by Arundhati Roy. Reading copy only, so I popped it into the 30p bargain basket under the window, alongside the front door.)

My cat, Tara, and I lived a cosy life for many years. She greeted me with good grace every day when I returned from work, and curled up on my lap on Sunday afternoons while I read or watched the occasional film. She was faithful and devoted, unlike most cats, and I almost believed she loved me as much as I loved her. But last Saturday, I arrived home to find Tara stiff and cold on the doormat. I had to pick her up before I could get in the door.

After dark, when nobody could see me, I buried her under the plum tree in my tiny back garden.

It was with a large measure of serendipity that I stumbled upon the vacancy in the Old and New Bookshop. Philip had plans to open up a further room of the shop, to sell a decent range of new books. He needed somebody to manage that side of the business, as well as helping him with the second-hand books. I like to think my newly acquired degree in English Literature helped me to land the job. Philip tells me he liked my friendly, non-pretentious manner and my willingness to clean. He felt I would slot very nicely into his bookshop.

We were a small, tight-knit team, Philip and I, in those early days. Just the two of us, in the shop from nine to five (often much later in his case), both of us for six days a week, most weeks. I have not minded giving up my Saturdays. My social life is sparse. But Philip has always been good company, funny and witty, and observant of his fellow man, if a little too critical. I have enjoyed his company since day one.

As the shop grew, the need for another member of staff became apparent, and Sophie became the third employee. A lovely girl, inside and out – intelligent and kind – perfect for the shop. I think I resented her, at first. I wanted the shop, and Philip – I wanted it all to myself. Sophie was new and pretty and I was jealous, of all things, which was utterly ridiculous. I got over it.

Sophie's boyfriend, Matt, collects her from work on Saturday evenings, and they often ask me to 'hang out' with them. They are getting a Chinese, or a pizza, they're watching a film. I'm welcome to join them. I always decline.

'Oh, come on, Roberta. It'll do you good,' says Sophie.

'No,' I always say. 'Tara needs feeding.'

A soft shake of Sophie's head. 'You need to get over it!

Go home and feed her, then pop round to ours. Stay the night. It's just a cat, not a child. You should live a little. For God's sake.'

Philip and I have a professional relationship, but we can laugh and joke together, and often we do. We rarely talk about our lives away from the shop. Philip bought the eighteenth-century building housing the Old and New twelve, thirteen years ago. I believe, I get the feeling, there is no mortgage, there are no loans to repay. Sophie and I speculate that he may have won the lottery. Or inherited money from a dead relative. Of course, we never ask. Some months, I know the Old and New is lucky to break even. It often makes a loss, and usually only makes a profit in December – and even then, only in good years. Yet Philip continues to run his independent bookshop as a going concern, and he has converted the uppermost floor into his comfortable and handsome flat. He is simple in his tastes. Books, obviously, lots of books in his personal collections. And paintings, mostly prints, but I suspect a few originals too, all nicely framed. Plants, lots of houseplants – unusually, for a man, I think. That lovely sofa in the roomy lounge, an old rocking chair. A small television in the corner. No game stations, no Xboxes or whatever they're called, just a handful of well-chosen DVDs. A clean kitchen, small and functional. All is simple and old-fashioned – or, at least, pretending to be simple and old-fashioned.

One of Sophie's recent ideas (Philip values her 'fresh' input) was for one of the book rooms to be given over to a coffee shop. Philip vetoed this immediately. I am secretly thankful for this. But bless Sophie. She is so . . . modern.

'We're not bloody Borders!' spluttered Philip. 'There's a reason they went to the wall, you know!'

And Sophie poked out her tongue at him.

Of course, he was joking. But he's right. We are small,

independent. We are unique. We deal in books. We deal in the written word.

I'm preparing a simple dinner to share with . . . who? My boyfriend? Lover? The man I sleep with?

We are having triple-glazed chicken in honey, with salad and herby potato wedges. I am not a great cook, finding the whole process rather tedious. A bottle of Pinot Grigio is cooling in the fridge. There is a lemon sorbet in the freezer. Wine is unusual for us because his wife mustn't smell it when he gets home. She thinks that every other Thursday he attends a yoga class, straight after a staff meeting. This blatant lie, so bare and transparent, frightens me a little. Subterfuge I abhor, although sometimes it is necessary. But I do wish his ideas were a little more inventive.

Of course, I feel awful. I never thought – or planned, or expected – to end up in a relationship with a man already married. I think I suffered a moment of weakness, a lapse in my normally quite good judgement. And now I seem to be living with the consequences. He's not happy with his wife, he says, and hasn't been for some time. She's 'difficult', whatever that means. I don't press him on this or anything else. I wouldn't blame his wife for being angry with me if she were to find out, truly I wouldn't. And maybe she would expel him from their home and he would turn up on my doorstep, bedraggled and tearful.

Would he expect to move in with me? Would I owe him that?

I think not. I certainly wouldn't *want* him to move in with me. And I know I shouldn't be carrying on with a married man twenty-two years my senior. It isn't nice and it isn't fair and it will all come to nothing. I know this.

His name is Charles. Old-fashioned, but that's the kind

of woman I am, attracted to older men with older-men names. I find them comforting, with none of the rawness and threats of a younger man. They are civilised.

And you don't have to love them, if you don't want to. They are flattered enough if you like them, invite them into your home and listen sympathetically to their woes. That's the drawback of older men: the woes are endless.

My older man – who, of course, isn't mine at all but belongs to her, his wife, the woman whose name is Francesca and who, he tells me, smells like Febreze – has bought me a cat. She's a replacement for Tara. He knows, as all the regular customers of the Old and New know, that I lost Tara. Their sympathy is enormous, and I believe it is genuine. The death of my cat is a subject up for discussion.

Our first date was, of necessity, some way off from our hometown. He could not afford for anybody to see him on a clandestine date with that woman from the bookshop. (What's her name? The plain one. Rebecca?) Mr Charles Dearhead, Head Teacher at Northfield Primary School. He had too much to lose. And so did I, only I wasn't as scared of losing it as he was. 'We' are a secret, and he trusts that I will always, always keep our little secret.

But I haven't kept it, not completely.

'Are you seeing somebody?' asked Sophie.

It was a quiet Saturday afternoon, a week or two ago. Fax-man had been in, and out, once again reminding me of the ongoing offer of a date. I politely laughed him off, as usual, and continued to look up the difference between swallows and swifts in *Birds of Britain: An Illustrated Guide*. Sophie asked her question, turning to me hastily before another customer arrived at the till.

'Why are you asking?' I said, grinning at her. I wasn't

exactly bursting to tell anybody about my fling. But it would be quite nice, I thought, to tell somebody, if only to get another perspective. I realised that we had swifts swooping around the Old and New in the summer. Not swallows. And definitely not house martins.

'You are,' she said, triumphantly. 'Aren't you?'

'I might be,' I replied, and winked at her.

'Who? Who? Who is it?'

'He's married,' I warned. I had hoped it would sound sophisticated, but it didn't.

'Really? Oh! Well, that doesn't necessarily . . . who is it? Does he come in here?'

'Yes.'

A pause. A customer inconveniently filled it, and Sophie hastily, politely served her.

'Who is it?' Sophie hissed at me as soon as the customer was out of earshot.

'Charles Dearhead.'

There was no mistaking Sophie's disappointment. I wanted to reach out and gently swipe it away, as I might a stray strand of hair from her face. I hold a great deal of tenderness for Sophie.

'It's all right,' I said, and shrugged.

Of course it wasn't all right. But it was better than nothing. I'd had rather too much of nothing, and Charles had become my 'something'.

I didn't love him. I would never love him. Sophie and I both knew it. And all this passed between us in those few seconds, telepathically, a silent conversation in which nothing was said but everything was communicated.

'He's a lot older than you,' said Sophie, breaking our spell.

'Twenty-two years older.'

'Too old?' she asked.

She made me think. But not for long.

'Maybe. But he's nice. I like him. He's kind to me. And he is handsome, for his age,' I said, my vanity coming to my defence.

'He's married to his wife,' said Sophie, and our eyes widened and we giggled.

'I know what you mean, though,' I said, and I whispered, 'Mrs Francesca Dearhead, no less. Have you ever seen her?'

'No, I don't think so.'

'He says she's difficult.'

'Aren't you worried that you'll be found out? Philip might sack you. Scandal at the Old and New?'

'Philip wouldn't sack me. And he'll never find out. Nobody will. I don't make a song and dance of it, and neither does he. It's all okay, Sophie. Okay?'

Jenna emerged from the children's book room, where she had been busy putting out the new books delivered that morning. She is a neat person, when she tries, and putting out new stock, arranging shelves, especially in the children's section, has become one of her particular duties. She smiled at us as we cut short our conversation. I don't think she heard any of it; perhaps she thought we were talking about her.

Jenna offered to make coffee. As the kettle boiled loudly in the kitchen, and we could hear her clattering around with cups and saucers, Sophie said my affair with 'the Dearhead', as she called him, was okay, if I said it was. And it was none of her business, which was obviously true.

But I care for her opinions. I know she knows I cannot be truly happy with a man like Charles Dearhead, even if he is handsome. She thinks I deserve better, and maybe that is so. But, living as I do, alone, Charles feels right for me, and he is a sweet man in his own way. And I quite like his way, the fact that he never really wants to speak about me. I can lose myself in his life, and it means I don't have to think too much about my own, which, I convince myself, is infinitely better than his.

Ah, but here he is now. Hassled. Frowning. I've put my Billie Holiday CD on for him. He likes jazz, and so do I. It's good to have that in common. If I sit him down in my small but comfortable lounge, massage his shoulders, pour him a glass of wine . . . there. That's better. Is he? Yes, he is, he is actually smiling now. And asking me what is for dinner because it smells delicious and he can't really believe that he will be able to stay here for the night, our first night together. He sips wine and looks smug. He parked his car two streets along. You never know who might be prying, he says.

Her mother is ill, you see. Francesca's. She's knocking on, he told me, and keeps falling over. She hurts herself, breaks her bones. This latest issue is nothing serious but she needs an operation, he thinks. And there's talk of a home, but she won't go into one. Which isn't really terribly fair on Francesca, who has her own life down here and can't keep dashing up to the Dales every time her mother sneezes.

'Anyway, stroke of good luck, eh?' he said when he telephoned me with the news.

I don't like him to telephone me at work. He rings my mobile, never the shop telephone. On my mobile I have him listed under the name of Ashley.

I leave 'Ashley' in the lounge. In the kitchen I cook, and sip my own glass of wine. I consider showing him my grandfather's letter. But I decide against it. The Dearhead would probably not be interested, and I would feel I was somehow betraying both my grandparents. Especially Babunia. It's private.

I'm luxuriating in fine silk underwear, purchased only yesterday for the big occasion. In a dark red colour, like blood from a deep cut. It looks pretty, but it's all rather uncomfortable; I'm ignoring that, and projecting ahead to his delight later when he removes my clothes to reveal the lingerie. I hope it's his thing. I hope we have a wild . . . no, not wild – what am I thinking? – a nice time.

We deserve it.

We do have a nice time. Charles is good in bed, and I may as well be honest about that. It's a very major part of his charm, and one of the reasons I remain his . . . other woman. But, somehow, there's a cynical emptiness to it all.

There's something missing.

'What do you expect?' Sophie, hands on hips, irate, hearing my tale.

'I don't know.'

'Come off it.'

'I thought . . . I don't know what I thought. It's good to have a lover, for want of a better word. Actually, it's fun.'

'Yes, of course it is, and you deserve some fun. But you won't get it from him, not long term. Being involved with a married man is rubbish, constantly looking over your shoulder. You can't relax, you can't hold hands in public unless you're, I don't know, three hundred miles away, and you can't be normal. There's more to a good relationship than just sex, you know?'

'I know. I do know that. It's all a bit . . . soulless, I think.'

'Whatever. If I were you, I'd drop him. Get your life back. That's the way forward.'

And I think. I hear and rehear Sophie's words, and I end my relationship with the Dearhead. Two days later, over the telephone. Like this.

'Charles? I'm sorry to ring you at work. But it's important. Look, Charles, I don't think we should see each other any more. It's got to end. I think things have . . . have fizzled out, rather.'

Of course, he is excessively polite. And after pondering for several moments upon his own shortcomings, he apologises for screwing my life up.

I tell him my life is not remotely screwed up. I'm just uncomfortable with the whole thing; he's a married man, after all. And I'm a little bored, if I'm honest.

He's less polite now and says he's boring, is he?

I say no, he is not boring. But the relationship is, frankly. It's getting tiresome. And it's hardly right, is it?

He says I'm not very sensitive, and he always thought that of me. I'm brusque.

I apologise. I try again. The thing is, Charles . . .

The conversation ends with a promise from him not to attempt any further meetings. Of course, we will both be cordial and professional within the confines of the Old and New. And thank God, that is the only place we are likely to encounter each other.

So now the relationship is over. I can keep the cat. He hates cats, anyway. Bloody butchers.

And we shall be happy together, she and I. Of course, I won't miss Charles at all, not even on alternate Thursday nights. I shall, instead, make myself useful. I'll catch up with housework. I'll tackle that ironing pile before I really do run out of things to wear. I'll decorate my flat. I'll take my new cat to the vet. I know I'll miss Charles Dearhead, despite the shortcomings. I'll miss his urbane presence. But I won't feel sorry for myself, I won't allow my essential aloneness to bring me down. Aloneness is the shell in which I gratefully hide. And it's not the same thing as loneliness.

Aloneness is what I've always felt I deserved; I choose it, prefer it and want it. You can't be hurt if you are alone. Perhaps that was how my mother felt the day she decided enough was enough. I'll probably never know. But I wonder how alike we might be. I wonder what she is doing, I wonder how she lives her life; how she lives with herself. Guilt is a terrible burden. So, I'm Doing The Right Thing. All is well.

I wish him all joy of this world, as my grandfather might have said.

And I so want to talk to my father about the letter.

I'm visiting him. It's a Sunday afternoon, it's pouring with rain – the heavy type that clashes on to windows and roofs like stones thrown by children. My grandfather's letter is nestled snug and dry in my handbag, and Dad and I are drinking tea.

'Have you visited Babunia recently?' I ask my father.

It's a start, an innocuous enough question.

'No. I haven't felt up to it much,' says Dad.

He looks wan today. Tired. I want to ask him about his pain management, I want to hear about the outcome of his last visit to the hospital. We have rarely talked about his illness. He broke the news to me several years ago, but he insisted that we shouldn't discuss it any more, unless it was 'absolutely necessary'. He vaguely refers to visits to the hospital. He mentions a Dr Moore, but it's pretty much a closed subject and one he usually forbids me to even try to discuss with him. So I don't. Of course, he's known for many years, but being the stoic he is, he was determined to keep it from me. Babunia still doesn't know about it. He doesn't want to burden her.

'I'm thinking of visiting her tomorrow,' I say. 'I haven't been for a month or so. I really should go.'

'Good. I'm sure she'd be pleased to see you. I can't go at the moment. She'll know straight away . . .'

'I know, Dad. I'll tell her you're busy. Actually, I might have a couple of questions I'd like to ask her.'

'What sort of questions?'

'Well, I'm thinking of doing a family tree thing.' I'm pretty good at thinking on my feet. 'Everyone else seems to do one, so I thought I'd give it a go.'

'Oh. I see.'

'I'd like to ask Babunia about your father.'

'Well, we don't know much about him, do we? He died during the war, before I was born. You know that, love. I don't know much else about him. He was Polish, that's about it. Your grandmother likes to remind us that he was a squadron leader in the Battle of Britain, God bless her. But you know that already.'

'Do you know exactly when he died? The date, I mean? It might help me to trace him.'

'Mum always said in November 1940. She was expecting me. Hard to believe, isn't it?'

'What?'

'That I was ever a baby. And so long ago.'

'Oh, I see. I thought you meant . . . never mind. Does Babunia have her marriage certificate?'

'She told me she thought it was lost years ago, I think.'

'But I could look that up, couldn't I? In a register?'

'I . . . well. Yes. I suppose you could.'

'Do you have your birth certificate?'

'Oh, somewhere. Although I rather think that might have gone missing too. I haven't seen it in years.'

We drink our tea and nibble on a digestive biscuit each.

'Your grandmother might have it,' says Dad. 'She likes to keep things safe for me. I haven't seen it since I started claiming my pension, I think. And that's longer ago than I'd like it to be.' Dad winks at me.

'Do you recall ever seeing their marriage certificate?' And now I am beginning to press, just the thing I must not do.

'No, love. I don't think so.'

'But you think Babunia *might* have it? She probably keeps such things all in one place, doesn't she? She's pretty methodical.'

'You'll have to ask her.'

'Is there a death certificate? For your dad?'

'I don't know, Rob. If there is, I've not seen it. At least, I don't think I have. You'll have to ask your grandmother about it all. But, darling?'

'Yes?'

'Don't let on to her. About me, I mean.'

'I won't, Dad.'

'It would break her heart. Always assuming she'd be with it enough to understand.'

'I know.'

'You're a good girl.'

'Maybe.'

'Do you fancy staying for your tea? We could watch *Antiques Roadshow*. I've got crumpets.'

'And gooseberry jam?'

'Sadly not your grandmother's. But I've got Tesco's mixed fruit jam, if that's any good. There might be gooseberries in it.'

And now I feel deflected, stalled; I know my father well, and I think he's hiding something.

Should I show him the letter? No. I'll keep it to myself for now. I don't want to upset him, any more than I want to upset Babunia.

We eat our crumpets and jam, and nothing further is said.

7

Nina eyed the bunch of wild flowers on the mantelpiece. Following her gaze, Dorothy noticed how they burst forth from the enamel jug, a little vulgar, a little showy. She watched her girls as they swiftly ate fried potatoes, fried eggs and broad beans – small, soft and sweet, early beans picked that afternoon by Dorothy under the unblinking sun. Far too early, of course, but there wasn't much else to choose from, yet.

Nina nudged Aggie, and raised her eyebrows.

'You been picking flowers, Dot?' said Aggie, winking at her friend.

'No.'

'Someone picked them for you, then?' said Nina.

'Yes.'

'A bloke?' said Aggie.

'A bloke. Yes.'

'Which bloke?' said Nina, through a full mouth.

Oh, how genteel, thought Dorothy. And: which bloke? Did Nina know all the 'blokes' in the world? Actually, Dorothy thought, there was quite a good chance of that.

'Squadron Leader Jan Pietrykowski, no less. He flies a Hurricane,' said Dorothy, more to herself than to the girls.

'Squadron leader, eh?'

'Is he a dish?' asked Aggie, gleefully.

'I don't know. I haven't really considered. A dish? Yes, possibly. Probably.'

'Well, if he is, you would have noticed, wouldn't you?' said Nina. 'You're not that bloody old. What's he like? Where did you meet him?'

'I met him today, here, in this kitchen.' Dorothy surprised herself. Was it really only this day and in this kitchen? 'And he's very nice, very polite. Foreign, of course.'

'What did he want?' said Nina. 'Apart from the bleeding obvious.' Aggie kicked her, and she squealed. 'I'm only asking, aren't I? You don't mind, do you, Dot? It's just, you've got to watch them Polish ones, they've got hands like octopuses. We had fun with them, though, didn't we, Aggie? Blimey, you'd think they'd never seen a girl before. They've got girls in Poland, though, haven't they?'

'Yes. Of course. But these men, you must understand. They've had a difficult time. They're in need of . . . diversion. The squadron leader had to flee his country in pretty ghastly circumstances. They all did. But I'll remember that warning, Nina. Thank you.' Dorothy hid a small smile behind her teacup. It was the cup that the squadron leader had drunk from, and she hadn't yet been able to wash it.

'Well?' said Nina.

'Well, what?'

'Do you fancy him?'

'Of course not.'

'Liar,' they chorused, delighted.

The squadron leader returned the following day, in the heat of the afternoon. The first day of June and, this year, flaming. Dorothy heard his confident, sharp rap on the kitchen door.

She had hoped he might return, yet she couldn't imagine why he would. She smoothed her pinny, tucked loose hair behind her ear, cleared her throat. She stood still for a few

seconds, breathing in and out, a mechanical effort, con-
sciously performed. She felt a crippling tightness in her
throat. Yet she had to be a picture of composure. It didn't
do to be anything else. And her knees almost buckled beneath
her. She breathed, deep and loud, she tucked more hair
behind her ears. She hummed a tune she had heard on the
wireless. She would appear normal. On no account could
she . . . she yanked open the door.

The squadron leader pushed past her, grinning, carrying
a box, bulky and heavy-looking.

'What on earth is this?' said Dorothy, hands on hips, head
on one side, while Jan Pietrykowski placed the box on the
kitchen table. Her curiosity emboldened her, if only tempor-
arily, and she forgot the tight throat, the quick breathing,
the sweat pooling like oil slicks behind her knees.

'A gift for you. For you, Mrs Sinclair.'

'Oh. Why, thank you. What on earth is it?'

'A gramophone.'

'Oh.'

'You like music, no? I think so, because you always hum.
At least, these two times we have met you have been
humming as I walk down your path. So I bring you music.'

She did like to hum – just simple tunes, half heard, half
remembered – and perhaps she liked to dance too, in her
mind, humming her tunes, performing her duties, trying not
to think about war and absconded husbands, dead babies
and dead pilots. It was only natural.

Jan carried the gramophone through to the parlour, at
Dorothy's request. She cleared the sideboard and blew off
its thin layer of dust. He returned to his car – 'Not my car,
our squadron car' – and came back in with a box of records,
which he placed alongside the gramophone.

'I can't accept all this, Squadron Leader,' said Dorothy,

collecting herself. 'I'm afraid you can't leave this here.' She hated to sound disapproving.

'Then it is a borrowing, from me to you, and you will return it to me when I have to depart, when I return home, whenever that shall be.'

'A borrowing?'

'Yes. Actually, it is not mine. It belonged to another man, a good pilot, an Englishman. I met him when I first arrived in your country. A generous man, of good spirit. He told me if anything were to happen to him, I must make sure his gramophone is looked after and is enjoyed. So I think of you, in this quiet cottage, and your girls who you tell me about. Girls, they love to dance, I think. And you too?'

'Dance? Me? No.'

'Yes.'

'No.'

'We shall see. Anyway, this is yours for as long as you want it, and to enjoy and to use.'

'Don't your men want it? For entertainment?'

'We have wirelesses. We have dances. In fact, next Saturday. I invite you and your girls to the dance, as my guests.'

'But I don't dance. Especially at dances.'

'No need to dance. We can sit and talk. Be like friends.'

'That sounds very nice. I'm sure Aggie and Nina would be thrilled. They so enjoyed the last one.'

'We must have fun when we can get it, in times like these. If my men can't fly yet, we can drink, eat, make joke, no? No need for guilt.' And the squadron leader smiled at Dorothy. 'I shall collect you next Saturday, at seven o'clock,' he announced.

'All right,' said Dorothy, smiling broadly despite her misgivings. 'I'll go, as you have been so kind as to ask. But I shall not dance.'

★

The girls, tired and grubby, arrived back at the cottage around half past five. They took one look at the gramophone and the records, and it seemed their world was complete. They searched eagerly through the stack of records, digging out their favourites. Aggie was delighted to find some Billie Holiday songs – 'You must listen to her, Dot!' – and that odd, brittle-strong voice was now flowing through the house, the jaunty music restoring something to them all. Dorothy immediately liked the joyful-joyless sound of the American woman's voice. And, for an evening, they forgot about the war. There was none of their usual talk: In a year it could all be over, in six months it could all be over, six weeks even, and Hitler will be here, and we'll have no freedoms, and Churchill will be strung up, and . . .

'Dance, Nina!' cried Aggie, pulling the heftier girl to her feet, and spinning her around, laughing, red-faced.

Dorothy sewed and watched. She smiled. It was an inspired idea of the squadron leader's, she thought. Of course, young women like to dance. They like music. Why wouldn't they?

'There's more,' said Dorothy, remembering the invitation. 'We are invited to the dance next Saturday night. Special guests of the squadron leader.'

'Oh, we know all about that,' said Nina, throwing herself down on to the settee, still red-faced, her mousy hair clinging to her face. 'Already invited, we are. All the Land Girls are going.'

'What are you going to wear, though?' said Aggie. 'I've got my blue frock.'

'I don't know. Don't much care either. Might just wear my uniform. All that lovely food up there too! They put on such a spread last time, Dot. You should've seen it. Cakes. Jellies. All sorts of sandwiches. Lovely, it was.'

'Yes, but that's why your dress won't fit you any more!' said Aggie, moving rhythmically around the room, arms held out as though dancing with a partner, her blonde curls flying behind her.

'It's all right for you. Just I've got a healthy appetite, haven't I, Dot?'

'Indeed you have. Why don't you bring me your dress, and we'll see if I can let it out for you?' said Dorothy.

The dress was a pale green lawn, with a matching fabric belt. Rather old, and in need of a darn or two, as well as letting out. Dorothy examined the seams, which were mercifully generous. After suggesting Nina try it on, she unpicked and pinned it, and managed to let it out to the required size. Nina looked well in it. Green suited her nondescript, pale brown hair, her country-tanned face and arms. Not exactly pretty – and, frankly, fat – but Dorothy still felt something akin to a mother's pride looking at the smiling girl wearing her newly altered frock.

The day before the dance, Dorothy examined her own wardrobe and pondered what to wear. She had three 'special occasion' frocks. The first was red, woollen, with long sleeves, more of a winter frock. It was a little close-fitting, but not too tight. She had never regained the weight she'd lost in the weeks after giving birth to Sidney. The red dress was of a pleasing length, just below the knee, and would show off her calves to advantage if she were to wear her black court shoes. She still had reasonable-looking calves. This she allowed.

She also had a green and blue patterned dress in a crisp cotton, which creased easily and was, besides, too young for her now. She would see if Aggie might like it. And lastly she had her summer frock, with a tiny flower print in pink, black, white and orange. It was undoubtedly her favourite with its summery, short puffed sleeves and its comfy, faded feel. It was perfect for a June dance. She had her pink cardigan she could wear with it, and her brown shoes looked smart with it too. Understated and admirably appropriate for a woman approaching forty, childless, and, for all she knew, widowed.

Her dressings had been removed, and the skin on her face was pink, no longer red and angry. It was still slightly sore to the touch when she covered it as best she could with her powder, just to see how it might look the following evening. It looked acceptable, she thought. She considered her frocks, hanging over her wardrobe door, draped across her bed. She liked them all, but at the same time she couldn't care less if she never wore any of them again. It was indifference, she knew – a horrible, blank feeling that she had become accustomed to over the past year. But still, she would have to choose.

Three dresses. One dance. One decision. There really was only one contender.

Nina had been right about the food. Trestle tables were loaded with plates of sandwiches, jellies, trifles, sausages, even cakes. There were large tea urns. And there was mild, if you wanted it, and cider. Some folk even had bottles of wine on their tables, Dorothy noticed. She took a cup of tea and a modest plate of food, and found a chair in a corner. Music erupted all around, loud and insistent. British and Polish airmen and their guests were dancing and laughing. Swing, Dorothy thought the music was called. She liked it, the soaring movement of it, the brashness. She watched the young people dancing, keeping a distant eye on her girls, who were oblivious of her – at least, for now – as they danced and laughed, cheeks rosy, freshly curled hair bouncing on their firm young shoulders. Dorothy felt weak as she compared herself to all these young people; she felt inconsequential. How glad she was to be sitting in the corner.

Dorothy liked to sit in the corner at parties. There was nothing worse than sitting with a large group of people, feeling left out. Or, even worse, trapped. Stupid people, asking stupid questions, interfering. Laughing at jokes that she was not privy to. No, she would take her own company any day. She nibbled at a fish paste sandwich, and wondered why on earth she had agreed to come to this dance. Squadron Leader Pietrykowski had duly arrived at the cottage at seven o'clock, driving the squadron car. He had smiled broadly at her, told her he liked very much her dress. Dorothy felt both elated and shameful. The girls, dolled up and excited, giggled and chatted in the back seat. Nina had her eye on a chap who she hoped to 'talk to' at the dance. The interior of the squadron car smelled of straw and leather and cigarettes, and Dorothy felt dizzy as they flew along the lanes, the hedges and trees and flowers, the cottages, people and bicycles all flashing by them.

The room swam with pulses and energies and jealousies, with chatter and spite and laughter. Dorothy, from her seat in the corner, continued to watch Aggie and Nina, and the other young women and men dancing, laughing, flirting. The squadron leader moved around the room, talking to people, ensuring the music was loud enough but not too loud, chatting with his fellow pilots, with the British pilots. There was talk of the Polish squadron being formed soon. And Dorothy thought yes, how useful it was that he could speak and understand English so well. It seemed that everybody wanted to speak to Jan Pietrykowski. He had that magic, that allure. So whatever she felt – what she thought she might have begun to feel – was nothing, was of no import. Dorothy watched him, her eyes roaming inconspicuously from her girls to him, and back again, and again. She watched as he spoke to the ladies of the village, who were eating greedily, nodding and smiling and gushing.

A couple of them, vaguely known to Dorothy as Marjorie and Susan, marched over to her corner. Dorothy smiled at them as they sat either side of her.

How was she? Everybody was talking about her recent escapade, did she know that? Her heroics?

'It was nothing,' said Dorothy.

'Nonsense!'

'Really—'

'And you seem to have made quite an impression on the Polish squadron leader!'

'I—'

'He is a very handsome man, isn't he? And such a gentleman.'

'Yes, if you say so.'

'And he speaks such good English!'

They smelled of mild and wine. And were far too loud, even for them, she thought, although she barely knew them and had no desire to know them better or speak to either of them. She thought they were friends of Mrs Compton, if Mrs Compton had any friends.

'Marvellous English, yes.'

'And, Dorothy, how are you keeping these days?'

'I'm fine, thank you. The girls keep me busy,' said Dorothy, pleased to come up with a change of subject.

'We always meant to say – didn't we, Susan? – how sorry we were to hear about—'

'These things happen. Don't they?' said Dorothy. She wasn't certain if they were about to talk about the loss of

Sidney, or Albert's desertion of her. But she would not talk about any of it with these women. She would not.

'But you must miss him,' said Marjorie. 'And we never see you any more. You do keep yourself to yourself, Dorothy, don't you?'

'I think it's best.'

Susan, more astute than her friend – and bored, or uncomfortable, or both – murmured that Mrs Sanderson had arrived and she should very much like to talk to her, and she and Marjorie excused themselves and returned to their side of the room. They whispered to their friends, among them the newly arrived Mrs Sanderson, Mrs Pritchard, Mrs Twoomey. Perhaps Mrs Compton was with them? But Dorothy had not noticed her. The women looked over at Dorothy from time to time, turning away hastily if she caught their eye. She was being talked about, she knew, but it didn't matter. Let them talk.

Perhaps she should give them something to talk about?

Scanning the room, she smiled brightly at Jan Pietrykowski. He joined her, pulling out the chair recently vacated by Marjorie, and smiled back.

'You are enjoying, no?'

'No. Not much.'

'I'm sorry. You are tired?'

'It's those women. Nosy things. I don't like them.'

'I shall sit with you now. And we shall eat. Can I get you some more food? Your plate is empty.'

They ate. He asked her who various people were. That ugly woman in the grey dress? The group of girls looking daggers at Nina and Aggie and the other Land Girls?

'The fat woman with . . . what you call? . . . jewels?'

'Nearly. Jowls. She is not very nice. Another nosy parker, I'm afraid. The world's full of them.'

'You like very few people, Mrs Sinclair?' said Jan.

'Is it so obvious?'

'Yes, I think so. Some of these people are probably very nice, if you give them a chance.'

'I'll reserve judgement on that, thank you. It's not that I dislike people. You must not . . . please don't think that of me. I'm just tired of it all.'

'Yet I hate to see you so lonely,' he said.

She blushed and looked down at her hands. They lay twisted in her lap, fingers intertwined. The squadron leader apologised. He changed the subject, to music, to the dancing. They ignored the quizzical, envious looks from the villagers. Dorothy reflected, as he left her for a moment to replenish their teacups and choose a cake for each of them, that she was getting almost as many disapproving looks as the Land Girls. It didn't do, she understood. A married woman, of a certain age, wearing a figure-skimming red dress (so *obvious*), and hogging the handsome Polish pilot to herself all evening. No. It didn't do at all.

. . . and her husband, poor Bert Sinclair, you couldn't blame him for running off like that, could you? She couldn't furnish him with a child, and no man deserves that. She couldn't even furnish him with a smile, in the end. And she never joined in, did she? She was a loner, she was snooty. Not much company for any husband. Too wrapped up in herself, that one. Not one for friends. A cut above, she fancies herself. Jane Frankman's niece, wasn't she? That's how she met poor Bert. They say her mother hasn't spoken to her since she married him. Lives in the south, the mother, doesn't she? Reading? London? Oxford? Must be lonely for Mrs Sinclair, in that cottage, and all that laundry to do. Doesn't seem right, a woman like that taking in laundry. Still, it keeps a roof over her head. Goodness knows what might happen if Bert were to be reported missing. They'll turf her out.

Then where'll she go? She has no friends round here. Is the mother still alive? Goodness knows. We're not allowed to know anything, are we . . .

This is what Jan Pietrykowski heard as he made his way to the trestle tables loaded with food, negotiating ladies with jowls (an amusing word, new to him, that he would try to remember), ladies wearing austere dresses, ladies who were determined to engage him in conversation.

But he escaped from the attention, and he returned to Dorothy.

Before she knew what was happening, before she could protest, before they could even eat their cakes, Dorothy was steered towards the dance floor and the Polish man's arms were around her, on her, gripping her waist, her shoulder, lightly at first, then more firmly. Around they went, locked together, and they moved in secrecy and silence as if nobody was watching. And yet to Dorothy it seemed that the whole world was judging, but she did not mind. The world could go to hell. She was without a care, for the first time in a long year. And the music seemed to go on forever – in her heart, this music would play forever – and when she looked at the man and he smiled and squeezed her waist in affection and understanding, she let her head fall on to his shoulder and she let herself be danced. And the nervous stirrings in her stomach, her bowel, her groin, the unfurling going on inside her, she accepted with a tacit grace. She was an adult, after all.

Too soon the lights were up, people were standing and shaking hands, couples were linking arms and preparing to leave, some drunk, others yawning and tired. Cigarette smoke hung over the room like a coarse blanket. There was a babble of goodbyes, and the squadron leader stood aside to allow Dorothy to collect her bag, and to see how Aggie and Nina were to go home.

'We'll walk, Dot!' shouted Nina, as a Polish airman – very young, perhaps eighteen – grabbed her face and kissed her, then released her with loud laughter. She hit him on the back of his head. Dorothy wondered if this was the young man she'd had her eye on.

Aggie agreed, yes, they would walk, and she too was with a young man, who whispered to her. Aggie giggled.

And the group of village girls, one of whom Dorothy recognised as Mrs Compton's oldest granddaughter, called out, 'Tarts!'

Dorothy looked at Jan. 'Do you think they will be all right?' she asked.

'They are not children,' he said, and shrugged.

Dorothy hesitated and he waited, politely.

'All right, then,' she said. And she advised the girls to be home within the hour, as she would wait up for them with a pot of cocoa.

The squadron leader was silent, lost in calm concentration, during the twenty-minute journey back to the cottage. There was a strong moon, and the evening was warm, and the moonlight was enough to see by, if he drove slowly. Dorothy too was silent. The road looked like a slick oily river. She watched him drive, confidently, safely. He was a man accustomed to being in control.

'Thank you, Squadron Leader,' said Dorothy, as he opened the passenger door.

As she got out of the car, he kept his hand on the door and blocked her way. But Dorothy did not feel threatened.

'You use my title all of the time,' he said. 'But my name is Jan. I lead a squadron, yes, and I am a member of the Polish Air Force and that is my job, that is my role, but I am Jan. That is my name. That is the name I wish to hear you call me. I make a point. That is all.'

'I see. Jan. Thank you, then, Jan, for a pleasant evening.'

'Merely pleasant?'

'Enjoyable. Hot and noisy, but fun. Actually, I had a marvellous time with you.'

'That is better. Thank you for being my guest. I am sorry you were so uncomfortable. Those gossiping ladies do not like you, I see. But I do.'

'Thank you. I don't mind being not liked. I prefer it.'

'Why?'

'Because I don't have to spend time with those gossiping women. My life is my own. Do you see? I don't want them to befriend me. I like my quiet life in this cottage, with just the girls for company.'

'You are like a mother for them?'

'Perhaps.'

'They are very fond of you.'

'Well, they give me a reason to get out of bed in the morning.'

'Then it's what I say. For them, you are a mother.'

'Jan, I don't wish to appear rude, but . . .'

'You are tired?'

'Yes. Rather.'

Jan released his hold on the car and walked Dorothy to the cottage door, and he waited while she struggled to unlock it. The lock had been stiff for months, she explained. He said he would bring oil for it on his next visit. The kitchen was dark and warm and smelled of bread, fresh laundry and, faintly, of fish. Dorothy was struck by the smell, as if it were new to her, and she realised suddenly how much this cottage *was* her – not just her home, but her life. Solidly built of red bricks, with square rooms, neatly plastered walls, high ceilings. She felt as though she had betrayed the cottage by staying away for so many hours. She felt like a stranger standing in her own kitchen, listening to her clock on the mantelpiece – tick, tick, tick – and she resolved to reacquaint herself with her home.

As soon as the squadron lead—

As soon as *Jan* had left.

He didn't want to, she could tell. Probably he wanted a kiss. Possibly he wanted more. But she wouldn't, and she couldn't, do any of those things. He was a man whom she could imagine herself kissing and touching, enjoying his body. And the thought of doing that did not make her blush or feel ashamed. But she would not do any of it. And she could not tell herself why, because she didn't know. It was certainly not a moral objection. It was not mere rectitude.

'Goodnight, Mrs Sinclair,' said Jan. 'I will leave you now. I may visit again?'

'Oh, please do. But my name is Dorothy. That is the name I would like you to call me. Now that we are on a more . . . friendly footing.'

'Dorothy,' he repeated slowly.

'It's such an awful name. I absolutely loathe it.'

'No. A good name, very English, I think.'

'Goodnight, Jan. Thank you for a lovely evening.'

'It's true. The British are so polite!'

'Come for tea? Tomorrow, at four o'clock? I can't promise a big spread, but . . . tea and sandwiches. Perhaps cake.'

'English afternoon tea? Yes, I will be here. Thank you.'

Jan stared at Dorothy, and she smiled at him, fixed, obtuse. He smiled back at her – resigned, she guessed – and he took his leave with a slight, stiff bow.

After watching the car drive away, Dorothy roamed through her house, ignoring the marital bedroom, now the girls' room, where her only child had been conceived and born. She entered her own small bedroom under the eaves and removed her red dress, her shoes, her stockings, corset, knickers and bra. She put on her nightdress and dressing gown, and with her cold cream she scrubbed her face free of its lipstick and powder.

She returned to the kitchen and made cocoa, stirring the milk slowly, and then she sat and waited for the girls, who returned two hours later, breathless, dishevelled and drunk.

8

'Dorothea, your tea is different.'

Jan had arrived at exactly four o'clock, on his bicycle. Despite the heat, he was unflushed, not even sweating. True to his word, he'd brought an oil can, and he oiled the lock, catch and hinges on the kitchen door. In preparation for their tea together, Dorothy had placed her wooden table and chairs under the shade of the silver birch trees in her back garden. The trees rattled and whispered in the warm breeze. She'd invited him to sit under them after his handiwork, while she prepared the tea and brought it out into the garden.

'How is my tea different?' she asked, sitting down at last.

'It is very tea-like. Very refreshing. And you have a pretty . . . what is it?' He gestured at the tea-strainer.

'Oh, the tea-strainer? It belonged to my mother.'

'She is dead?'

'No. I took it when I left to marry Albert. I'm afraid I took some rather odd things from my mother's house. It was rather sudden, you see. I thought certain items might come in useful. And some of them have.'

'And some of them have not?'

'Quite.'

'Why did you marry him?'

'Why?' She laughed, a little flustered. 'Because I wanted to.'

'And why did you want to?' Jan stirred sugar into his tea, slowly, looking at Dorothy.

'Well, I suppose the right answer would be that I loved him dearly, I simply had to be his wife, he could offer me a wonderful life and eternal happiness. That I fell in love.'

'And the actual answer?'

'Oh, I don't know. Escape, I think. I wanted to escape from my mother. I wanted to strike out on my own and I had no means of doing so, other than marrying. I thought his life sounded interesting, and he was kind to me. There.'

'A sad tale, Dorothea.'

'Dorothea' watched Jan take a bite from a sandwich. His teeth were small, even and white. She noticed the way his fingers curved lightly around the sandwich. He was an elegant man.

'Perhaps it is sad,' she replied.

'Were you ever happy?'

'Oh. What a question. Perhaps I was happy when I was very young.'

'Not since then? I am sorry to hear it. You deserve happiness.'

'I'm not sure what happiness would mean to me, anyway.'

'Perhaps a child?'

'Yes. Oh yes!' Dorothy realised she was leaning eagerly on the table – brazenly, she thought – squaring up to this man, engaging with him in a way that could be considered literally 'forward'. She checked herself, sat back in her chair, and sipped her tea.

'You have regrets, no?' said Jan. He raised his eyebrows at her encouragingly.

'I have regrets, you could say, about certain things,' said Dorothy.

'I have heard talk of it.'

'I expect you have.'

'You lost a baby?'

'I lost more than one.'

'But you gave birth to a child?'

'You are very full of questions!' Dorothy picked up the plate of cakes and offered it to Jan.

She watched him eat, and he seemed unabashed, eating under her scrutiny. She, for her part, always ate guardedly. She hated the way eating contorted her face, and it made her feel exposed.

'I ask too much,' said Jan, wiping his mouth with a serviette. 'Forgive me, I am sorry. I like to know, that is all. You are an interesting lady and I would like to hear more about you. Sadness turns us into people, surely you understand? People with hearts that thump in our chests, and souls that dream. You see?'

It was becoming increasingly difficult to hold off from Jan.

She took a deep breath. 'Sidney. That was his name. A dear little boy. He was taken away. They – Mrs Compton and Dr Soames – thought it best. But I didn't want them to take him away. I wanted him to stay with me. I wanted to hold him and comfort him and tell him how sorry I was to have let him down.' She was breathless and close to tears, but it felt right to have said such things – things that she needed to say. Things she had never said.

'The child was born dead?' Jan asked. The birch trees swayed softly around them, gently rattling their silvery leaves.

'A stillbirth, yes. He was silent, no crying, you understand? There was just this dreadful quietness. The stillness was terrifying. He was blue, I shall always remember that. Translucent.'

'Trans . . .?'

'. . . lucent. As if I could almost see through him.'

'Ah.'

'Not like a little human being at all.'

'I wish it had not been so.'

'Thank you.'

'And now I have upset you.'

'No, no. Truly. I think I need to talk about it with somebody, from time to time. It doesn't help to bottle it all up and try to pretend it didn't happen. It did happen. And it's with me all the time, I can't stop thinking about my little Sidney . . . his little body . . . what became of him? He was a person, you see. A dead person, but he had been alive, kicking inside me, I felt him kicking every day. I so wanted to be his mother.'

Jan said nothing, but he passed her a serviette. Dorothy took it, wiped her tears and blew her nose, then apologised.

'Fate played a cruel trick on you, Dorothea. Or God did.'

'God?' said Dorothy.

'You believe in God?'

'No. I do not.'

'You never pray?'

'I have done.'

'But you prayed to an empty sky, no?'

'Of course.'

'So for what did you pray?'

'For my babies. For Sidney, in the last few days before he was born. I thought it might make a difference. I thought prayers might keep him safe.'

'But the prayers did not work.'

'No.'

'There are no gods. This I know. There is no sense to this life, what we call life. All around is madness and cruelty and things that are unfair. That which pleases one person dismays another. Nothing is personal, no great being is up there or down here, plotting against us. Everything that happens, happens because it can. There is no meaning beyond life itself, the breathing and sleeping and eating and talking and loving and hating, all of this. And the losses, we lose from the minute we are born, or whenever life begins. I do not know when life begins. Does anybody know? But life, it is hard. It will always be hard. This I believe, Dorothea.'

'I see.'

'You do not like?'

'I think I do. It makes far more sense.'

'More sense than what?'

'Oh, Sunday sermons. The bleatings in church.'

'You go to church?'

'No. Not now. It's ghastly. I was forced to attend every Sunday as a child. Jan? Do you mind if I ask why you are calling me Dorothea?'

'Because it is an even prettier name than Dorothy. You *are* a Dorothea.'

'I think I like it. Say something to me in Polish. Please.'

'*Ty jesteś piękną kobietą.*'

'Such a strange language!'

'No, simple. Much simpler than yours.'

'You think so?'

'Of course.'

'So what did you say?'

'I said this is a beautiful garden, this is a beautiful afternoon, and all is perfect here and now.'

'I'm not sure I believe that.'

'Well. You will have to wonder, then.'

'I shall.'

'My wife was always "wondering". I think I am not easy to understand. Not translucent perhaps?'

Wife? But she thought . . .! You ridiculous woman. Oh, goodness, had she—?

'Jan, I . . . I'm sorry. You are married.'

Dorothy berated herself. Of course, but of course. Did she really think a man like Jan wouldn't be spoken for? Oh, how awful—!

'I am not married,' he said. 'I *was* married.'

'Your wife died?'

'No. She was young – a beautiful, young woman. We married when we were both eighteen. My mother said no, not to marry, but we didn't listen, we married, we were in love.'

'What happened?' She barely dared to ask, so her words were whispered, and were lost in the swaying of the trees.

'We lived happy, for a few months only, we made a pretty home. But I was not enough for her. She was restless. She wanted more. Other men. She took other men. I angered, I shouted. I was betrayed and I made her out of the house. And I was lonely. So I too left the house. I joined the Air Force and I have not seen her since. She returned to the house of her father. We have divorce.'

'I'm sorry, Jan. It must have been difficult for you. I know how fragile a man's pride can be.'

'A woman's love. That is the fragile thing.'

'All love, surely?'

'No. Some love is solid and is not breaking.'

'Does not break,' she corrected, and immediately wished she hadn't. 'But you have been disappointed in love?'

'As you have.'

'Yes, and everything can be broken, Jan. I've accepted that in my life. You cannot trust anyone or anything, it just doesn't do.'

'You think not?'

'Why don't we talk about something more cheery? I know, your music box. The girls are enjoying it so much! They love to sing and dance and they whirl around in the parlour of an evening, so lost in themselves and the music. It's priceless.'

'And what do you do while they dance?'

'I sew. Mending, of course, and alterations. Nina, the bigger girl, she eats like a horse and her clothes need letting out constantly, it seems. She can't have had much to eat back in London. She's from quite a poor family, I think.'

'Yes. She is one of many children?'

'She has two elder brothers, I think, and a little sister and brother – twins, I believe. I so envy her! The twins have been evacuated from London, to Wales. She tries to write letters to them, but I have to help her. She's hopeless, she can barely read or write. She says she misses London, but I rather think she should be glad to be away from it. Why volunteer for the Women's Land Army if you would prefer to stay in the city?' She stopped abruptly, aware that she was talking rather rapidly, and not making much sense. 'But perhaps you like city living?'

'I have not lived in a city. You have?'

'I lived in Oxford, as a child. It was too noisy and crowded and busy for my liking. And that was in the days before there were so many motor cars.'

'How old are you, Dorothea?'

'Why, I . . . well, since you have asked, and you did tell me how old you are, I shall tell you. I'm thirty-nine years old. I shall be forty in November.'

'A young woman.'

'Nonsense. Too old. Too old for babies, anyway. Perhaps that was my mistake with Sidney. Trying for too long, allowing myself to fall pregnant so late in my life. It was stupid of me. So I was punished.'

'Punished by whom?' His clear blue eyes were fixed on her.

'I don't know. My mother? She may have cast a spell on me.'

Now his eyes crinkled with mirth. 'You are not serious?'

'I suppose I'm not. But she is a witch.'

'Why do you say such a thing?'

'Because she had no right to motherhood,' said Dorothy, standing and beginning to clear the table.

Jan sprang up to help her.

'She was hopeless, just utterly hopeless. It's been five, six years now, since I heard from her. She was furious with me, you see.'

'Because you married Albert.'

'Yes. I left her home, my home, to marry a man "beneath me". She couldn't stand it. She thinks we still live in Victorian times. Well, we don't. It's the thirties now. Actually, it's the forties already, isn't it? Modern times, modern women. Look how they go on these days! Look at my girls. They're shameless at times. But I don't blame them. I really don't. You only get one life. And times are hard, they're frightening. God only knows how this will all end.' Dorothy turned towards the cottage, holding the tray. 'Would you like more tea?'

She insisted that Jan stay where he was, and enjoy the afternoon's peace while it lasted. She replenished the tray with a fresh pot of tea and clean cups and saucers, and topped up the milk jug and sugar bowl. Today she would not spare the sugar. Then she popped upstairs to look at herself in her dressing-table mirror. She was tempted to apply lipstick, but she resisted.

On her return to the garden, she found Jan recumbent on the ground, his legs crossed, one hand behind his head, the other holding a blade of grass that he chewed. He smiled broadly at her as she placed the tea things on the table.

'Are you all right down there?' she asked. She felt bemused, but she could not say why. Perhaps because Albert had not been one for lying around chewing grass. Albert had been anything but nonchalant.

'I am perfectly all right. Dorothea, do you fear this war?' he said.

'I hoped there wouldn't be another one. We all did, surely?'

'Of course. But it was always coming, I think. It was going to happen sooner or later. And now it has, and we must fight again for the good.'

'I hope we'll win. All of us. Somehow! It's really starting now, isn't it? Churchill in charge at last . . . it makes it all seem more real somehow. You feel that something will *happen* now. And you Polish chaps arriving. But we need a miracle. Don't we?'

'We need a miracle. And yes, the war it is coming. Hitler will not stop short.'

'Will there be one, do you think? A miracle?'

'I don't know,' said Jan, and for the first time he sounded sad.

'Are you afraid?' she asked him.

'In my heart lies hatred. I want to kill these Nazis. The biggest pleasure, no, the next biggest pleasure in my life is killing Nazis.'

'Have you killed any yet?'

'Yes.'

'Really? Is that murder?'

'No. It is justice. Those monsters have destroyed my country. They kill children, they kill women, like you, women in their gardens, in the fields, they shoot down, there and then. They forced me to flee my homeland and so they should expect me to kill them. They destroy my country. I have no mercy.'

'I see. I'm sorry, Jan. It's all so bleak. And all these soldiers returning from France. The newspapers can dress it up how they like, but it's a defeat, surely?'

'Defeat? No. A tactical withdrawal, I have heard it said. Many are rescued, don't forget. They can gather themselves, rearm themselves, start again. Like me, leaving *Polska*, getting here eventually, my men and I, all of us with one aim, to kill the bastards that took over our country. Dorothea, has my fighting talk alarmed you?' He sat up, discarding his blade of grass.

'No, I'm not scared. I've given up being scared. I've feared so much in my life, and my worst fears came true. The spell of fear has been broken somewhat. There's no fear left in me.'

'That is hard talk for a woman.'

'I am weary, but that's all.'

'World-weary?'

'Yes, I suppose so. Nothing much shocks or surprises or delights me any more.'

'Nothing?' He moved closer to her, and perched at her feet like a dog seeking affection.

'Don't you know that feeling?' said Dorothy.

'I think I do. But I don't like it.' He frowned when she shrugged. 'You do like it? You like being, in Polish is *cynik*. Is it the same in English?'

'It is. But I'm not a cynic.'

'But yes, you are *cyniczny*. It's understandable. Hard times bring hard reactions. This is war. This is life, all our wars and battles. Nobody will blame you.'

'Blame me?'

'For feeling as you do. You are not alone, Dorothea. Not you.' He put an odd emphasis on the last word.

'You say that . . . are you alone?'

'In my thoughts and my heart, yes. But I am surrounded by men, some of them boys, who look to me, who listen to me, who rely on me. In that way I am not alone.'

Dorothy was suddenly very aware that Jan was a mere inch or two from her knees, which were bare and quivering. Really, it was . . . inappropriate. Why on earth had she not put stockings on? She tried to pull her skirt down a little, but Jan appeared not to notice her discomfiture.

'But you are lonely?' she asked.

'As you are,' he replied.

'Loneliness can be a good thing. Sometimes.'

'How is this?'

'It makes one think properly, and understand things. When you have time to be alone, to think, to just cogitate.'

'Cogitate?'

'Cogitate . . . um . . . mull things over. No, that's no good . . . consider? Anyway, I think we are all essentially lonely, don't you? Nobody can really understand another's mind. We're all inside our own heads and minds and hearts. But that's how it has to be. We can only reach out so far to others. Maybe our fingertips will meet somebody else's, and that will be a beautiful moment. But it can never be more than fingertips.'

The squadron leader was examining his hands. Dorothy felt as if she had stopped breathing. She inhaled deeply, and sighed.

'You are a philosopher,' he said at length.

'Goodness me, no. I'm just a woman with time to think. Mundane tasks lend themselves well to thinking. Washing, ironing, mending.'

'You are "just a woman"?'

'Yes.'

'But a thoughtful woman. A woman of intelligence. You see in clearness where others do not.'

'No.'

'I think so.'

They lapsed into silence, Jan resuming his prostration at her feet. He took up another blade of grass.

'This is nice, Jan. To sit quietly and not have to talk.'

The sun was beginning to sink, casting a golden glow over the Long Acre, over Dorothy's garden, over Jan as he lay now on his stomach, examining the earth beneath him. He looks like a child, she thought.

'I dislike too much talk,' said Jan. 'Too much of talk is nonsense. With you there is exception. But almost always I prefer my own company.'

'Yes. I understand. Where did you grow up?'

'In a small village. Near Krakow.'

'Yes, of course. You told me on the day we met. I'd not heard of it before.'

'As I had not heard of Lincoln before arriving here.'

'You lived with your parents?'

'I lived with my mother. The woman I called mother. I had no father. He was never known to me.'

'Ah, you said. Forgive me. But what do you mean, you *called* her your mother?'

'And so we get to it.' Jan shook his head. 'She took me as her own child. My true mother was young when she became pregnant. Young and not married. I don't know too much about what happened. I was lucky, I have been told, to have been born. If you understand. I was brought up by my aunt, my mother's elder sister, a widow. My mother left the village, she never returned. I have not heard from her.'

'My goodness. But your aunt? Was she good to you?'

'Of course. Yes. She loved me. I called her *matka*. Mother. I was safe, I was fed and clothed and educated. I was bright. She had more children, after me. Two girls. But I do not regard them as my sisters.'

'Why ever not?'

'Because they were not the children of my mother. You understand? She left me, my mother, it doesn't matter who with. She did not want me. I was a shame. I am a person with no roots.' He sat up, stretched and stood.

She looked up at him. 'But she was your real mother's sister, you said, the woman who brought you up? Not so far removed from your roots.'

'But still removed. That is enough. I wanted to be with my mother. Ever since I can remember, since I could understand. If I was naughty, I would hear, "You are like your mother!" It was not said in cruelty, you understand. But it was said. My mother was not loved, you see, she was not respected for having a baby outside of marriage. I think she had to leave. But she should have taken me with her. She chose not to.' He sat in the wooden chair opposite Dorothy, sighed and looked deeply into her eyes.

'Thank you for sharing these things with me, Jan,' she said.

'We all need a friend, no?'

It felt as though the night would never fall, and Dorothy didn't want it to, but the sun finally dropped all the way below the horizon, and stars and planets announced themselves one by one, prompting her to rummage around in her kitchen for a candle. She brought it outside in tremulous hands. As soon as Jan had lit it with his cigarette lighter, moths and indeterminate insects busied themselves flying into the flame, their tiny bodies fizzling and dropping beside the candle. Dorothy and Jan looked on in speechless fascination, powerless to prevent the deaths. They heard owls in the distant woods, small scurryings in the hedges, and the eerie night-time rustle of the birch trees.

Jan rose to leave at thirty-two minutes past ten, and she rose with him, mirroring his movement. He did not say when he would return, but he held Dorothy's hands in his and kissed them, first one, then the other. She stared at him. His kiss on her mouth, when it came, was the most alive thing she had ever known. His lips moved soft and hard on hers and she felt a rush of white heat, like nothing she had ever imagined. His teeth were like tight, hard pearls. She found herself, against all her sense of propriety, running the tip of her tongue over them. And as if waking from a stupefied and tropical dream, she stiffened, she became aware of the facts. Her hands rose up and she pushed at his chest, unsure, panic rising in her like vomit. He drew back, took her hands in his again and smiled at her. He said he was sorry. Mute, Dorothy shook her head. But she tried to smile at him, until her lips trembled and her cheeks stiffened. She felt like a young girl, sickened by the shock of her very first kiss.

They walked together to her front gate, and he took her hand in his as though they were taking a lovers' stroll past a duck pond. He whispered goodnight and rubbed her arm reassuringly. She thought he winked at her, but in the failing light it was hard to tell. She watched the Polish man and his bicycle disappear into the darkening night, slipping away from her like an apparition.

She stood alone for many minutes, staring after him into the gloom.

9

13th September 1947

Dear Marion,

I write to thank you for your visit last week, it was lovely to spend time with you and Lionel again. Peter had a marvellous time too. So nice to play tennis once more. We made a grand set, didn't we? Since your departure I have been bottling and jamming fruit, we have a bumper crop this year. And the weather has been so hot! I think of Denis always at this time of year, how he loved his fruit! And his tennis, of course. Peter played terribly well, didn't he? He grows more and more like Denis with each day that passes. Very soon he will be off to university, and I don't mind admitting, dear Marion, that I shall miss him dreadfully.

Do visit us again, dear, any time you can manage it, and please give my love to Lionel. I hope his tooth has stopped playing him up? And that your headaches are subsiding? Headaches are such a trial.

Yours, with love,
Hilda

(The first letter I found at the Old and New, and I can't remember in which book I found it. It's not the most fascinating of letters, but it has a sweet poignancy, and I took it home to begin my collection, which is now housed in Mrs

Sinclair's suitcase. I have formed a mental picture of Hilda, her teenage son Peter, her dead husband Denis. I see her with her hair scraped back in a bun, I see her face hot and red as she throws herself into jam-making. But I don't think it helps.)

There are changes in Jenna, changes only I notice. Hair not brushed so well, make-up clumsily applied, or missing altogether – something I thought I would never see. Her clothes are creased, her skin is dry and flaky across her nose. Her cheeks are hollowing, and she has shadows under her eyes, grey-purple shadows that speak silently, I think, of guilt. Of regret. Sleep-dust litters the corners of her eyes. These changes are subtle, you understand. She has hitherto been impeccably presented, and now she is less than impeccable. Now she is more like me. She is a seven out of ten.

I know exactly how she feels, and I know how much it hurts, though the circumstances were different.

It was at university. I hooked up with a student who was good-looking, clever and funny. I'll spare his blushes and keep his name to myself. I felt flattered by his attentions, and I fell in love, I thought. It was fun. It was bloody brilliant, in fact. Until my period was two weeks late. Panic. A solitary late-afternoon trip to Boots. A long wait overnight (because in those days you needed to test your first urine of the day). Two pink stripes. Not one, which is what I wanted, but two, very clearly, very pinkly. There was little discussion between myself and the handsome student. Just a conviction that it 'might be best to terminate'. 'We' were too young. 'We' were career minded. 'We' had no intention of . . . so I visited the GP, then the clinic, discreetly, swiftly, alone. Handsome Student said he was 'grateful'. I broke up with him.

I've never told anybody else about my termination. I've never felt the need to.

Does Philip notice the differences in Jenna? Surely he must. Does he *know*? Perhaps Jenna bled for days, prompting concern, which led to a confession? Perhaps she is still in pain? I hope not. And yet I feel hardened, somehow. Something has changed between Jenna and me.

I shouldn't have helped her. It was a mistake. It was all too raw, too close to my own experience. I could have told her it was something I had been through too; I could have told her in the car as I drove her to the clinic, or even on the way home. I understand, I could have said. It will be all right in the end. She would have nodded, maybe smiled. Instead, she smoked a cigarette, holding it outside the car window, and we spoke barely at all.

I can see that Jenna now wishes she had confided in anybody else but me. She's done her best to avoid me since the very day after the clinic. I try to be kind; I make her tea, take it to her wherever she is in the shop; I once went to hug her, because she looked so very sad. But there was no hug. Now, we speak only when we have to, in clipped, purposeful sentences. Neither of us alludes to that day. She doesn't look at me. I want to help, but I'm not sure how to, I'm not sure what to say. It is so much simpler to do these things alone.

Babunia's care home is serene and hushed. There are pretty gardens behind the building, and the house itself is reassuringly small. It smells nice. The nurses and carers are uniformly professional and kind. Dad and I, and Babunia, chose the home together, and I know we chose the right one. It's a pity it's not a little closer, but a thirty-minute drive is not such a big deal.

I have telephoned ahead, and I am met in the entrance hall by a woman who introduces herself as Suzanne. I don't remember meeting her on my previous visits.

'I'm the new Entertainments Manager,' she explains, 'but I do all sorts, really. I wanted to meet you. Your grandmother and I have formed something of a rapport.' Suzanne tells me what I already know – Babunia is the 'darling' of the home. She is no trouble, and not even incontinent yet. Probably she never will be. Dignity, that's what she has kept hold of, Suzanne tells me, glowing with pride, as though she is talking about a high-achieving niece.

'Can I see her?'

'Yes, come on, I'll take you down to her room.'

I follow Suzanne, who is slim and wears a purple dress with purple high-heeled shoes. She has masses of thick red hair, walks with a feminine wiggle, and it's impossible to guess her age. We reach my grandmother's room and Suzanne knocks. When there is no reply, she slowly opens the door.

'Dorothea?' she calls.

Babunia is sitting in her armchair, her back to the door, facing the large bay window. The garden is filled with flower beds, which look pretty in the height of summer, but are fading a little now that it's August. There are small fruit trees, a bird table, wooden seats. I look at her. She does not turn round. She is so still, she may be asleep. She may be dead.

Suzanne stands back to let me pass into the room.

But I hesitate.

'Go ahead,' Suzanne says, smiling at me kindly.

'I don't want to upset her,' I whisper. 'She's so . . . vulnerable.'

'Why would you upset her? She'll be delighted to see you.'

I slowly walk towards my grandmother and stop beside her chair, looking down at her grey hair, which is in her habitual neat chignon. She slowly inclines her head towards me and I smile at her. She opens her mouth and struggles to speak, tears pooling in her green eyes as she searches my face. She looks utterly dismayed.

I had not expected this. I've stayed away too long, a month is too long. I should come every week, as I used to do.

'Who are you?' she says.

Despite our reassurances that I am her granddaughter, Babunia continues to ask me who I am. She wants to know what I am doing here. It feels like an accusation. I can see real fear in her eyes, which is horrible.

Suzanne and I sit either side of her, holding a hand each.

'It's me, Roberta. I . . . I love you.' It seems an odd thing to say in the circumstances; but it's the right thing to say, all the same.

She shakes her head, and Suzanne tries to explain. But Babunia, panicked and tearful, is not listening. So we sit, the three of us, in silence.

When, eventually, Babunia dozes off, Suzanne and I converse in whispers.

'She's not always like this,' I tell her.

'I know,' says Suzanne. 'Only yesterday we were doing a crossword together and she got some of the answers.'

'Why doesn't she know me?' I ask.

Suzanne shrugs. 'I don't know. She gets easily confused some days,' she says. 'You must try not to worry.'

I am at work when I get one of the calls I have been dreading.

'Is that Miss Pietrykowski?' says a female voice, navigating my surname with some difficulty.

'Yes.'

'Oh, hello, I'm a staff nurse from the ward where your father . . . Mr—'

'Yes? Is he all right? What's happened?'

Philip, talking to a female customer, looks over her shoulder at me and raises his eyebrows enquiringly.

'He's okay, Miss Pietry—'

'Look, I know it's a bloody mouthful. Why don't you just call me Roberta?'

'It is rather, Roberta, yes. Thank you. Your dad had to come into hospital, an ambulance brought him in an hour or so ago. He's all right, a little uncomfortable, but stable.'

'But what's the matter?'

'Breathing problems. He's on oxygen. The doctors are hoping to change his medication and send him home again, but not today. I know his wish is to be at home as much as possible.'

Dad made me swear he will be allowed to die at home, and I have promised him. But I don't think he's going to be dying any time soon, as I frequently remind him.

I thank the nurse, finish the phone call, and tell Sophie I must go. I grab my bag and jacket and, as I hurry to the door, Philip calls after me to take all the time I need.

10

Mrs Compton smiled at Dorothy as they sipped tea and avoided, as usual, talk of any importance. Dorothy – also as usual – had not actually invited her visitor, and she wished the older woman gone. She was trying not to look at her, not to gaze too long into those eyes that were as cold and hard as a bathroom in winter. Perhaps if she stayed silent long enough, Mrs Compton might take the hint, and go away. How Dorothy wished now for the simple presence of her two girls, with their loud, frank talk, their apparent lack of fear, and their no-nonsense attitude to life. Dorothy was 'too nice', they often told her. You just have to stick up for yourself from time to time. It won't do you no harm. But the girls were across the fields, at the North Barn, up to their elbows in cow shit, straw, milk, calves, cauls, blood. And Dorothy wasn't sure what 'sticking up' for oneself could really mean.

She had no idea why Mrs Compton had called round again so soon after her last visit. The woman was asking her inane questions. Was she coping? How was the wound on her tummy? Healing up by now? Her face was certainly looking better, and she would not scar, anybody could see that. Such a relief, wasn't it?

Dorothy gave perfunctory, correct answers, and drank her tea.

'And how are you keeping, nowadays?' said Mrs Compton, with crushing predictability.

Dorothy gave whatever answer was expected, barely regis-
tering the words. She had not seen Jan for three days.
Something was happening, there were aeroplanes coming and
going. There were rumours that the Germans were poised to
attack, they were going to gas the entire country, they were
going to invade any day, and soon. They were slaughtering
people on the streets of Warsaw. They were 'rounding up' the
Jewish people. Perhaps in Krakow too?

Dorothy didn't join in with the rumours. She laundered,
she sewed, she cooked, she tended her hens, she thought
about how much she wanted to see Jan, she wished for him
to appear in her wash-house doorway, solid and strong,
looming through the moisture like a saviour.

'The war news isn't good,' announced Mrs Compton.

Dorothy made no reply. She could think of none.

'I reckon we're for it,' the older woman went on, leaning
forward, inviting Dorothy to speak, to open up, to smile at
her.

Sullen, rude, stand-offish, Dorothy didn't care. She knew
she would be described as all these and more later, in the
village, Mrs Compton shaking her head, gossiping with the
other women. Dorothy knew she was something of a mystery,
and therefore unlikeable. She knew she was without friends.

Eventually, Mrs Compton rose to leave, promising to
return the following week.

'There's really no need,' said Dorothy in what she hoped
was a determined, assured tone.

'Oh, I like to keep up with all my ladies!'

'But I am not one of your ladies. I am my own lady. Now
please go, and don't bother to return. Ever. You nosy old
witch. You baby-stealer.'

Of course, Dorothy didn't say these things. She only
smiled a dry, scornful smile. And said over and over to

herself, in her head, her head that seemed to be stuffed with cotton wool, with wood shavings, with pure white flour: Leave me, woman, leave me alone.

A further week passed with still no word from Jan. Dorothy, resigned, deduced that she had put him off forever with her reaction to their kiss. Perhaps he thought her immature, or neurotic. Perhaps he thought she did not like him and no longer wished to see him. Perhaps he had simply not enjoyed kissing her as much as he hoped he would.

Oh, it was disappointing, and she berated herself, over and over. What else did she expect? What else did she deserve?

But in the end, he came. There was the confident knock at the door, another bunch of wild flowers, another smile that seemed to welcome her, even though he was the guest. He entered the kitchen, he put down his hat, he loosened the top button on his tunic as he took the chair she offered him at the table. She wanted to ask him why he had not visited for almost a whole fortnight. But she could not. It was not her business. It was not important. So she made tea, while he watched her wordlessly. She wished he would speak, though she half enjoyed the intensity of the silence between them. It was another hot day and he rolled up the sleeves on his tunic, revealing brown, lean, strong forearms.

Dorothy tried not to notice. Really! It was all so inappropriate but . . . oh, heavens. It was out of her control, and she had not admitted to herself, despite her longings, what had happened to her. She had not yet accepted the state she was in.

His arms were poetry.

'I bring news,' said Jan, eventually, after clearing his throat and taking a cup and saucer from Dorothy's hands. 'Thank you.' He sipped.

'Good or bad news?' said Dorothy.

Now they were talking, it was all right again. She could now be the polite, interested, middle-aged, educated woman, befriending the foreigner who could speak her language so well, and was a long way from home. Propriety came rushing through her door.

'Ah. That is for your own interpretation.'

'It's not good so far. Go on.'

'I am leaving Lodderston. Not just me. The men. My men. We have formed a proper squadron.'

'Where are you going?'

'Kent. Closer to the fighting.'

'It makes sense.'

'It makes perfect sense, dear lady, no?'

'Would you like a biscuit? I made them this morning. A little lacking in sugar, but they're perfectly acceptable. At least, Nina always says so.' She slid the plate across the table.

'Thank you.' Jan took a biscuit, ate it quickly and took another.

'When do you leave?' Dorothy asked, not wanting to hear the answer.

'Today.'

'Today! Oh. I see. Things happen so suddenly these days, don't they?'

'I apologise. I should have let you know this was likely. But we have been busy, training, flying, negotiating with the RAF.'

'No, no, please don't apologise. You owe me nothing, Jan. And I did think something like this would happen.'

'It's going to get worse before it gets better. You do realise that, Dorothea?'

'Of course. I'm not a fool.'

'No. You are not a fool.'

There was a pause.

'I hope not,' she said, to fill the silence.

'So I must take my leave. But I vow to return, whenever I can. I will return to visit my friend in her little house made of bricks.'

'You make me sound like a character from a fairy tale.'

'You are.'

Dorothy felt herself redden, all over, a strange, hot, thrilling rash seeping over her body. Her spine tingled.

'I see,' she said. 'Well, I'll certainly be here. I hope.'

'That is good, as it should be. Now I must go. Thank you for your tea.'

'You have to go right now?'

'Yes. I'm sorry.'

'But you'll be safe, won't you?'

Jan leaned across the table, took Dorothy's face in both hands and looked into her eyes. She dared not blink.

'I give you my word,' he said, and let her go.

So he would not kiss her again.

He stood up and put his hat back on. Dorothy walked once again to the front gate with him, and watched him mount his bicycle.

'But shall you truly be safe?' she said.

She put her hand on his arm. She wondered at his bodily strength, his solidity. She fantasised their skin might meld together and they could disappear into the red and bloody safety of each other's bodies. But she had no right to think about this man in such crude terms. She was a married woman.

'But yes,' he said, 'I have told you. I have good luck, always. Polish luck. Can I write to you? Please?' And at last he sounded not like the confident 30-year-old man he always projected, but like a young boy. He placed his other hand over hers.

'Yes, of course. But I don't write letters,' she replied, blushing again; he was rather too good at embarrassing her.

'Why do you not write letters?'

'I don't like the way I write them.'

'You are a strange lady. Now is a good time to make an exception, no?'

'Perhaps.'

He removed his hand and looked down at hers where it still rested on his arm. Hastily, she used it to tuck a stray hair behind her ear, flushing even more fiercely. He seemed not to notice.

'We leave in two hours, three at most. We shall fight, eventually, when your compatriots wake up and see what we can achieve. Perhaps in France, perhaps in England. So I must return and prepare. I got away, to say goodbye to you, my new friend. But I must now return quickly. Look out for me. We will fly over. You must wave to me. I will be in front.'

Jan started to ride off. He looked back and waved, which made him wobble. 'Mrs Sinclair?' he shouted over his shoulder. 'Your biscuits definitely need more sugar!'

Dorothy laughed.

But when he was gone, the laughter drained from her throat, tears gathered in her eyes, and real fear crept into her blood, despite her claim to no longer feel it – an idle boast, of course. And so already she was no longer Dorothea to him. Their fledgling intimacy had taken a step backwards, and it was her fault. She was his 'new friend'. She was Mrs Sinclair again. Fear she would conquer. Because if he could, she could. He had good luck, he claimed. Was there such a thing as Polish luck? Such a notion! But it was something to cling to. He would be safe. There was no room for fear.

She returned to her kitchen and, against all her thrifty impulses, she broke up the remaining biscuits, carried them on the rosebud serving plate out into the garden, and scattered what remained on to the ground for her hens.

Dorothy lingered in the garden, slowly gathering in her laundry. It was stale-dry and stiffened by the sun. The sky was pure blue, and the sun beat down on her like a public flogging, so she stripped down to her blouse and skirt, and undid her two top buttons, confident that she would not be visited again today. She removed her stockings – something she had done often this summer – and she felt the sun's fierce heat on her bare legs, like the caress of a giant.

She admitted to herself that she was enraptured. Alone in her garden, unwatched, unshackled, she could open up to herself, and she did. She wanted to kiss Jan, hold Jan, she wanted Jan to—

She just wanted Jan.

And then, hearing the distant roar as the squadron of Hurricanes started its engines, Dorothy ceased her work and looked towards Lodderston. She left her laundry and the sanctity of her garden and wandered out into the Long Acre, where she watched as the Hurricanes appeared from beyond the elm trees on the far side of the field, one by one, and fell into formation. She shielded her eyes from the sun, and within seconds the large formation was heading her way. The Hurricane in front suddenly dropped, low, lower, flying towards her as though to crash, and for one awful moment it seemed to Dorothy that he *was* going to crash, and suddenly it was that day in May all over again, only this time Dorothy felt no need to end her life. And of course it was Jan – in absolute control, as one would expect – and he waved, he actually waved to her, and he was so low that she could even see his large grin, his gloved hand waving to and fro like a mechanical puppet.

This was their time, theirs alone, and she felt this moment could never be taken from her. This smiling, gentle man, flying over her, was preparing to kill other smiling, gentle men, to actually kill and maim and injure other men. And he was looking forward to it, she knew. He had already killed.

It was all so peculiar. He was brave, or he was evil, or perhaps he was both – one doesn't necessarily preclude the other, she thought, does it? – and Jan was gone, off ahead like the lead in a skein of geese. And Dorothy waited and watched until the whole growling squadron had flown over. And soon it was out of earshot, it had flown beyond the horizon, and she knew that she might never see the squadron leader again. He could be gone forever, snatched out of her life, out of their burgeoning friendship, after such a short beginning – like Sidney, her darling little purple-blue-dead Sidney. Jan could be plucked from the sky by a capricious quirk of fate, or more likely just a belligerent German. Things happen because they can, he had said, and although this idea should have been a comfort, it truly wasn't.

Fighting her tears, she took down the remaining rows of laundry and folded it, pressed it, aired it, and while performing these familiar tasks she trawled through each and every moment of her time with Jan – their conversing, their kissing, their dancing. She vowed to pray for him every day, to pray to that wide, empty sky that Jan occupied, even if God did not.

Jan saw her, a small figure, not among the white sheets and pillowcases and tablecloths billowing in the breeze in her garden like gigantic white flags, but standing starkly in the field like a lonely scarecrow. He had wanted her to surrender, this strange Englishwoman he might never see again. He had forewarned his men that he would be flying down towards her garden to keep a promise, and he ignored the smiles, nudges and winks that this prompted. It was an open secret that their leader had fallen in love with this (widowed?) Englishwoman, for he was a soft bastard, despite being a hard bastard. They indulged him, and made jokes over their radios as he swooped down, ahead of the rest of the squadron. He turned off his set, because this was his moment and hers. He wanted to be alone with her. He saw her face turned up like a child's as she stood, minute and alone, in the field, looking at the sky, expectant and awed. He smiled and waved, and he was convinced she had clearly seen him and waved back.

Once past her, past her garden and the surrounding fields, he allowed himself a sob, two sobs, strangling a third before switching back on his radio and telling his men to be vigilant, to be safe; they would all be needed in the coming days, weeks, possibly months. God forbid, but yes, perhaps even for years to come. If they were to spot any Luftwaffe aircraft on this journey – which was unlikely, but possible – they were to shoot the Germans down; they were to show no mercy.

He knew it hardly needed saying, but still he rallied his men. 'Remember,' he said in his native tongue, 'the Nazi bastards deserve everything they get.'

11

Dear Dorothea,

So this is the first of the letters I am to write to you. I hope there will be many more – although, of course, that means we shall be apart. But better that than dead, no? Did you see me wave to you last Tuesday? You looked so sad. I hope you are happier now. I would have written sooner to you, but every day there is something to do.

Do not fear for me. I have not yet met danger. My men and I are taking part in exercises, always we are asked to do that which we can do already. It is frustrating! And we are humiliated. But we are not allowed to argue. But I do argue, because I speak English. I reason, but to no good yet. I do not give up. Already they are sick of my pestering. Some of these people, they are arrogant. Only English people can fly, they think. Oh, forgive me, but I am cross. But we shall succeed in the end.

We live in nice quarters here. Food is good, lots of it, beds comfortable. I have my own room, of course, quiet, at the end of a corridor. I can shut the door and shut out the world, and write to you. I wait for your letter,

Jan

2nd July 1940

My dear Dorothea,

*I have had no word from you, but I trust you received
my letter. I now send another. Badly written, I expect, but I
am tired. I argue still. Sometimes I wonder if I should have
bothered coming to England. But I had nowhere else to go. Still
it is disappointing. My men are in fury. But what to do? The
wheels of English minds turn slowly, it seems. They do not trust
us, but I think they should be glad of our help, our experience,
our skills. They now talk of giving my squadron an English
leader. So it seems even my English is not good enough.*

*But what of you, dear friend? What is happening? My
guess is that you carry on as you were? And the girls?
They still work hard, still amuse you? They are good young
women, good company for my friend, lonely in her red
house, hiding in the Lincolnshire fields. I think about you
often. I do not know when I shall return to see you, but I
hope it will be soon.*

I miss you. Please write to me.
Jan

6th August 1940

Dear Dorothea,

*Sometimes it is easier to write down on paper our deep
thoughts and feelings than it is to speak of them. I have to
tell you that the few weeks we enjoyed were the best of my
life. Despite everything that has happened, is happening, and
will happen, whatever it is that brought me to England and
to you is something I will always be grateful for. I have had
no time to write. Every day it seems we must practise, practise,
practise. And for why? The British officers, they do not like
me, I know. My men are desperate to fly, to fight the
Germans. We need combat. I think soon we will, they will*

see they are wasting our talents. The days are long and most are warm and sunny, so there are many battles. The Luftwaffe gives the RAF no peace. But today has been quieter and all have had opportunity for rest.

I am scared, Dorothea. For when you have found the one great joy and comfort in your life, it is hard to say goodbye. So there will be no goodbyes for us. I will return, my death only can prevent it. Can you write? Often? As often as you can? Until I can visit again?

I do not want to say goodbye, so I will not. This is temporary. We shall sit and talk in your garden, we will talk again of this God we do not believe and we will drink your nice tea.

Until then, think of me often, as I will think of you.

Your Jan

12th August 1940

Dear Dorothea,

I hope you received my last letter? Finally, we are in operation, in real combat! Our squadron has been recognised and we fly every day. My men are happy at last. And I am in charge. Remember I told you they wanted an English leader? Other Polish squadrons have a Smith or a Jones, but ours has Jan Pietrykowski. I am trusted! Already we have shot down Germans. I shot down a Stuka myself, I chased it from the sky. It was a moment of pure joy for me. The RAF has suffered great losses, no doubt you have heard the news. Each day we trust we will survive, but for many, they wake to their last day. I cannot see how this can end well. Yet we must believe. The Luftwaffe is strong and persistent and we cannot easily match it. What this will develop for my men I dare not think, nor do I want to think. We can but fight, and hope, and at last we do, and it is so much better than those stupid exercises. Yet already I write too many letters to mothers and fathers of dead sons.

I tell you a little of my day. This is what we must do. Awake and out of bed at four o'clock, half past four. Early, but necessary. We eat breakfast, good bacon, eggs. Sometimes kippers. Always toast with butter, and lots of tea, only not as nice as yours. We go to the dispersal hut and we wait here, we wait for the telephone to ring. The call can come at any time. Sometimes we are waiting for hours, on bad weather days. I play poker with the men, I win often. But play only with matchsticks. We play chess. We lay on the grass, we have deckchairs, we read newspapers, books. Rainy days, clouded days are the best, we get rest, perhaps we do not fly at all. But mostly the weather is fine and we go out early, often twice, three, four times, any time. My men are exhausted, they sleep when they can, if on leave, they sleep, all day, all night. But there is little leave. Sleep has become a luxury. Some men cry at night, I hear them. I try to comfort, but the fear and despair are too strong and not until morning can they again take hold of their courage and eat, and fly, and fight. When we scramble, some men are sick. We all leap from our skin when the telephone rings. The little click before the ring begins, it is a bad sound. All are nervous, waiting is horrible. You must imagine this.

Yet we get good hits. Yesterday my squadron shot down two Stukas. A good day. One of them was mine, as I told you. Yet I find myself sad at causing death. I don't know why. The Stuka crashed into the sea. Nothing left of the German crew who I thought I hated. Do I hate? Am I a murderer? I do not know. I can only say I am a fighter.

How is life with you? And the skies above you? Has harvesting begun yet? Aggie and Nina, they continue as normal? They still enjoy the music box?

I must finish now, Dorothea. There is much to do and so little time to do it. I have reports to write. I keep the squadron diary too, which needs to be written while the day is fresh in my memory. It is half past one in the morning. I am tired, but I am alive. Do not fear.

Until next time,
Your Jan

19th August 1940

Dear Jan,

You may not believe me, but it is so. This is the first letter I have written, aside from the three or four I sent to my mother after my marriage. I don't count those. I apologise for not writing to you sooner. I have no excuses other than my own stupidity and reticence. Things that are written down are so permanent and that always frightens me somehow. But I write to you now in friendship and trust.

Thank you for all your kind words to me in your letters, which come thick and fast and are a joy to receive. The last few weeks have been a special time that I shall always remember. You are a good man, Jan, far too good for a woman like me. Please don't trouble yourself with thoughts of me while you are down there in the thick of things. You have more than enough on your plate. I am absolutely not worthy of the depth of feeling you express. I am conscious of your feelings and I should like to return them. But it is hopeless.

I trust that you will remain safe. I hope and believe that you will. Any time you can, if you get enough leave, please visit. The girls and I will be pleased to see you.

Dorothy

25th August 1940

My dear Dorothea,

Your letter was a joy to receive, all 225 words of it. But you are wrong. You are worthy. And there is always hope. Hope is all we have now – everyone, all of us. I fear your cities will be next, of that I am certain. Did you not say that your girls are from London? They have families living there? The Luftwaffe bombed London last night. I hope that it will not happen again. Our losses continue, but I think we are still enough, with the RAF, to fight. And your Winston Churchill says such good things about the pilots (the Polish ones too). You may have heard him on the wireless? We are become heroes! Not murderers at all. Our mood is high, despite death all around us. And it is a miracle that we seem to be holding on. But, of course, everything has its price.

What of you? Do you continue with your laundry, your sewing? You are a woman of industry. I think if you don't work, if you are not busy, you will allow yourself to think too much, and fret?

Now I must write to a mother in Polska. Her son died yesterday, lost in the sea. I do not know if my letters arrive. But I must send. I wish for courage to do a good job and be a small comfort to the boy's mother.

Your Jan

16th September 1940

My dear Dorothea,

So autumn arrives, and with it a change of tactic, as I thought. Do you recall I said this would happen?

Are you safe and well? I doubt very much the Luftwaffe is interested in bombing Mrs Dorothea Sinclair in her little cottage, lost among the fields of Lincolnshire. But you must be vigilant, being so close to the aerodrome, as the Germans will attack anyone – women, children, it means nothing to them. I told you of that. It has happened. These Nazis, these Germans, are cowards. But they are dangerous cowards. Yesterday, we are told, was a good day for the RAF, we fight on, we score hits. The Luftwaffe are not having it easy.

I hope to get some leave in the next few weeks, perhaps in October. If that is so, could I visit you? To sit with you again in your cottage is a dream I hold dear.

Until then,
Your Jan

20th September 1940

Dear Jan,

Poor Aggie has had word that her fiancé has been killed. His name was Roger and he was a pilot in a Spitfire squadron. I didn't even know she was engaged to be married. She met her young man shortly before leaving London, and she was in love, she tells me. She is desolate. Nina and I try to cheer her up, but she talks of going home to London – a thought to make one shudder in light of all that is happening there. She will be far better off staying here and enjoying the relative safety of the country. She still goes to the dances and the pub regularly.

Aggie's news made me think about Albert, my husband, and whether the same will happen to him. Although, of course, he is in the army. As we are still married, I suppose I would receive a telegram? I think of you, every day. I must confess, I've started to pray for you, prayers of a sort. Is that silly?

The weather grows colder, and I can smell winter. The trees are becoming bare and such a wind blows, howling around the house at night. Please visit in October. I can make up the bed in the spare room, it is rather small but comfortable enough. Do let me know in advance, if that is possible? So I can make all the preparations. Do you think you may have leave over Christmas time? A long way off, I know, but we need to look forward to things.

Nina is well, although she took a funny turn yesterday evening. She was trying to cheer Aggie up by getting her to dance – you know how those girls love to dance – well, Nina keeled over, out cold for a minute or two. We put her head between her legs, and later we got her to bed and I made her drink a hot toddy. Aggie tells me she slept well. And this morning, when they both went off to work, Nina was cheery enough. She works too hard, I think.

Bombs fell on Lodderston aerodrome last week. Nothing much – some damage, we hear – and two ground crew were killed. The noise was indescribable, so how it must be in London or Liverpool, I cannot imagine.

I have no other news. Mostly day follows night here, and things go on in the old familiar pattern. I suppose there's a comfort in that.

Dorothy

12

For my best friend, Charlotte, on her 30th birthday,
because she also loves to shop!

(Inscription found on flyleaf of Penguin Classics edition of *Madame Bovary* by Gustave Flaubert. Evidently, Charlotte does not love to read. Inscription aside, as new copy. Placed on classic fiction shelf in entrance lobby, price £2.50. I bought it myself after a few weeks and have since read it twice.)

D ad was okay in the end, thank God. After three days in hospital, during which his breathing stabilised, he was allowed home. I visit him each day after work. He needs rest, and plenty of it, but he won't let me 'do' for him. He never will. We chat, drink tea, eat crumpets or muffins – 'There's only so much brown rice even a gravely ill man can eat!' – we watch the news, we watch *Pointless* and he always beats me. But I know that I cannot ask my dad any questions about the letter. It isn't fair to bother him, and it would be nothing short of cruel to potentially turn his already troubled world on its head. Yet I wonder . . . I wonder if his world *would* be turned upside down? Or would it be mine?

And my visit to my grandmother, although it was a pleasure to see her once her initial confusion had passed, was unproductive. In the end, Suzanne left us to ourselves, and I simply sat with Babunia, holding her hand, commenting on the garden. I'm still not sure that she realised who I was.

But in subsequent visits Babunia recognises me, and smiles, and asks me when that son of hers is going to deign to visit. I am going every week, as I resolved, and it's a joy to meet up first with Suzanne, who tells me about how Babunia is getting on, the things she says, her preoccupations: these are often unfathomable, Suzanne explains, and I nod in understanding. She's always been like that, I say. I tell her I'm immensely grateful that she has taken the time to befriend my grandmother; it's a relief to have somebody looking out for her, somebody we can all trust. Suzanne says it's a pleasure. Of course, Dad wants to go – and will go with me, when he's up to it – but it's hard to think up excuses. Babunia is not a stupid woman. She might guess straight away that something is wrong; he has changed so much, and for the worse.

I have not mentioned Jan's letter, not yet, to either of them. I need to find the right time.

I am in the Old and New, the place where I am always to be found. Philip and I are undertaking the task of rearranging some of the shelves in the large old books room. He also wants the French windows to the patio to be polished, closed and locked, as it is late September, and so we are closing up the garden for winter. Jenna is not at work today. Philip explains to me she is unwell, and in bed with a whisky and hot water – a cure-all his mother always swore by. I have my own thoughts regarding this illness, but I say nothing. I hope she is okay. But she will not let me know. Our friendship, I fear, is finished, turned in on itself.

At the desk, which is manned by Sophie, a woman is

asking for me. She has a cultured voice, educated, confident. I know who she is instantly. I freeze. A surge of bad adrenaline flows through my veins, the dread-rush of certainty. I look at Philip, who looks back at me quizzically. A roar starts up in my ears, a cacophony of cursed voices. This cannot be happening. Oh no, no, no, not this, not now.

'Roberta?' calls Sophie.

'Don't worry, I'll find her,' says Francesca Dearhead.

Slow, deliberate footsteps in high-heeled shoes become more pronounced as they tick through into the back room. She has come in search of me, as I knew she would one day. And now she stands in the doorway.

Like a child, I hope that if I close my eyes this will stop. If I concentrate hard enough this won't be happening, the roaring in my body will end, here and now. But nothing stops. The roaring becomes louder.

Mrs Dearhead's scent floats around her, and it is not Febreze at all, but something expensive, and tasteful. And as I open my eyes again she is upon me, slender hands on slender hips, a queasily triumphant smile revealing even, white teeth. She seems taller than me, although she is probably around my height, elegantly dressed in a cream wool coat, her black hair immaculately styled. She is invading my personal space and I take a step backwards, intimidated.

'You . . . *shameful* little woman,' she whispers, staring at me as though I were a tarantula.

'Hang on a minute,' says Philip. He puts down his pile of books on a footstool, takes off his spectacles and glares at her. Almost imperceptibly, he moves an inch or two closer to me.

'Are you aware that this . . . employee of yours . . . has been carrying on with my husband?' says Mrs Dearhead. 'Do you know who my husband is?'

'Vaguely,' says Philip as he wipes his spectacles and puts them back on. 'Are *you* aware that this is my bookshop, and are you further aware that I do not tolerate any form of abuse, physical or verbal, towards myself or any member of my staff? Is that clear? Nor do I listen to . . . loathsome tittle-tattle.'

The few customers, formerly leafing through books, chattering, murmuring, are inexplicably quiet. There is a marked silence in the Old and New. Somebody coughs. I even think I hear a muffled 'Shh!'

'This woman deserves to be sacked!' she shouts, her composure finally slipping a little as she indicates me with a dismissive wave of her slender hand.

I find myself wondering whether she has recently touched her husband with those hands. She's a lot more attractive than I had imagined, and younger. Did they still . . .? Of course. Don't be so naive, Roberta. My God, Jenna had a point.

'I do the hiring and firing around here,' says Philip, flustered, and both myself and Francesca Dearhead stare at him, wrong-footed. Did he really say that?

She turns back to me. 'Do you have anything to say?'

'I think I do, actually.'

'Then please say it. I am all ears.'

'I am not carrying on with your husband.'

'Of course, you would deny it. But I know you are.'

'But I'm not. Whoever told you such a thing?' I know, absolutely and certainly, that my former lover would not reveal our affair to anybody, least of all to his wife. It would make no sense for him to do so. Especially now that it was over, and I had been the one to finish it.

'That's my business,' says Mrs Dearhead.

I take a deep breath. I can see she has the bit between her teeth and she's not going to give it up. I don't have much choice if I am to salvage anything even resembling dignity. 'I *was* seeing your husband. For a while. But it's over now. It's been over for some time. I can assure you that is the truth.'

'I see. Is there anything else?'

'Only that I'm sorry. I am truly very sorry. I'm not sure what happened, really. To me, I mean. It was a mistake.'

I am aware that Sophie and Jenna are in the doorway, watching us, Jenna obviously roused from her sick bed by the commotion. There's a look of fascinated, intrigued horror on their beautiful young faces. I look at Sophie. She grimaces. Jenna avoids meeting my gaze. Behind them, dear little Mrs Lucas – a regular customer with an inexhaustible appetite for second-hand Mills and Boon – is peering over their shoulders, aghast.

And Francesca Dearhead's face is calm again, her smooth, tanned skin unpuckered. She studies me, her curled lip betraying her thoughts before she voices them.

'Well. You're not quite as I pictured you. You are younger, I suppose, just about. But what else? I can't see it.'

'That's enough!' says Philip.

Jenna reddens, glaring at Philip. Sophie looks at me, raising her eyebrows.

'I really am very sorry,' I say, 'but it truly is over. And not much happened, anyway, if I'm perfectly honest. Your husband is in love with you. Not me. I'm too shallow for him. I'm no good for a man like him, not good enough, as you seem to be suggesting, and you're absolutely right about that. And if it took a stupid . . . pseudo-affair for your husband to find out where his true affections lie, and to appreciate what he already has, that's not such a bad thing. Now, if you don't mind, Mrs Dearhead, I'd like to get on with my work.'

Francesca Dearhead turns and pushes past Sophie and

Jenna and Mrs Lucas, all of whom gape after her, open-mouthed. I hear her high heels tap-tap-tapping on the flagstones in the foyer; I hear the front door open and close. A pause; then the silence breaks, customers murmur again, there are sniggers; a throat clears. Sophie and Jenna recede like discreet angels. Mrs Lucas stays a moment or two longer, then she too evaporates, and only Philip and I remain.

I can't look at him.

'Put the books down, Roberta,' he says.

And I realise I have been clinging on to a large pile throughout the whole episode, hiding behind them, barricading myself in. I am trembling, so Philip takes the books from me, and sets them on the floor. He leans towards me and suddenly he gently moves aside a stray strand of hair from my face. He looks at me warily, as one would stare at a troublesome wasp, deliberating whether to kill or rescue it. Our heads have never been so close. But I won't look away from him, I will not twist my eyes to the side like a person ashamed. Even though I *am* ashamed, horribly so, and my face must be reddened and anguished.

'Go upstairs and get a drink,' he says, looking away from me at last. 'Tell Jenna to leave you in peace.'

'Good for you,' Jenna says, handing me the brandy I have requested.

I take it, gratefully, with a shaking hand. The brandy is hot and angry in my mouth, in my throat, belly, legs.

'Good?' I say, between mouthfuls.

'You told that silly cow where to get off. That's exactly what I would have done.'

'I've been seeing her husband. She has every right to be angry.'

'But causing a scene in public like that! I'd be ashamed to make such a fool of myself. Wouldn't you?'

'Yes, of course, but she's upset, isn't she? She's half Italian, and you know what they say about Mediterranean temperaments . . . I thought she was rather cool about the whole thing, really. She just wanted to have it out with her rival. And when she discovered I'm not actually much of a rival . . . I don't know. I got the impression she was relieved, more than anything. It could have been worse.'

'Have you really been seeing him?' Jenna asks. 'Was it all true, what you said? What she said?'

'I was seeing him, kind of. But it wasn't a grand passion by any means. If that's what you're getting at.'

'He's a bit old for you, isn't he?'

'Yes. But it's over now, anyway.'

'God, it was funny. I heard her shout. I should think the whole bloody town heard it! And I just had to come down and see what all the fuss was about. You've caused quite a scandal, Roberta P.'

'Jenna?'

'Yes?'

'I wonder if I could be left alone for a few minutes. I just need to recover myself here. You know?'

Jenna looks like a child scolded in public for picking her nose, but she shrugs her shoulders nonchalantly enough. 'Of course,' she says.

And leaves me.

13

12th November 1940

My dear Dorothea,

I find myself realising today that I have not heard from you for a while. And I remember that today is your birthday. I send you many greetings. I trust all is well with you? I am satisfactory. We are kept busy trying to defend London, but it does not always go well. We are helpless at night-time, the frustration is unbearable.

I hope to be visiting you soon, perhaps the first week in December? A day, maybe two, no longer. I had no leave in October – disappointing for me, and for you, I have to hope. I am tired and I need the rest. I need time to be relaxing and spending time with my friend with her good food and tea and conversations. The room with the little bed, it sounds like a wonderful place to be. I need peace, Dorothea.

Until December,
Your Jan

The evenings were drawing in, and Dorothy was finding it difficult to sew without the aid of sunlight. She huddled under her oil lamp, she lit extra candles and she peered more closely at her work, frowning, pins in her mouth, her familiar tarnished thimble a comfortable fit on her middle finger.

She listened to Billie Holiday, she listened to the chatter of the girls, she thought about Jan, away from her, in danger, all his strength and maleness no protection against the vulnerability that threatened to take him – at any moment, day or night – one bullet, one destroyed engine, one plunge into the cold, dark sea. The possibilities haunted her.

She was making a set of antimacassars, using an old linen tablecloth with a stubborn stain she hadn't managed to wash out. She was embroidering on each one a circular rosebud pattern, using green and pink threads. This was the third; the first two were already adorning the settee. It was satisfying work. It kept her busy, and it allowed her to climb into herself, to lose herself in thoughts of Jan. For he was all she wanted to think about. The black hair, the blue eyes, the smile, the near-perfect English, the clear-thinking ideas so similar to her own. His hard-soft face, his foreign accent, faltering, polite. His mile-high laugh.

She read and reread his letters. She was keeping them in a small bundle, one on top of the other in the order she had received them, tied together with a dark blue ribbon; they nestled among Sidney's clothes in the suitcase. She had a dozen or more letters, all on pale blue paper of an ethereal thinness, all written in a neat hand, recognisably *his*, smudged here and there, all in blue ink. To see the postman open her gate, stride down the path whistling, and then laugh when she rushed to the door to relieve him of his delivery, was the highlight of her week.

'You've got it bad, love!' he would say. But there was a shrewd look behind his twinkling eyes that spoke of gossip and suspicion. Goodness only knew what tales he told of her in the village, in the pub, everybody mocking her – 'Falls over herself, she does, for letters from her Polish lover boy!' She knew she was the subject of talk among people who were friends of her husband, people who had known Bert Sinclair all his life.

What a fool she must appear to everybody.

Yet the letters arrived. She snatched them from the postman, she read them eagerly, once, twice, three times. And then the unbearable wait for the next one, occasionally punctuated by her own inadequate replies – short, but not succinct, not interesting or funny, not even particularly informative. The immense disappointment on the days when the postman failed to arrive. These were long days.

Thank God, she thought many times, for the girls. Like birds of paradise, they coloured her life. True, Aggie was more sombre these days, but she tried hard to be cheerful, and sometimes succeeded. Nina and Dorothy tried hard to rouse her, talk to her, and console her when the tears flowed. Both girls lived in daily fear of bad news from home. The bombings were continuing, and the news was no comfort. All three women listened in respectful silence to the wireless each evening. Both girls talked of visiting their families in London, but the estate could not spare them, and Dorothy was secretly glad.

Another washday, a dull mid-November morning, winter hanging over the world's window like a threadbare curtain. The girls were long gone, hiking off across the fields wrapped up in their coats, hats, scarves, gloves, boots, each with a bag of lunch prepared by Dorothy – sandwiches with fish paste, a boiled egg, slices of pickled beetroot, a Thermos of tea and, for a treat, a home-baked biscuit. It was the least Dorothy could do. She had eggs – plenty of eggs compared to most – flour, some butter. Even sugar. She always made sure now to put enough in her biscuits.

There was a breeze, cold, but strong enough for drying, if only partially. Sheets flapped and slapped on the lines, gulls and rooks circling, cawing and fighting, the clouds racing by as though late for an appointment. Hens, earth-bound like Dorothy, clucked and pecked at the hardening ground. And Dorothy, alone, was lost in hot water, in soda crystals and soap, lost in her longings. So many longings that she couldn't tell them apart, couldn't separate them any more.

Suddenly aware of a presence, she turned from the copper, wiping her hair back from her face, and there he was, a man in the doorway, a heavy-looking kitbag slung across his shoulder. He was leaning against the door frame, a cigarette protruding from his lips and the smell of the smoke breaking through the steam.

She stared.

'Hello, Dot.'

'Albert.'

Aggie and Nina returned at dusk and seemed surprised to see this man, Albert, sitting at the table drinking tea. He was brawny, muscled, yet his eyes were pale and insipid, and appeared not to focus on anything. Even so, he looked the girls up and down, lingering on Aggie.

The evening meal was a stilted affair, punctuated by awkward conversation and long, impenetrable pauses. Under Albert's unnerving scrutiny, the young women ate their dinner slowly, propriety replacing their usual abandon and appetite. Even Nina, perennially hungry, finished second. They all listened politely as he told jokes and stories none of them wanted to laugh at.

After the meal, after their tea and the daily dose of news on the wireless, the girls yawned and said an early night would be just the ticket. And Dorothy and her husband were alone in the lounge. If he noticed the changes she had made – the rearranged furniture, the crazy-patchwork cushions she had made last winter, the antimacassars – he didn't comment.

'You got a gramophone?' he said.

'Yes.'

'Where d'you get that, then?'

'A friend gave it to me. It's a . . . borrowing.'

'What friend?'

'You don't know him.'

'Oh, it's like that, is it?'

'No. It's not "like that", not at all.' Keeping her voice light and steady, Dorothy explained the events of May and June, and the respect and friendship she had earned from the squadron leader. She did not mention the letters. She did not mention the kiss, or how much she missed him, or his lean, strong, brown arms.

'Well. That's all right, then,' said Albert, leaning back on the settee with his hands behind his head, his legs stretched out in front of him.

'Can I ask, Albert? What . . . why are you here?'

'A man can come home, can't he?'

'I suppose so. But you have been gone for over a year with no word. I had no idea if you were alive or dead. And I am your wife.'

'I'm not dead, am I?'

'No.'

'Those girls give you the runaround?'

'No.

'Just make sure they don't. You're not their bloody mother, are you? Don't worry, Dot, I'm not hanging around for long. I've got four days' leave. Then I'm back to it. But I want to come home after the war, if it ever bloody ends. I want to come back and . . . I was unfair, a bit. But I want to make it up afterwards, when we get back to normal. Perhaps we could try again? Have a baby?'

Her stomach roiled. 'Albert.'

'Yes?'

'I'm forty years old now.'

He waved a dismissive hand. 'My Aunty Lou had her last when she was forty-two, or forty-three. Can't remember which. But she was an old bird. And I've been thinking, I should send money – for your keep, like.'

'No.' Her voice was tight and clenched. She would not take money from him, not now.

'A man should support his missus.'

'I have all the money I need, thank you, Albert. I launder for the estate and get paid by them. I'm independent now.'

'Oh. I see. Doesn't seem right, though.'

Dorothy allowed herself a smile. Albert wasn't a malicious man. He was just a man. Simple. There was no hatred here, on either side. Yes, she had been bewildered and disappointed when he had abandoned her. But all was well. Because she had found her life after he had gone. She was his wife, but in name only.

Albert seemed disappointed but resigned when she firmly showed him to the small bedroom with the single bed. The bed was made up with brisk cotton sheets, two woollen blankets and her favourite quilt. Albert, who had no reason not to imagine the room was made up in readiness for his anticipated return, made no comment. He sat on the small bed, looking up at her, as she stood in the doorway. His eyes were dispassionate. He never had been able to read her. They were, and always had been, utter strangers.

'Goodnight, Albert.'

'Goodnight, Dot.'

14

Albert kept out of her way for much of the following day. She made him breakfast, which he praised highly. He spent the morning pottering around in the garden and the shed, tinkering with his bicycle. After lunch, he slept. And when he awoke at around five, he said he would go down to the pub. She made some sandwiches, and watched him eat his before he went.

He left, negotiating the November fog and the blackout on his bicycle; with relief, she made herself a fresh pot of tea and ate her own sandwich alone in the parlour as the girls had not yet returned from their day of work. She listened to the wireless while the fire crackled in the grate, warm and glowing and safe. Yet she felt uneasy. What if there were *talk*, in the pub? From Albert's friends – those still there, at least? He would hear things.

. . . your wife and the squadron leader, the Polish one. Friends, eh? Come off it, Bert. Very friendly, they are. Postman says she fair climbs the wall waiting for letters from him.

She's head over heels. Got the goat of girls around here, set their cap at him some of them had, but he didn't seem to notice. You missed the boat, mate. Bad luck . . .

Albert would drink his mild. He would listen. He would say little.

*

The girls returned, tired, cold and hungry, putting an end to Dorothy's uneasy thoughts. They ate their evening meal in the kitchen, and then the three women retired to the lounge with their cups of tea and listened to the wireless. The girls seemed as relieved as Dorothy that Albert had gone to the pub. They stayed home and kept her company while she sewed, and later they listened to the gramophone, and none of them mentioned him.

Albert reeked of alcohol, the mild he had always favoured. It was late, and there was an edgy new rawness about him that Dorothy didn't like, a flaming in his face that spoke of anger. It spoke of danger, and she was on her guard. She had hated those nights, which became more frequent as their marriage went on, when he returned from the pub drunk and stinking, loud and often obnoxious. It looked as though those nights had returned.

The girls were in bed. Dorothy was in her seat by the window, sewing by the light of the oil lamp, peering from behind the wire-rimmed glasses that she wore only for close work, only at home. For Dorothy was still vain, in her own quiet way.

Albert threw himself into the settee and sat wordlessly for a few minutes, crossing his legs, uncrossing them, sighing, clearing his throat.

Dorothy continued to sew. Perhaps he would fall asleep, and wake up in the morning hung-over and forgetful. She would say nothing to him.

He glowered, shifted and cleared his throat again.

Still Dorothy did not speak. If he had something to say, he would just have to come out with it. He was a grown man. He must act like one. She would say noth—

'You going to tell me what's been going on with this Polish cunt?'

Dorothy continued to sew, not daring to look at the man who was her husband, but not her husband. She wasn't even sure she had heard him correctly. Albert was an earthy man, she knew, but he had never sworn around her (apart from the occasional 'bloody'), not once. He had never said anything so crude.

'Well? You not going to tell me about your fancy man?' Albert sneered.

'My what?' she said. She glared back at him.

'I've been hearing all about it. Seems that everyone knew but me. Flowers, letters, this fucking gramophone!' Albert sprang up and made a lunge for the music box.

But Dorothy was there first. 'No, Albert. Leave it alone. If not for me, then for Aggie and Nina. It's not yours. It's ours. Your argument with me has nothing to do with those girls. It gives them such pleasure. The music—'

'And how much pleasure does your fancy piece give you, eh?'

'I will not be drawn into this nonsense, Albert. I will not. You're drunk. Please go to bed.'

'Don't tell me what to do in my own home, woman.'

'This is not your home. You haven't lived here for months. This is my home.'

The slap came hot and sharp and hard, and it knocked her off her feet. She staggered, righted herself, and put her hand to her cheek. The blow had awakened the pain from the May day – was it really that long ago? – when she had tried to 'save' the young Polish pilot. Everybody had made her into a heroine. But her husband now, slapping her in the face, drunk and panting, had no respect for her. He stood before her, his eyes as wide and empty as the Lincolnshire sky. And when he grabbed at her and ripped her blouse open it came as no great surprise. And his mouth pushing on to hers, his breath sweet and sickly and acrid with tobacco, and their teeth clashing as she tried to twist away from him. He gripped her face with one hand, and pulled her skirt up over her hips with the other. He was strong and relentless, and in another era, an earlier life, Dorothy would almost have been thrilled. His fingers dug into her cheek.

'No, Albert. Please!' she gasped, before his hand covered her mouth.

He didn't hear, or didn't listen, she was unsure which. He spun her round and pressed her face into the settee, his large rough hand pushing her neck down. She could barely breathe, let alone cry out, as he knelt behind her, thrust aside her knickers with his bullet-like fingers and, after a few misdirected thrusts, broke into her body, piercing her. He released her neck and she suppressed the urge to cry out in pain. She would keep still, she must not move, let it be over with, let him do this thing he was determined to do. Please don't let this wake the girls, it mustn't, it mustn't. Be quiet, Albert, please, for God's sake. If the girls were to hear and come down the stairs . . . she must make no noise. She bit her lip so hard she tasted the brutal tang of blood. Albert grasped her hips and held them firm, and his movements slowed and became rhythmical, as though they were actually making love. He was pulling her on to him, harder, slower, but he was mercifully quiet, and each thrust told her: *You are mine, not his, not that Polish bastard's. My wife. You are my wife.*

And when it was over, he crept away from her and she remained on the settee, face down, frozen. She could not think, or move, or absorb what had happened to her. After a few minutes, she pulled her skirt down. She stayed on the settee until she heard his breathing become slow and gruff, like a heavyset dog's. Turning her head, she saw he was in her chair by the window, legs and arms at strange contorted angles, his bullish head lolling to one side.

Dorothy slowly twisted herself round so that she was sitting on the floor, and leaned back on the settee. She had married this man. She had *loved* him, once. She stayed motionless and without further thought for an hour, perhaps two, eyes wide open, until she became too cold, until the need for sleep became apparent. She raised herself from the floor and, without a glance at the man snoring in her chair by the window, she quietly left the parlour. Closing the door behind her, she dragged herself to her room, not bothering to visit the privy first, nor wash or brush her teeth. She climbed into her narrow bed, wrapping herself up under the sheets and the blankets and the quilt. It was a freezing, foggy night, but she must have fallen asleep and dreamed, because in the morning she sprang awake with a bright sun streaming through her window. She remembered her dream and in it she had held a young baby, she had kissed a baby's soft head, and he smelled of musk, of lavender, oranges, honey.

Albert was gone.

Nothing of him remained. Nobody would know that Albert Sinclair had returned to his abandoned wife, accused her of adultery, and assaulted her in a few unremarkable moments of rage and jealousy, a common fit of pique. To the world – that is, to her girls and her hens – Dorothy presented her usual face, free of make-up and pretensions, and followed her usual habits, making tea and breakfast, packing lunches, scattering grain for the hens, setting the fire under the copper and watching the girls set off for the North Barn. She found herself thinking about the possibility of a baby who may even now exist in what remained of the red, lush warmth in her womb.

She found herself also thinking about Jan.

Jan so far away, in all ways, always.

Day piled upon day, heavy, grey, those bedraggled days of winter. She was afraid to find blood with each visit to the privy, frequent fevered interruptions to her days. In the two weeks since Albert had left she'd felt no cramping pains, no tension, no anger or clumsiness or weepiness, all of which regularly accompanied the machinations of her monthly cycle. Hope was once again looming in front of her, large and fat, obvious as a prostitute and just as mysterious. She told herself it was almost worth it, those few minutes of Albert's rage and aggression, the few minutes of pain and humiliation, his lust – as greedy and short-lived as a child let loose in a sweet shop – her shock, and her dread not of what was happening to her, but of being discovered. The hideous thought of Aggie and Nina flinging open the door, their shocked faces, Dorothy, despite herself, crying *Help me!* And sometimes it seemed to Dorothy as though these things had actually happened; she thought she could remember the girls' faces, their shock and disgust. And sometimes, while feeding the hens, while darning stockings, she would shudder at these quasi-memories, sick at the thought of being caught.

Was she caught? No! No. But if she had been . . . and the possibility now opening up in front of her, despite everything, was thrilling. But she tried to remain unaware, to ignore the secret drama that could, *could*, be blooming inside her. She tried not to think too much, yet it was impossible not to think about it, and not to dream.

She tried not to be intimidated by fears, real fears, the fear of blood and failure and of life being washed away along with the precious egg, the lush preparations of her womb, the spring of life itself. The life-spring was in her, on her, around her. It was her, but she had no power over it, she had no control, only hope.

15

Jan flew steady, keeping his course, waiting for the enemy. Yesterday, he'd picked one off, a Dornier. He'd fired at it repeatedly, trying to kill the gunner first, as you should. He'd strafed the aircraft and with sweet satisfaction he'd watched as it spiralled towards the ground, caught in the earth's inexorable pull. There was nothing like it, he thought, nothing as satisfying as killing your enemies. He thought the crew had stayed in the Dornier, he had not seen any of them escaping. Perhaps he had shot them all. That was a small justice. The only good German was a dead German. And one way or another he'd killed four in one attack.

The day was bright, and so cold that there was no need to climb to any sort of height before the frozen air gripped him. But cold was the least of his worries. The squadron was flying day and night, supposedly protecting the city of London from the German bombs that continued to fall, relentlessly. Sometimes he and his men did all right, sometimes not. Men were lost almost daily, good Polish men. Somehow, today, he was alive. And today, he knew, he would kill again. But he himself would not be killed. It was a matter of faith.

His gaze flicked around: here, there, above and below. He always used his eyes, his own perceptions. He could not bring himself to trust this new 'radio direction finder', nor did he enjoy giving trite, dry orders to other men – even though that was his job, even though they were his sub-ordinates. In the air, in battle, after his initial instructions, it was every man for himself. On the ground, he could be the boss, but not up here, in this diaphanous space that belonged to nobody. Up here was chaos, flight, adrenaline.

He saw them, a skein of bombers, the hated Dorniers, ugly, elongated, with death written all over them. He pulled his Hurricane round swiftly and gained as much height as he could. Up . . . up . . . he wanted the sun behind him, always it was best to have that advantage. It was impossible to get to the bombers this time, he realised, flanked as they were by wearisome Messerschmitts, vicious little aeroplanes, quick, deft, deadly. Admirable too, Jan had to concede. A formation of Spitfires flew in under him, picking off the 109s. But two were on him, he knew it, breaking off from the main group and heading for him, escaping the Spitfires. The 109s split. He could only keep one in his sights.

Swinging round, he steadied his Hurricane, aimed, fired his guns for two seconds. Missed. Where was the other? Was somebody on him? He thought so. Two seconds again. Missed, missed, *damn*! His guns pummelled nothing but sky, and the 109 flew on towards him, firing back.

Had he been hit? The smell of hot oil swamped his cockpit, and all was clatter and panic. He worked always within panic's stabbing confines and the fear, he knew, kept him alive. He banked right, gained height, pulled round, levelled, aimed, fired, fired, running out. And yes, as he predicted, the familiar scene of smoke, death, and the welcome sight of the enemy aircraft twisting towards the earth. The pilot bailed out, his parachute opened like a huge silk moth breaking out of its cocoon, and Jan, grimly enraptured by such a perfect target, took his time, slowly flying lower towards the German pilot dangling helplessly in the sky under his huge parachute.

Jan's flight officer (English, as the Poles were not entirely trusted to manage their own squadron effectively) shouted over the radio: Where the bloody hell was he? They'd lost one, bloody hell, they'd lost him and the rest of them needed orders. Now!

Jan carried on, barely listening to the pompous and panicked Englishman. He had the parachute in his sights. He knew he was acting against the Geneva Convention. Would he be court-martialled? Perhaps. But he knew of at least two other Poles in his own squadron who had performed this act, and countless more Germans. Everybody seemed to get away with it. So would he. The British didn't seem to approve. But so what? And the Nazis had trampled over the Geneva Convention every day of this war. Rumours out of Krakow spoke of them shooting hospital patients as they lay in their beds and forcing men to dig their own graves at gunpoint – and not only men. They were throwing sweets on to the ground, and as the children scrambled for them, the Nazis laughed and kicked them to death. Jan doubted none of these rumours.

Nazi bastards get all they deserve.

Jan fired. His last ammo, he knew. And no real need to waste it in this fashion.

The parachute shut up on itself, disappearing into a thin silver column, lethal as a blade. What did the British call it – the Roman candle? And the German who had been dangling aimlessly beneath it suddenly shot earthwards to his death. His name was Hans, or Dieter; he had a sweetheart in Berlin, or in Munich; he had a mother, a father. For just a few more seconds, they had a son. It was a cruel death, Jan knew – but was not all death cruel?

And what would the Englishwoman say? He could imagine her, if he allowed himself to, her stray hair being pushed back off her face, but he did not allow himself to think of her while he was flying. But the killing – murder? – of this young German, it stuck in his throat, it stalled him, just for a moment, and he feared her reproach more than anything, this woman who had lost her own precious son. And he understood what her son had meant to her. He should have told her how he—

And for a moment, two moments, he lost concentration, he didn't look.

Jan felt an explosion in his arm. He caught the stench of pumping blood, of something else, something chemical. God, not the cooling fluid? He felt a torturous, burning sensation, although he felt – he knew – there was no fire. He had to fight the fog that threatened to close in on him, and he struggled to pull his Hurricane round, one-handed and bellowing in pain. He radioed he'd been hit, and then he remembered there had, of course, been two 109s. He'd made the indelible mistake of focusing on the one, one he had already rendered harmless. And where now were the bombers? They were gone, they had got through, and they were going to release their terror, as Jan had released his.

He looked around for the other 109 and he saw him in his mirror, on his tail, so close, so fast, he swore he could see the whiskers on the German pilot's face. Jan dropped his aircraft – a useless manoeuvre, he knew, but at least it brought him closer to the earth. He was determined he would land this stricken aircraft. The RAF could not afford to lose it for no good reason, and pain was not a reason. He was damned if he was going to simply sit there and die. He could barely breathe. And suddenly he saw the 109 aflame, black smoke, a shrill whine, a twist, a turn, and it was gone.

And Jan's flight officer gloated over the radio that he'd got the bastard, and for Christ's sake get down, Pietrykowski. Now, if you can. Get back, man.

16

3rd October 2010

Dear Philip,

I hereby give you one week's notice of my intention to leave my employment at the Old and New Bookshop. I have enjoyed the past eleven years in so many ways, but now I feel it is time to move on.

Yours,

Roberta

(Letter written and waiting in my handbag to give to Philip tomorrow.)

At least now the customers have got over The Scene. The gossip has subsided, nobody is talking about me any more. For a while there I was a scarlet woman, but my infamy has been short-lived and now I am plain old Roberta ('Rebecca?') again, Philip's right-hand woman and stalwart of the Old and New. It's a good place to be.

But Philip has not forgotten. He is keeping his distance and avoiding any mention of The Scene. I don't blame him, of course, but I do wish he would forget about it – like everybody else seems to have done – and I wish he would forgive me. I apologised, of course, the same day. Fuelled by my hastily downed brandy, I sailed back down the stairs to the shop, and found Philip continuing with the rearrangements in the back room, pencil in mouth, frowning, his hair perhaps a little more dishevelled than it had been, his cheeks a little pinker. He looked at me, as I stood in the doorway.

'I'm sorry, Philip. I never thought . . . I didn't think she would ever . . . but she has. I don't know what else I can say. Really. I am so very sorry.'

He looked at me with what I can only describe as dissatisfaction. He didn't seem to hear my apology. He sighed, he looked away, he scribbled a price inside a book cover with his characteristic flourish. I have never seen anybody look more disappointed.

'Perhaps you could take over here while I grab some lunch?' he said wearily. 'These need pricing, those over there need dusting, and these need putting on the lower shelf, as we discussed this morning. Oh, and could you remember to clean the windows too, please? Or get Sophie to do them. Thank you.'

He hasn't spoken to me since.

Getting home from the Old and New, to my flat, to my cat bought for me by Charles Dearhead – the cat I call Portia – is a relief. I tell Portia all that happens each day, and she listens and asks for her supper, and I cook mine, or more often I butter some bread, splash milk over cornflakes, nibble on chocolate digestives and sip coffee. I'm not sleeping, I'm tired, I look washed-out and lank-haired, and I'm so sorry all this has happened.

I'm lonely.

That's the bottom line. Lonely and, I believe in my heart, a little messed up. Charles Dearhead meant nothing to me. In fact, I didn't even like him. Boring. Self-centred. Urbane? Did I ever truly believe that? I put his poor wife through a terrible time, their marriage perhaps irreparably damaged.

And that was a matter of choice, my choice. I shall not do that again, I promise myself.

And now my friend – the only person, I have realised, whose opinion is essential – appears to despise me. I have been thinking, and thinking, I can't stop thinking, and I have to leave the Old and New. Philip does not want me there, he has made that clear. I shall write a letter of resignation tonight. I think he will be shocked, though probably relieved, and will thank me for my integrity. Except I have none. This I have proved to myself, to Philip, to Sophie and Jenna, to various intrigued and scandalised customers. Thank God my father hasn't got wind of it.

Did I 'invite dishonour', like my grandmother before me? Yes. Of course. And I have brought dishonour to the shores of Philip's life too. Oh, I should live a little! Not hide away in a bookshop all my life, dipping my toes into the murky waters of sex with a man so much older and so much more married than me. Sophie was right.

I am not scared to hand in my notice tomorrow. I'll find another job. I have savings, I am frugal with clothes and food, I run an economical car. The Old and New is more of a home to me than anywhere else on earth, but I am resolved now to leave that place of warmth and humour because that is what must be done.

But it will kill me.

In the morning, I ask to speak to Philip. He is accommodating, as usual, and we go to his small office at the back of the shop. I take my time in closing the door. When I turn, I see that he has retreated behind his desk, the expansive but cluttered desk that he was sitting on, relaxed and interested, on the day he 'interviewed' me for the job.

'Philip,' I begin, not looking at him, 'I want to give you this.'

'What is it?'

'It's my notice.'

He takes it from me. He eyes me, opens the envelope, reads the note, rips it in two, and throws it into the bin. 'Let's start again, shall we?' he says.

'What do you mean?'

'Do you love him?'

'I'm not sure what love is.'

'Don't be ridiculous. Do you love him?'

'Charles Dearhead?'

'Are there others?'

'No! And no. I don't love him. Why would I?'

'That's precisely what I've been pondering. So what on earth are you playing at?'

'I'm not playing at anything. It's finished. I . . . I stepped outside myself. That's all.'

'Yes. I think you did, rather. You see, I keep asking myself . . . I keep asking why a woman like you . . . why are you wasting your life on a man like him? I mean, come on. He's a complete twat. Sorry.'

'You think so?'

'Yes, I do. Frankly.'

'Whatever you think, it's none of your business.'

'Oh, but it is.'

'It isn't.'

We stand, facing each other across the huge walnut desk, this gigantic obstacle it seems we shall never be able to surmount, in a pantomime of our own making. But neither of us is laughing. Philip removes his glasses, cleans them awkwardly on his shirt front, puts them back on and clears his throat. It is a familiar routine. His face twitches with a strange kind of pleading innocence, willing me to do what he wants me to do. Philip's eyes are fixed on me, and my heart—

Oh, but surely. Surely? No. I'm crazy to even think it.

What is it that holds me back? Am I shy? I'm not *shy*. Am I not good enough for him? Whatever, none of it matters any more. It's over. And it didn't even begin.

'Look,' he says. 'You can't leave.'

'I can.'

'Yes, yes, of course, you can, what I mean is . . . I don't want you to.'

'Why on earth not? I've embarrassed you horribly.'

'You've embarrassed yourself, that's all. But nobody cares. This sort of thing always blows over. I forbid you to leave, actually. You do remember that I defended you? Utterly?'

Of course I remember. 'Philip—' And to my surprise I start sobbing, loudly. I didn't want to cry. I hate to cry.

'Oh no,' he says. 'For God's sake, here, take my hanky.'

Only a man like Philip would have a clean hanky in his pocket. I blow my nose. Pull yourself together, Roberta, I tell myself. Sort this out. 'I thought you would be used to crying women. With Jenna around, I mean.'

Not for the first time, I regret my thoughtless words. Philip stares at me, he feels the need to remove his glasses again, he runs his hand through his hair. He puts his glasses on the desk. I hope he doesn't sit on them in that absent-minded way of his. It wouldn't be the first time.

'Jenna and I are none of your business.'

I know this is true. I hate myself. And I am wrong, of course, quite wrong. Philip regards me as an employee, and only an employee. He is in love with Jenna, not me, and I cannot believe I even framed such thoughts, admitted such hopes to myself.

'I'm sorry,' I say, blotting out my dreams. 'I didn't mean to intrude.'

'Forget it, Roberta. I understand. And you shall stay. I

absolutely depend upon you. This place would fall apart but for you.'

'What about Sophie?'

'She's capable, a sweet girl, she knows well enough what to do. But you . . . you lend this place some gravitas. You *are* the Old and New. Don't you get it?'

'Gravitas? Me? Causing scenes like last week's? Come off it, Philip. You are the Old and New. It's your shop.'

'Then, *we* are the Old and New. One of us can't operate without the other. And you didn't cause a scene, that ghastly woman did. So I ask respectfully and in all sincerity, please will you reconsider, and please will you stay? Please, Roberta.'

The fact that we are even having this conversation is enough to convince me. I have to leave. I have to leave now. Sod the notice period. If I don't leave now . . .

'I am leaving, Philip. I'm so sorry. I'll go now.'

'Right now?'

'Yes.'

If I think Philip is about to clamber over the desk, grab me, kiss me on the lips, shake me by the shoulders and beg me even further to stay, I am mistaken. He holds out his hand and I shake it. It is warm, his grip is firm, yet his touch feels somehow fragile. His eyes are vague, as though he is peering into a murky and troubled future, and I fear he is close to tears. And I fear my rising desire to comfort him, so I release my hand and leave the office.

I'm aware of him, standing alone, receding from me as I leave, watching me go in silence.

17

Dear Jan,

I am sorry not to have written to you recently. But as
you know, I don't like writing letters. And I have been so
busy with one thing and another. The war and its ruination
of this world may as well be happening on another planet.
We see and hear so little of it now that the squadron has
gone. Of course, there is still activity on the aerodrome, just
not as much as before. But no more bombs. No more
Hurricanes landing just a whisker from my house! Thank
goodness for that. You know, I still think of that young pilot
and I feel sorry that he died in that way.

Well, December has arrived. I do hope you can make it
up here to see us, I'm sure Aggie and Nina would be
pleased to see you again. Aggie goes on all right, missing
her chap and dreadfully sad, but she soldiers on. Nina and
I both do our bit to cheer her up. I hope Christmas will
restore her spirits and despite all that is going on in this
world, I shall do my best to make the day a happy one for
her.

As for your needing peace, Jan, I am possibly the last
person who can offer you such a thing.

Yet, I am your
Dorothea

*

Two weeks and five days after Albert raped her, the familiar cramps began. For a day she managed to ignore them. But the following morning, the blood began to flow, and she had no choice but to acknowledge once again the bitter disappointment that blighted her life.

She knew he would never return, and that was one small consolation. She hoped he would be killed, really, to make everything easier. And because he deserved to die after what he had done to her.

He had abandoned her, knowing how much she wanted another child, knowing full well that if he went away there could be no further children. But hadn't she abandoned him too, setting herself up in the tiny bedroom at the back of the house, shutting the door on him night after night? There could be no child if she didn't—

It was hard to believe that she once fancied herself in love with the man. He could offer her nothing. But she had not thought him a bully. Had he done this to other women? She thought not. No, it was just her, his wife. His anger was directed at her, nobody else. She could imagine him, in a different home, with a different woman; she would be younger, simpler, they would be happy together, and he would even be loving, in his own way.

But still the thought nagged at her, should she report him? What exactly would she report? A soldier returning home on leave and having relations with his wife? Who would believe there had been any wrongdoing? And now it was surely too late. Perhaps he didn't even understand that he'd done anything wrong, although he had gone a day earlier than he'd said he would. Out of guilt? Perhaps he had learned his lesson.

And what if she *had* fallen pregnant? How on earth could she have begun to explain to Jan? Because she knew – yes, she was absolutely certain about this – Jan would come back, she would see him again. She could have told him the truth, but would he have believed her? Perhaps he would think it only natural. After all, Albert was her husband.

But no matter. There was no baby. There was just her – empty, hurt and bloodied. Nothing to tell, no confessions to make.

Try as she might, Dorothy could not get her words to rhyme. So she ceased trying and she let her words take shape on the page as they would, as they seemed to want to do, with a life of their own. And at last this small collection of words seemed to her a poem. She felt that she had written her first, perhaps her only, poetry. And she would be the sole judge, she knew that she would never share her writing with another.

But her words, as she shaped them, read them, over and over, in snatched moments, late at night, early in the morning, startled her, gave her a strange unearthly sensation of power, like running along a wide, empty beach on soft-firm sand with youthful and boundless energy. It was a small liberation, but from what, she could not comprehend.

18

S uch lurid dreams!

The woman was on her hands and knees before him, her eyes closed – this, the most ladylike of the women he had loved, the most demure. He cried out – he must have cried out often – and one of the nurses would be by his bedside, as suddenly and silently as an apparition. Oftentimes it was the nurse named Sylvia, nineteen years old, he guessed, pure-skinned, angel-white, soothing him with a quiet word, a soft murmur, a cool hand on his brow. She would check his pulse, holding his left wrist, checking his dogged heart-beats against the little watch strapped like an amulet to her breast pocket.

Was he in pain?

Yes, but not the kind she talked of, not the kind she even knew of, he thought.

The pain in his arm was nothing to the pain in his heart, and that in turn was nothing compared with his physical desire. Love, at this stage, was secondary. He acknowledged to himself that he was once again in the grip of pure lust, the most vulgar emotion. Sylvia and the other nurses must have noticed. They bathed him and dressed him, they were familiar with his body. But it mattered not. Where was the shame, in truth? He was born a man.

He longed to clamber back into his Hurricane, to be back among his men. He wanted to kill more Germans. And that was a lust too, and sometimes it was difficult to define where each lust began and ended. He even wondered, in tortured lucid moments, if his aroused state was entirely due to thoughts of the Englishwoman.

Dorothy. Dorothea. Hardly could he bring himself to think her name.

Mrs Dorothy Sinclair.

The hospital bed was comfortable enough – white and firm. His sore, aching arm was broken. Smashed in several places, the doctor said. It would give him 'gyp' for the rest of his life, and by that Jan inferred it would give him pain, irritation. But he was alive, he was well. And he would return to flying, he proclaimed to the doctor, within the next week.

It was his right arm, which was unfortunate. He couldn't write. He had thought of asking a nurse to help him, but no, he did not want his words to one woman shared with another. The nurses were pretty, young, confident and – with him, at least – flirtatious. He flirted back too, a little, if he wasn't too tired, but only to be polite. They were gentle girls doing a difficult job. He did not desire them.

A new doctor came. He sat on the bed, introduced himself as Dr Burton. He wanted to talk, if that was all right. Jan was no fool, he knew he was a head doctor immediately. He told him so, and Dr Burton smiled. So, then. They could be frank.

It was not a good idea to return to flying too soon.

'We fear you are fragile, mentally. Exhausted. You need to rest longer,' he said.

'That cannot be done. I am needed,' said Jan.

It was a fine winter's day with pale diluted sunshine, small puffs of cloud skittering across the blue sky. Out of the window he could see other wounded men sitting in wheelchairs with blankets on their laps, being wheeled around by the pretty nurses, or sitting and smoking, contemplating the views across the hospital gardens to the fields beyond.

He had no idea, he suddenly realised, exactly where he was. Which hospital was he in? It appeared to have been converted from a grand house. But he did not know its name. He thought he was still in Kent, but perhaps he wasn't. Somehow he hadn't ever thought to ask.

'If you return so soon,' said Dr Burton, 'have you considered that you may be a liability? Your judgement impaired? Not to mention your injuries, which will not have healed fully.'

Jan found the young doctor smug, like most doctors. This Burton thought he was God, obviously. He looked dapper in a grey flannel suit. But he was not God, and Jan was determined to keep this young man in his place.

'I am not "impaired",' he told him. 'I shall return today, if you like. No? So I give myself three, no, two more days, and I return. I flew back to my aerodrome with one arm. Two weeks ago, I think? It is healed. I feel it is healed. It is very near to healing. I will remove this plaster myself if you do not do it for me. I will do this.' He made a violent tearing action at his injured arm.

Dr Burton shook his head. He asked Jan questions: Where did he come from in Poland? Where did he learn his English?

Jan, bored, defensive, said as little as possible.

The doctor reiterated his warning not to be foolish, to consider his squadron – its safety, his own safety.

Jan kept up his stubborn silence. He was behaving, he knew, like a spoiled brat. But he would not be bossed around by a doctor who looked as though he had never killed a rabbit, let alone a fellow human being. Jan could not communicate with such a man.

Dr Burton gave up, thanked Jan for his time and left him.

19

Dorothy smiled to herself as she basted the chicken, slaughtered just the day before by Nina. Dorothy could not bring herself to perform the task, and Albert had always been the one to snap the birds' thin tremulous necks. Last Christmas, alone, she had not bothered with Christmas lunch, but this year she had plucked, gutted and now cooked the bird with great pleasure. The smell was divine, she thought, the house was warm, the frost outside clinging to the world like washed lace, and she and the girls were cosy and contented. Dorothy was determined to make Christmas Day a good one for all three of them. Besides the chicken, there were roasted potatoes, Yorkshire puddings, parsnips from the garden. And port, a bottle hidden away by Dorothy for years, taken from her mother's house. Why she had taken it, Dorothy couldn't fathom; it was just another item in her strange and ill-considered trousseau. Perhaps, she mused, today was why: Christmas Day 1940, cold, but calm. And safe, for now.

The girls had sipped two small glasses each already and were lounging, listening to their favourite Billie Holiday songs. They had loved the presents Dorothy had made for each of them: simple linen handkerchiefs she had dug out from the bottom of her rag bag and which she had embroidered with their initials, pressed and then scented with a handful of lavender; a silk scarf for Aggie that Dorothy no longer wore; a red lipstick, barely used, for Nina. Not astounding gifts, but something sitting under the small Christmas tree for the girls to open, wrapped simply with brown paper and kitchen string.

Dorothy was glad there were no presents for her. She had never liked them. She would be expected to smile and say thank you; she felt obliged to be thrilled. Her mother's idea of presents had been *The Infant's Progress: From the Valley of Destruction to Everlasting Glory*, and other hideous books that Dorothy had never read but had hidden away under her bed. They were probably still there, she thought, as she took a modest sip of her own glass of port. The thrill of alcohol, its exuberance, was a sensation Dorothy rarely allowed herself. She loved too much the hot, glowing feel of it in her mouth, her throat, her gullet, through her stomach, down deep into her legs. She loved too much the feeling of losing oneself, of being buoyed up, and the opportunity it afforded for blurring and forgetting. But she could not forget the way in which Albert had acted towards her after he had taken too much drink. She would never allow herself to get into that state, to lose her mind completely to drink's calamitous charms. But today, this Christmas Day, she was allowing herself the pleasure of alcohol. December had been a month of further disappointments, and she needed to forget.

Despite his promises, his hints and suggestions, Squadron Leader Jan Pietrykowski had not visited. Indeed, he had not written for over a month. Was he dead? Dorothy thought not. She *knew* not. Was he injured? It was possible. It was probable. Perhaps the squadron had been moved again? Perhaps he was cross with her? Did he know, somehow, about Albert and her brief, shameful, blameless relations with him? Such a shrewd man, she would not have been surprised if he had guessed from the tone of her last letter, from her careful choice of words. But, of course, it was impossible. Wasn't it? Nobody was that intuitive.

'What's up, then, Dot?' Nina said. She was languishing on the settee, her port glass glowing in her plump hand, the glass rimmed by the red lipstick she had been unable to resist trying on.

Dinner was nearly ready, and Dorothy had emerged from the kitchen to take a short rest. 'Nothing at all, Nina,' she said. 'Dinner will be ready in ten minutes. I'm just letting the chicken stand.' Dorothy sank into her chair by the window.

'You're the best ever cook,' said Aggie.

'Oh no, but it's good to feel useful. You both looked so cold this morning.'

'It's bloody freezing out there,' said Nina. She shifted on the settee, wincing as she did so.

'Are you quite well?' said Dorothy.

'Yeah. Course I am. Just feel a bit funny. Can't get comfy. I'm ever so hungry. Can't wait for that dinner.'

Dorothy turned to the window. Slowly, she rose from her chair, transfixed, wide-eyed.

'What is it, Dot?' said Aggie, coming to stand beside her. She flicked the yellowed lace curtains to one side. 'Oh!'

Squadron Leader Jan Pietrykowski was opening the gate. He was carrying a bottle-shaped brown package and a kitbag. A small open-topped car was parked half on the road, half on the verge, crimson and bright as a brand-new toy. Dorothy wondered that they hadn't heard the car arrive. But, of course, the music was loud.

'You've been pining for months, and now he's here. And you're just going to stand there?' said Aggie, taking her glass from her.

As if in a dream, Dorothy made to go back into the

kitchen, to open the door and let him in. But her knees, disobedient, would not budge.

'I can't,' she whispered.

'I'll go!' said Aggie brightly, handing Dorothy's glass back, and she half ran, half skipped through to the kitchen.

Dorothy looked aghast at Nina, who grinned in her disingenuous manner, took a large mouthful of port and shrugged. Dorothy groped behind her for her chair and sat down. She stood again immediately as Aggie entered the lounge, followed by the unmistakeable smell of uniform, of hair grease, of kindness. And the man, more handsome than she remembered, the man she had longed for, stood once more in her parlour, smiling, unwrapping a bottle of champagne, no less, and looking at Dorothy as though she were Elizabeth Bowes-Lyon herself.

'I apologise for arriving without asking,' he said. 'I had a last-minute pass. Twenty-four hours only. Tomorrow, I must return to Kent.'

'I see,' said Dorothy. Her throat was so tight she felt she might suffocate. He was extraordinarily handsome. Had she not noticed this before? She thought she had. But there was something wrong, something amiss with the way he held himself, the way he moved. And it was still a shock to her that she cared so much.

'But for now, today, Christmas. Good times, good wine. Good company.' He looked at her, and smiled.

She smiled back.

Suddenly, it was Christmas.

Jan followed her into the kitchen where she helped him remove his greatcoat, which was wet and cold, and laid it over the clothes horse in front of the range to dry. Gentle plumes of steam filled the room. He opened and poured the champagne, with his left hand, holding the bottle awkwardly against his body. Goodness knows how he had come by champagne. But who cared? It was champagne! And Dorothy could see he was in pain. He held his right arm at a curious angle. Nevertheless, he helped her to dish up the dinner, putting the heavy plates on to the table one at a time, using his good arm.

'I'll call the girls through,' she said.

But Jan put a finger to his lips and shook his head. He gently took hold of Dorothy's waist with both hands. She looked away, embarrassed. He took her chin in his good hand and softly tilted her head towards his. He kissed her, soft and light. She did not want the kiss to end.

'You have lost weight, no?' he said, releasing her.

She opened her eyes.

Had she? Perhaps. Since Albert's visit she had certainly lost her appetite.

'I've been pining for you,' said Dorothy, and she smiled shyly at him.

He laughed his big, hearty laugh – the laugh of one who doesn't laugh as often as he should – and she blushed and pulled away from him, calling to the girls that dinner was on the table.

They ate the food and washed it down with the champagne and more port. Jan said he was hopeful that all was not lost; the death all around was not in vain. There had been a victory, of sorts, despite the bombings, and the war could and would be won. There had been no invasion, and there was no sign of one coming any time soon. They could all take heart from that.

'But I have no idea when the war will end,' he said, pouring himself another glass of port. The last glass. The women had insisted.

'Years?' said Dorothy.

'I hope not, but I suspect so. I do not expect to return to my homeland for a long time.'

After dinner, they listened to the King's speech, and then the girls made space in the lounge and insisted on dancing, giddying themselves until Nina, red-faced and full, plonked herself on the settee, laughing. Drunk and tired, she soon slept, and Aggie left the cottage to milk the cows alone. It would take three times as long, she said, but Nina was all in. Let her sleep. She deserved some time off. She worked like a bloody packhorse.

Alone in the house, apart from the sleeping girl, Dorothy and Jan cleared the dishes and washed up. Jan, ever mindful of his arm, winced once or twice.

'May I have a look at your arm?' she asked him as she put away the last of the dishes.

'It's nothing,' he said.

'But it looks as though you're in a lot of pain.'

He shook his head and changed the subject. 'May I stay tonight? On the settee will be all right, I have my kit. Only it is so cold, and colder still now it is almost dark. And I am not expected back until ten o'clock tomorrow morning.'

'Yes. Of course you can stay. You must. But in the spare room. I prepared it for you weeks ago.'

After Albert's departure, Dorothy had stripped the bed, turned the mattress, scrubbed the floor. She had remade the bed and scrubbed the settee, over and over.

Aggie returned, and Dorothy made sandwiches and tea. One of the cows had mastitis, Aggie thought. Nina, awake now and slothful, announced herself to be 'full to the bloody brim' but happy to accompany Aggie to The Crown, to 'see who was about'. The girls disappeared upstairs and returned, a few minutes later, changed and lipsticked. Jan offered them a ride, one at a time, in the little red sports car. It was an

MG, loaned to him that morning by his English flight officer. 'Take care of her, Pietrykowski,' he had said. Jan wasn't certain that he had meant the car.

Dorothy watched and waved from the parlour window as each girl was whisked away. And while Jan was ferrying for the second time, Dorothy made up a fresh tea tray and set it out on the low table in the lounge.

'Thank you for giving the girls a trip in that car,' she said. 'I'm sure they think it very glamorous.'

'It is glamorous, isn't it? And fast too. And red! But so cold, like flying. So I got here in time, in time for your delicious dinner.'

'You didn't write.'

'I'm sorry. I hoped a surprise would do. Besides, I could not write,' and he raised his arm.

'It's incredible to see you again,' said Dorothy. 'Please may I have a look at your injury?'

'There is no need.'

'What happened to you?'

'Nothing. Nothing to speak of. A small injury, a scratch. No need for any worry.'

Dorothy said nothing. She slowly sipped her tea, and concentrated on the tick, tick, tick of the clock, the crackling of the fire. She felt the man's gaze on her, unwavering. He perched on the edge of the settee, drinking his tea in long gulps. She had hoped he might be more comfortable with her. But, of course, she could not expect too much.

Truly, they barely knew each other.

He recalled these cups from their first meeting, when they had tea in her kitchen, all those months ago, in May, months that could just as easily be years. And yes, she had aged – imperceptibly to others, perhaps, but he noticed one or two new lines around her mouth, her eyes. She was definitely thinner. He noticed these things, because he looked. He looked at Mrs Dorothy Sinclair as only a man in love can look, with attention to detail.

There had been few women in Jan Pietrykowski's life: his young bride, lost to him after just months of marriage, followed by an intense but short-lived fling with a young woman who had bewitched him for a while; and once, once only, but shamefully, the wife of a colleague. Dorothy seemed to him, now he was in her presence again, to fill the world with womanhood. And he had missed her presence, reading over and over again the odd, stilted letters that had occasionally arrived from her. She was no writer, as she was quite possibly no lover. And if he found that out – if he pushed this woman beyond her endurance, if he tried to 'get into her knickers' (a peculiar phrase he had heard often since being in England) – then the spell between them would be broken, irretrievably and forever. At this moment he hated being a man, the ludicrous physical reaction that accompanied thoughts of her. And he had thought of her often, before and after his injury, alone, at night, in bed (and sometimes not alone, not at night, not in bed), imagined pleasure overtaking all sense, all reason. He imagined Dorothy above him, wide-eyed, sweating, hair crumpled, face flushed, breasts swollen.

And now, to be here with this woman, in her warm and safe home, was almost more than he could bear. The fear and exhaustion he had so long fought finally beat him, and his face caved in like a bullied child's. Rising from the settee, he stumbled towards her, knocking into the tea tray as he did so, and the tray swayed on the edge of the low table, and he waited for it to fall, but it righted itself.

Jan fell to his knees and Dorothy stroked his hair, cradling his head in her lap. And he was glad to feel her compassion, to know that hers was intact while his had been blown apart.

'Hush, Jan. Come now, it's all right,' she whispered as she tentatively stroked his glossy black hair.

He cried. Her hand found his neck and stroked back and forth, back and forth, a hypnotic movement that had the desired effect. She repeated her request to see his arm, and this time he allowed her to remove his tunic and roll up his shirt sleeve. The arm was reddish-purple and swollen, but surely less so than it had been. Still, it saddened her.

Even injured his arm was a work of art, and she could not stop looking at it. Gradually, his sobs lessened. The clock ticked, and the fire crackled. His head was heavy in her lap, he was perfectly still, barely breathing; she thought he slept. She looked down at his hair, the curve of his ear, the tiny birthmark shaped like Italy just beneath it, his cheek and his solid jaw. Dorothy ran her hand over the stubble that was beginning to shoot forth like small black arrows, then turned her hand over and stroked his face with the back of her fingers. She gazed down at the closed eyes of this man who was also still a boy, at the tear tracks crusting like fresh ice on his cheeks; she gazed at his strong neck, stretched across her lap as though on the executioner's block. His surrender, she realised, was complete. This was Jan, the person, the man. She kept perfectly still, save for her stroking hand.

He could be, she dared to imagine, her happiness.

And later, after an hour, perhaps longer, Jan raised his head to look at her. 'I'm sorry, Dorothea.'

'No.'

'I am a coward. You see, I am.'

'No.'

'I cry like a baby and sleep in your lap.'

'I like babies.'

'I know.'

She held his shoulders. The male strength flowed from him into her hands and up to her arms and flooded through her body, to her lungs, her heart, her stomach. She gritted her teeth and held him firmer still, and for a moment there was panic in his eyes.

'Jan.'

It was not a question.

He raised himself, balancing on his haunches, reached for her hair and loosened it from its chignon. He curled it around his fingers and smelled it, and then she was on him, her mouth grasped his, and she kissed him, she took control. He seemed stunned, and for a moment he did nothing, nothing at all, until he stood, pulling her up with him, and with one movement he gathered her up in his arms, wincing again, just for a moment, and then they were through the door, and he was carrying her upstairs, and grappling to open the door of a bedroom, any bedroom. The one he found was the little spare room made up for him, and he threw her on to the bed and kicked the door shut behind them.

20

Dearest Eliza and Bert,

Just a note to let you know I had the baby at last!
Four nights ago, just after midnight, so she shares her
birthday with me. I have named her Diana. My mother
has been helping with the housework while I rest and
nurse Diana and try to sleep. I read too, such a luxury to
lie in bed all day. Thank you for the Agatha Christie
books you sent for my birthday. I am enjoying them, and
quite see now why you are such admirers. Diana is a
wakeful baby and very hungry, which is not always
comfortable for me. I love her dearly and shall feel like
this for always. Is there a mother who doesn't? If only
Bob were around to meet his little girl. My heart breaks
each time I think of it and I cry often. Mother calls it
the baby blues, and perhaps it is, even though I think I
have reason enough to be crying. Wish me strength, dear
friends, to be both mother and father to this baby girl. Do
visit when you get the opportunity. You are much missed
down here,

Jean

(I found this letter inside a first edition of Agatha Christie's
The Moving Finger. Philip asked me to check the book over

and wrap the almost pristine dust jacket in protective cellophane. It was later placed in the locked antiquarian cabinet priced at £230, and it sold shortly thereafter.)

The day is bleak but the care home is warm and sheltered. Suzanne is there, greeting me with a smile.

'How are things?' she says.

I tell her almost everything. I like talking to strangers, or near strangers. They don't judge. I don't tell her about Babunia's letter from my grandfather, even though I can sense it burning a hole in my handbag, demanding to be set free. I do tell her a little about my stupid affair with Charles Dearhead, his wife's confrontation with me, my leaving the Old and New. I tell her about my father's illness. I tell her how Philip defended me.

Suzanne is a good listener. She says she likes the sound of Philip.

I ask her how my grandmother is.

'Not so well,' says Suzanne. 'Dorothea is confused more often than not. But I don't feel that it's senility, not as such. I feel that she has something on her mind, some burden, as old people often do. It's probably nothing at all, just something she has kept within her all these years and has now blown out of proportion.'

I don't know what to say. I'm not about to betray Babunia's secrets, even if I knew what they were.

'The name you call her, Babunia, where does it come from?' asks Suzanne.

'It's Polish for "Grandma".'

'I thought it probably was. Your grandfather was Polish, wasn't he?'

'Yes. I think she likes me to call her that in memory of him. He died when she was expecting my dad, you see. It was a wartime romance. They weren't married for long before he died.'

'Married?'

'Yes.'

'But Dorothea was never married to your grandfather.'

'They were married in 1940.'

'Oh. I'm sorry, Roberta. I thought you knew. It's just . . . she told me she never married him. She was married, but to somebody else. She changed her name to your grand-father's, though. I expect she was ashamed – in those days, it was a big deal to have a child outside of wedlock. And by another man. That could be what's troubling her . . . Oh. Now I've upset you. I'm sorry.'

'She just took his name, you mean?'

'It looks that way, yes.'

'Is there a deed poll certificate?'

'Yes. She showed it to me not long after I first started here.'

'May I see it?'

'Of course.'

Later, my mobile rings. It's Sophie. She telephoned me at home the day I walked out of the Old and New, in tears.

She couldn't believe I had left. When was I coming back? Couldn't I patch it up with Philip?

I told her no, I could not.

Now she is calling to tell me that Philip has been inter-viewing. 'There's a woman called Patricia, very tall, taller even than you, with very short grey hair, lots of beads and bracelets. Philip asked me what I thought of her after she left. I said she was nothing like you. And I'm sure he was going to cry, Roberta, I swear. He moped off into the office and I didn't see him for two hours.'

'What can I do about it?' I ask, crossly. None of this is my concern.

'Nothing, I suppose. He's interviewing again tomorrow. Jenna's helping – but to be honest, she's more of a hindrance. And she's acting weird. I'll let you know how it goes.'

'If you want to, that's fine.'

'You do know you could come back right now. I mean, you could walk into the shop this morning and he'd take you back like a shot.'

'I don't know that.'

'I think you do.'

I hate the word 'orphan'. I'm not an orphan, of course, not yet. And can adults be described as orphans, anyway? I sit alone in my flat, sipping a glass of Pinot Grigio, not getting drunk exactly but feeling sorry for myself, going over my pathetic life, hating myself. And, of course, regretting my hasty departure from the Old and New. I'm hoping to get a call from Philip, begging me to return. But the telephone in my hallway sits stubbornly silent, cold and inanimate, and the mobile phone in my handbag has nothing to say either.

I consider ringing Dad. I want to talk to him. Suzanne showed me the certificate from 1941, which proved to me that my grandmother changed her name by deed poll from Mrs Dorothy Sinclair to Mrs Dorothea Pietrykowski. So at least now I know the suitcase was hers, and hers all along, and now it's mine. And so what if Babunia had an affair and fell pregnant? It must have happened so much during the war. I wonder who her husband was? Did he die in the war? Is that why she changed her name? But why did she lie to us about it, to Dad and me? I don't care if she was married, or had an affair, or had a dozen affairs. I'm pretty sure my dad wouldn't give a fig either, he's pretty laid-back about most things. But of course, Suzanne was right, things were different back then. I understand that my grandmother is very much a product of her time.

And does Dad know any of this? My dear father, gradually dying from this hideous disease, refusing to fully accept his limitations. He has an aversion to hospitals, and I can't blame him for that. My mother, Anna, Dad's former wife – they are long divorced – is unavailable to me, for reasons entirely of her own making. My grandmother is confused and old, possibly weeks from death – even though we have been fearful of that for a decade, probably longer. It seems to me she has always been weeks from death. I've broken off my only proper adult romance (I don't count the unfortunate episode at university), which in itself isn't a tragedy, but it feels like one. I've been exposed in public as a homewrecker (although the Dearhead marriage, from what I've heard, appears to be intact). I've cut myself off from the person who is surely my best and most reliable friend. And this letter, this stupid letter that I wish had not fallen out of *The Infant's Progress*, seems to refute all that my grandmother has told me about her early life.

I sip my wine. I read the letter again, although I know it by heart now, but I read to search for clues and answers that I will not find. I can't think ahead. I can't think sideways. All I can think about is the past, which is unravelling slowly. All I can do, it seems, is wait for it to reveal itself to me.

21

Dorothy awoke and realised it was snowing. The bedroom was too light, the world too still. It was but five o'clock, and she guessed she had slept for three hours, perhaps less. She sat up and pulled back the curtains. It was cold and white, so she lay down again and snuggled into the arms that had held her through the short night, and the owner of those arms stirred, and kissed her head, and told her to go back to sleep.

'It's snowing, Jan.'

He sat up then, leaned over her and looked out of the window. He exclaimed in Polish. 'I have to get up. The car . . . before there is too much snow. I'm sorry, my darling.'

'It's perfectly all right. I know you have to leave early.'

She watched as he climbed out of bed, and marvelled that he was not at all abashed by his own nakedness. It was funny to think how familiar she had become in one short night with his body, when this man was really still a stranger to her. She could not recall all that they had enjoyed together; it was as though she had been drunk, which she certainly had not been. Were they lovers? Yes. Of course. He was her lover. All the rumours were true.

He dressed, and left the bedroom to use the privy. She climbed out of the bed, and tiptoed through to her own bedroom where she watched him walk along the path to the outhouse, his breath billowing in the morning snow-light.

She roused herself then, dressed, and in the kitchen she cleaned out the range, reset and lit it and boiled the kettle for tea. She set out some bread, some butter, some gooseberry jam. Jan must eat before his long journey. She boiled more water so he could wash. He performed his ablutions and dressed himself properly in the spare bedroom while Dorothy sat in the kitchen and sewed the buttons back on to his shirt.

If the girls knew that Dorothy and Jan had spent the night together – and, of course, they must know – they said nothing. Dorothy had heard them come in the night before, late. This morning they were preparing for a long day of work, all the more arduous after the previous day's festivities. As she sewed, Dorothy listened to them all as they ate bread and jam, drank tea, exchanged subdued niceties and talked about the day's work ahead. She knew Aggie and Nina were watching her mend Jan's shirt, and she could feel the weight of their intrigue.

'Christ, my belly hurts,' announced Nina, rubbing her stomach and waving away a second slice of bread and jam.

'I'm sorry to hear that,' said Dorothy. She looked over at Jan. He was about to leave. She was dreading the separation, trying to spin out these remaining moments left to them. Yet she could think of little to say.

Nina rushed to the privy, looking wan and cold on her return.

'So did you girls have fun last night?' asked Dorothy, to break the unusual silence.

'Not as much as—' began Nina.

But Aggie shook her head.

Dorothy smiled sweetly and avoided the cool gaze of the squadron leader who, she could see, had finished his breakfast. She glanced at the clock. It was very nearly six o'clock.

He must leave. She could not contemplate how she would bear this. Five minutes of separation would be too long, she thought, and she suppressed tears.

He put on his greatcoat, scarf, hat and gloves and picked up the kitbag he had packed before breakfast. He cleared his throat. Taking the hint, Aggie harried Nina to get ready, and the older pair watched as the girls trudged out into the snow and moved off for the North Barn, across the Long Acre field. They made slow progress in the falling snow.

'I don't want to go, my darling,' said Jan, finally. 'But I must.'

'I know. I understand. But you will come back to me? As soon as you can?'

'Of course I will. And you will write to me? Properly?'

'Yes. I will. My letter will reach Kent before you do. How's that?'

'I am likely to have a new address soon. But write anyway, letters are sent forward. I'll let you know my new posting as soon as I can.'

They hugged, and Dorothy cried. And they prepared to part, Dorothy slinging her coat over her shoulders to walk down the garden path and watch Jan roar off in the car. He would ignore the snow, he said. It was nothing compared to the snowfalls at home. A last kiss, a wave, the cold engine growling and the crackle of snow as he drove through it, and he was gone.

Once again, she stood alone.

She waved until he had rounded the corner and was out of sight. Conceitedly, part of her had hoped he would stay, claim illness, incapacity. But she knew him better than that. The snow drove her back inside to her hearth, to her empty house. She cleared away some of the breakfast things. She found his shirt, on her chair where she had left it when she got up to prepare for the big goodbye. She had sewn all of the buttons but one back on, and she had forgotten to give it to him. She would have to send it on. She drifted upstairs to the spare bedroom, where the smell of sweat and maleness lingered. The sheets were crumpled. Dorothy lay on the bed and closed her eyes. She wanted to remember last night forever, so she would have to start remembering it now, before the memories began to fade. She luxuriated in the feather pillows, which smelled of him. She thought of his hard warm body, his soft mouth, his tongue on her and in her.

Later, after she had slept a little, she rose from the bed and tidied herself, and resolved to have a bath. But first she must let out the hens, the poor things, and bake bread, and begin preparations for that evening's meal for the girls. The washstand Jan had used that morning needed cleaning, the water disposing of. This she was reluctant to do. Even his dirt was desirable to her, sacred. She smiled to herself. She felt inordinately thrilled.

After tidying away the breakfast things, she set to making the bread. As she kneaded the dough, her mind dwelled on all that had happened in the last day and night. It was momentous, this she understood. To take a man like Jan into her life, into her body, into her very self, allowing him to possess all her emotions, to see her for who she was – it was new. She had not had that completeness with Albert even before the rape, the ugly name for the act she now accepted had been visited on her.

But life had to go on. Jan was gone, back to his work, back to play his role in the game they called war, and she was alone again. She would launder and sew and cook and play mother to the girls. Her life, her tiny life, punctuated at last by love, was not to change, could not really be changed. Perhaps, once the war was over . . . but she dared not think that any happiness of hers could endure. Happiness was an illusion.

She set the bread to rise in the linen cupboard. She would write to Jan, a wild, girlish letter proclaiming her love. He would be surprised to receive it so quickly, but she had promised. And she wanted to make him smile and remember, as much as she did. She would write to him every day!

She went to the small oak writing desk in the parlour and wrote feverishly for half an hour, perhaps an hour. About what? About joy. Between the lines, she wrote of her desire for wifeliness and motherhood. Ah, motherhood. Funny, but Dorothy had not considered the notion of falling pregnant, being pregnant now with Jan's baby. Their coupling had been about them, their love, their lust. She wrote in her letter about her desire only for Jan, her dreams for their future, if they had one. After finishing her letter, reading it, rereading it, she found herself wanting to write it again but knowing it would be ruined if she did. She took an envelope, kissed the letter, tucked it inside, and addressed and stamped it. Pulling on her coat and boots, she ran through the snow, her hair flying behind her, to the postbox at the top of the lane.

Returning to her cottage, slow and deflated, she ambled, enjoying the chill crispness. She felt cleansed. The snow was falling like graceful ballerinas, and the world was silenced.

Until she thought she heard a shout. Again. Her name.

Was it Aggie?

Yes, there she was, holding on to her hat, running across the Long Acre towards the cottage. Dorothy hastened, and made it to her front garden as Aggie came through the rear gate, red-faced, out of breath, eyes wide in panic.

'Aggie?' said Dorothy. 'What's the matter?'

'It's Nina. I think she's dying!'

'Dying?'

'She's up the North Barn. Can you come?'

'What's wrong with her?'

'She said she felt bad this morning. She feels sick, and she's getting awful pains. Shrieking her head off, she is. Please hurry, Dot.'

'My God, is she poisoned?'

'I don't know.'

Dorothy locked the kitchen door, and the two set off. The snow was thickening. Why hadn't she sent Aggie for Dr Soames? Dorothy wasn't a nurse, she couldn't help Nina. She wasn't even a mother. She had never mopped a sweating brow, spooned broth, or cleaned up vomit other than her own.

Dorothy struggled to keep up with Aggie, who ran ever faster as they approached the barn. The snow was now falling thick and fast. Aggie pulled the barn door open. Entering, panting, Dorothy felt a surge of relief to be out of the cold. Aggie pulled the door to behind them. The barn was dark, and as she waited for her eyes to adjust, she cast around to find Nina. Her gloveless hands were cold. It felt as though her feet were shrinking in her gumboots. She breathed deeply, getting her breath back.

Nina was in the farthest corner, curled up on a pile of straw. She moaned, a strange lowing noise. She was an animal. And she was in pain.

'Nina?' Dorothy knelt beside the stricken girl, and felt her head.

She was neither hot nor cold. Aggie knelt on the other side of Nina, and held her hand.

'Dot? Oh!'

'Where does it hurt?' said Dorothy, removing her coat and placing it over Nina's shoulders. 'Nina, listen to me. Where does it hurt?'

'Oh God, everywhere! So bloody much . . .' Nina squirmed and rocked, crying out.

Dorothy and Aggie stood up. Aggie looked small and lost. But Dorothy ignored her childlike trembling. 'Has she eaten anything strange? Anything she shouldn't?' she asked urgently.

'I don't think so. We all ate a lot yesterday—'

'But we all ate the same, and you and I are fine and so was Jan. I don't understand. Nina? Have you . . . you've been sick, yes? Oh yes, a little. No matter. Anything else? Have you . . . soiled yourself?'

'Course she hasn't!' cried Aggie.

'Nina?'

'I had to go to the privy three times this morning but nothing since then. Oh. Oh no. Oh my fucking God.'

'Aggie, run to Dr Soames. If he's not there, try Mrs Compton. She's better than nobody, I think she trained as a nurse once. And she has a telephone. I expect an ambulance will have to come. Something's obviously wrong. Appendix, perhaps?'

'But that can be dangerous, can't it?'

'I think so. She'll be all right. But go for help now, please.'

'You'll stay with her, won't you? Dot? She won't die?'

'Of course I'll stay, and of course she'll not die. The very idea! But I can't help her much. Run, Aggie, now.'

Snow hurled itself through the heavy barn door as Aggie pushed it open. With one last anxious look at Nina, she left the barn and pushed the door shut behind her.

Nina was sweating now, eyes closed, and she lay still and quiet. Dorothy crouched down and touched the girl's face.

'I can't bear it,' said Nina, and she began to cry. 'I'm going to die. I am.'

'Nonsense. Aggie has gone for Dr Soames. You will be perfectly all right, Nina.'

'Oh fuck, fuck, fuck!'

Nina flailed wildly for Dorothy. She pulled the older woman off balance, and Dorothy fell down beside her. Nina would not let go, gripping Dorothy's arm harder, screaming into her ear. Dorothy struggled to free herself of the desperate girl, and sat back on her heels. She swallowed hard. She stared at Nina, writhing in the straw in agony, convinced she was going to die, and understanding dawned on her, fierce as an Egyptian sun.

She ran to the barn door, thoughts piling on thoughts, realisation flooding into her mind and galvanising her like nothing ever before. It was all there, it was all clear, all of a sudden. Oh, but she had been so blind!

'Aggie!' she cried into the blizzard, more loudly than she had thought herself capable of shouting. 'Aggie!'

She waited, but Aggie must have gone out of earshot; her figure failed to reappear through the swirling snow. Dorothy slammed the door and threw herself back down beside Nina. She turned the girl's face towards her own and looked squarely into her wild, frightened eyes.

'Nina, when did you last bleed? You know. Your monthly? Can you remember?'

'Buggered if I can.'

'You've been putting on weight, haven't you? I've had to let out your clothes several times, haven't I?'

'So bloody what?'

'Have you felt any movements inside? In your body? Pokes and prods? Kicks? Somersaults?'

'I've felt lots of wind. Sometimes it hurts.'

'Nina. That's not wind. Well, it's not only wind. I think you have a baby inside you.'

'What?'

'And probably there's not much time. I think we're going to have to do this ourselves. It's all right, Nina, hold my hands, that's it. Hold tight. Bear with this one and we'll get you out of your underclothes. All right, don't panic, that's it. Breathe, Nina.'

Nina, crying, moaning, gripped Dorothy's hands.

'Don't fight it,' said Dorothy, lowering her voice to a whisper as the girl's cries subsided. 'That's it. My God, I can't believe how blind I've been.'

'What are you talking about?'

'You're having a baby.'

'Are you mad? A baby? Inside of me? A baby?'

'Yes. That's it. Hang on to me, there, that's it. Well done. It will pass, all of this.'

Nina screamed, then gradually she calmed, and lay still again. 'I'm expecting?' she said.

'Why didn't you tell us?'

'I didn't realise. I swear.'

'How could you not know you were pregnant?'

'I don't know. I just didn't know. That's all I can say. Are you sure?'

'Nina, you're in labour. I think these are labour pains, coming in waves. It's your body pushing the baby out. You're giving birth!'

'I'm having it now? But I can't. Oh no, it's coming back. Help me, Dot, please!'

Dorothy held the girl, and rocked her through the pain until it subsided.

Nina relaxed again.

'How could you not know?' scolded Dorothy. 'Oh, you

silly, blind girl. Didn't you even suspect? Didn't you think this might happen? Listen to me. You're at the end of your pregnancy. You're getting labour pains. They come and they go, and they are very, very strong. Yes? I know. Hold on again. That's right, Nina. Breathe. Breathe. There's a girl. Well done. Now, I want to take off your clothes, just your bottom half, and have a look. Because I have the feeling you may be having your baby quite soon. I . . . I know these things.'

Nina looked wildly at Dorothy, searching her face as if she could not speak Dorothy's language, and did not understand.

'Nina. Can I take off your trousers and your underclothes now, please?'

'I can't,' moaned Nina, the agony seizing her again, and she writhed and thrashed and moaned.

The pains were coming so quickly, one hard on the back of the other, and Dorothy knew birth was imminent. She took off Nina's boots and pulled down her breeches, which were wet. As if in a dream, Dorothy gently parted the girl's thighs. Peering at her, she could see that Nina was, indeed, in the throes of labour.

'You're going to have a baby, Nina, that's for sure. I can just see its head. Listen to me now. I know it hurts but you *are* having a baby. You're in the thick of it. And it's supposed to hurt and you are not poorly and you are not dying. I promise you. You must know that. Oh, why on earth didn't you tell us?'

'I didn't know, I swear,' she panted.

'So you keep saying, but . . . Well, never mind now. Keep my coat around you, Nina, if you can. That's it. Hitch up! That'll be nice and warm for your baby when he comes out. We'll have to keep him very warm – as warm as we can manage, at any rate. You'll need something underneath you. Is there anything in here we can use? Anything at all?'

Dorothy looked around and spotted a tarpaulin in the opposite corner. Rushing over to grab it, she saw a line of cows in their pen, ephemeral breath floating out of their nostrils as they lowed softly, nibbling hay, staring as though in fascination at the drama of human birth unfolding before them. So focused on the labouring girl, Dorothy had not noticed them before. But now their presence was an unexpected comfort. Dorothy grabbed the tarpaulin, unfolded it and shook it out. Where on earth was Aggie? Hopefully reaching Dr Soames by now, or Mrs Compton. But even as she thought this, Dorothy shuddered inside. She wanted to do this herself. The intimacy of the barn, the inquisitive cows, the poor hapless labouring girl, and her – and her alone – to help bring this child into the world. And Mrs Compton . . . the woman was not to be trusted around newborn babies. Mrs Compton would ruin everything.

Dorothy rolled Nina on to her side, spread the tarpaulin out underneath her and rolled her back on to it. She knelt beside Nina, and urged her to hold her hands, to squeeze tightly.

'Nina, listen to me. Next time you get the pains, I think you can push. Push as though you were . . . how can I put it? . . . as though you were in the privy. Do you understand?'

'Shitting, you mean?'

'Exactly that. Don't hold back, Nina. It's all perfectly natural. We're both women here. There's no shame even if you do—'

'But the baby won't come out of that hole, will it?'

'What do you think? Surely you've seen enough cows giving birth? Good God, Nina.'

'Don't half feel like I'm going to shit myself. Oh, Dot. Don't leave me. Oh God, oh God, oh God!'

And Nina pushed – for she was strong, if exhausted. And she was capable, if shocked.

'That's it, Nina, keep going. My goodness, there's not much longer to go now. Try to breathe, breathe now before the next pain. That's it.'

'I can't be having a baby. I'd know, wouldn't I?'

'Never mind about that now. You are having a baby, trust me. Are you ready? Hold my hands, don't let go. See? Aren't they warm and strong? Now gather yourself, breathe deep, and push, Nina, push.'

Nina stared at Dorothy, the girl's wild eyes locking on to Dorothy's. The baby's head began to emerge, and Dorothy removed Nina's hands from her own. She moved to kneel before the labouring girl, hands outstretched, waiting. And it seemed to Dorothy that the sun was about to shine on her, stronger and brighter than ever before, it was going to burst out from behind thick and dark clouds, and her life would become at last a life of illumination and warmth. But she could not truly tell why she felt this.

Nina, red-faced, sweating, threw back her head and bellowed. And from her body erupted a head of dark hair, a pinched-up little red face, shoulders, white-purple arms, belly, legs, twisted slime-grey cord, and blood, mucus, a gelatinous flood of indeterminate fluids. Dorothy gasped, and Nina sagged back on to the tarpaulin, and the baby cried, loudly, and Dorothy saw the baby kick and flail, strong like his mother. Strong like he should be.

'Oh, you're beautiful!' cried Dorothy to the baby, enchanted. She hastily removed her cardigan and wrapped it around the baby, and placed the little boy in his mother's arms. She drew up the mercifully large tarpaulin over the mother and child, and she repositioned her coat over Nina's shoulders. It was as warm as she could make them. It was enough, she reasoned. It would have to be. The baby, cries soon subsiding, lay quiet and calm, and Nina leaned back on the straw, exhausted, eyes closed as though asleep.

'He's truly perfect, Nina,' said Dorothy.

Nina made no reply.

Dorothy, sitting back, breathless, stared at the scene before her. Thoughts fired through her like a speeded-up newsreel. Nina was a mother. She had a baby, red-faced, angry, vigorous. Living. Very much living.

She noticed the girls' packed lunches and Thermos flasks.

'Nina, love, I'll get you some tea in a moment. Come on, sit up a bit, that's it. I need to cut the cord.'

Dorothy pulled the tarpaulin up over Nina's legs. She had no means of cutting the umbilical cord. She looked around the barn, but nothing was to be found. Yet it must be cut; it was bloody, and dirty, and bad luck, she thought, if not cut free of the baby soon. Could it even be dangerous? The thought sickened her, for a moment, and she wanted to cut the cord now before . . . before . . . even though this baby was free. Free of his mother's body, safely. The cord now simply trailed between mother and son like a question mark. She had to be calm. She must look after Nina. If the after-birth would only come away, all would be well, probably. She pressed down on Nina's belly as hard as she dared, and the afterbirth gushed out in a bloody pool. Leaving it lying in the straw between Nina's legs, she pulled the tarpaulin back over the girl and her baby, poured tea from one of the flasks she had made up for the girls only that morning – a mere few hours ago, fresh then from her intimate encounter with the squadron leader, blissful in the short-lived afterglow of a momentous night.

Nina sipped tea, her hand trembling so much that Dorothy had to hold the cup for her. Piling up more straw behind the new mother, Dorothy helped her to sit up, lifted up her jumper and helped her to undo her shirt and bra so she could feed her baby. He suckled immediately, eyes closed, a picture of peace and joy. Nina stared down at him, half in horror, half in wonder. Dorothy wrapped her coat more firmly around Nina's shoulders, covering the baby as much as she could, tied the sleeves of her cardigan together so the baby was swaddled, and finally helped herself to a cup of tea. She realised she was trembling almost as much as Nina.

The barn door creaked open and Aggie, drenched in snow, entered, alone. She closed the door, headed towards Nina and Dorothy and stopped dead.

'What the blazes—?'

'Nina had a baby. She was in labour. It's a little boy,' said Dorothy, and she could feel a wide and stupid grin slicing her face in two.

'A baby?'

'Yes.'

'A real *baby*?'

'Shut up, you bloody idiot,' said Nina. 'Can't you see it's a real baby?'

'But . . . but you're not . . . I mean, you weren't pregnant.'

'Oh yes, she was,' said Dorothy. She refilled the cup from the Thermos and handed it to Aggie.

Aggie took it, staring at Nina and her baby. 'You kept it a secret, Nina?' she said, breathless.

'I didn't bloody know, did I?' said Nina.

'How could you not know?' said Aggie.

'Aggie, she claims not to have realised. It can happen

sometimes. It's not unheard of. Nina's not regular like you. It can happen.'

'I can't believe it,' said Aggie, shaking her head.

'Did you suspect?' said Dorothy.

'No.'

'No more did I. It happens.'

'Let's have a look at him, then,' said Aggie, leaning over her friend to see the baby, who had ceased feeding and was asleep, swaddled tight in Dorothy's gorgeous – and ruined – pink cardigan.

'Oh, Nina. He's beautiful . . .' and Aggie cried, softly.

The cows shuffled their hooves, and Dorothy sat before them all, surveying this holy tableau. Nina, perennially unmoved, shrugged. The girl was pale, exhausted and in shock.

Dorothy recovered her senses. 'Where's Dr Soames, Aggie? Mrs Compton?'

'I tried both their houses, but nobody was in. Boxing Day, isn't it? They must be visiting.'

'I see.' She said this with a surge of something that felt oddly like relief. 'Look, we need to get Nina and this little chap home and in bed. How on earth are we to do that?'

'The tractor? I can hitch it up to the trailer and they can sit on the back. But shouldn't they go to hospital?'

'What?'

'Shouldn't they go to hospital?'

'No,' said Nina quietly. 'I'm not going nowhere. Get me back home, that's all I want. No one is to know, all right?'

'No one is to *know*?' echoed Aggie.

'Of course not. I'm nineteen, I'm not married. I've just had a baby. I don't hardly know who the father is.'

'Since when do you care about that sort of thing? Mary Knibbs had a baby, don't you remember? When she was only sixteen?'

'I do bloody remember. And her mum and dad booted her out and she went to a home for unmarried mothers. Don't *you* remember? And everyone called her a tart. And all her friends dropped her just like that, including you and me.'

Aggie looked down at her feet, sobered. Dorothy listened intently.

'Nobody is to know!' hissed Nina. 'Nobody.'

'We could ask Mrs Compton?' said Dorothy, wanting to be helpful. She felt she ought to be solicitous.

'That old gossip? Good job she wasn't in,' said Nina.

'But you might need medical help,' protested Aggie.

'No. I won't need help. Tell people I'm ill. That's it. I'm ill. I can't work for a few days. That's all.'

'But what about the baby?' said Aggie, wringing her hands.

Her anguish, Dorothy thought, was understandable.

'Dot will take care of him. You'll take him to the adoption people, won't you, Dot? Nuns? Somewhere?'

'Of course I'll help you, Nina,' said Dorothy. That feeling again – was it exhilaration?

'I can't keep it,' said Nina.

Aggie looked from woman to woman.

'I need to cut the cord,' Dorothy told her. 'Do you have a knife?'

She did. Dorothy held the cord and sawed at it with the knife, and at last it slipped apart, jelly-like, a strangely lifeless amputated limb.

'Aggie, go and get the tractor ready, will you? Aggie? Go on, it's nearly dark now. It must be done. We need to get these two in the warm, in bed.'

'I don't like this. Promise me, when we get back, promise me we'll send for Mrs Compton? If nobody else?'

'First things first,' said Dorothy.

'If she dies or the baby dies, how are you going to feel then?'

'Neither Nina nor her baby are about to die, what a silly notion. You're being melodramatic. He's as vigorous as hell and so is she, despite appearances. But they need to get warm. I'll talk to you later, tomorrow. But now we must act. Please, Aggie.'

Aggie shook her head and left the barn without another word. She returned with the trailer hooked on to the tractor, the cold engine of which grumbled and whined like a child suddenly awakened from a deep sleep. She and Dorothy helped the exhausted new mother on to the trailer, hushing her cries of pain when she stood up, Dorothy murmuring to her that, yes, everything 'down there' would feel bruised, battered, tender, for a few days. But not to worry, soon you will be in bed, and warm, and safe. Dorothy handed the tiny baby to Nina, covered them both in coats and the tarpaulin, gathered up the afterbirth and cord and scattered the bloodied straw around the barn. She climbed up beside the mother and child, placing the detritus of birth at the far end of the trailer. She would hide it under the hedge later.

Aggie drove them home, stealthily and slowly. And God Almighty, Dorothy was cold, perished, she realised, in just her skirt and blouse. But what could be done but get everybody home? Aggie drove on – no headlamps, of course, but the eerie light given off by the snow showed them the way – across fields, down the track, across the Long Acre and back to the cottage. Dorothy took the baby from Nina, and Aggie helped her to clamber down from the trailer. The party made their way gingerly and silently along the frozen back path to the kitchen door, Dorothy and Nina looking around furtively in this strange evening, snow everywhere.

In the dark, empty kitchen Dorothy switched on the

electric light. 'Sod the blackout,' she said, but she instructed Aggie to make sure all the curtains in the house were drawn tightly. She lit candles, ready for when she would turn out the light, settled Nina on the settee with her baby, tucked them up in blankets and lit the range in the kitchen.

Aggie returned the tractor and trailer to the yard. Still Dorothy could not believe it: Nina, expecting all that time, and nobody had known? Nina hadn't known? It seemed impossible – but, of course, there was a new baby boy to prove it.

Nina was a mother!

Dorothy shuddered.

Nina was not a mother. But she would learn, she would have to learn. Nobody is a mother until they have a baby, are they? she reasoned. That little boy, small and helpless, lying against his mother's breast, so peaceful, so oblivious.

Lighting fires, making tea, Dorothy's head pounded with fear, with shock, with unquestionable but baffling delight. She was feverish in her work, and this long night was only just beginning, she knew.

22

Dear, darling Jan,

Oh, my love, life sparkles today! You have been gone for three hours now. It feels like three decades. I hope you are enjoying a safe journey and are not stuck in the snow somewhere between here and Kent. I miss you already. I missed you before you left, before you got out of bed this morning. I even missed you while I slept alongside you last night. I shall never forget. I shall miss you always, while you are not here with me. This cottage felt like a home until you left this morning. I long to share my home with you, to share my life with you, to be all that my womanhood will allow. And dear man, I do not pray, as you know, but if I did I would pray each and every day for you, for God to return you safely to me. And I would pray that I could be here for you and be the woman you deserve. And I would pray for this war to end soon. Darling, I feel alive. Do you remember when I said that falling in love was like touching finger-tips? It has happened, for me, and I hope, for you too. I am the most fortunate of women. Please write, and soon.

Yours forever,
Dorothy

★

Jan drove through the white landscape, faster than he should. He was very cold but he ignored that. It was so early and dark on this 'Boxing Day', as Dorothy called it. She was a beautiful woman, Dorothy Sinclair. Strangely girlish and ripe, and not young. Dorothea. Maybe, he dared to hope, Mrs Dorothea Pietrykowski, because he knew already, he had decided long ago, that she would be his wife – a feeling as immutable as the moon. There was no alternative for them. And she felt it too, he thought. Only a catastrophe could keep them apart. She could do no wrong. And so, he would not return to Poland. He would not, even if he could, which was impossible to foresee. He would stay here in England, this austere country, where people laughed, like his own people, where they had a strong sense of humour, despite all that was threatening them. He liked it here. He could speak the language well enough. And, he thought, this country would owe him after the war. The Polish squadrons were contributing so much at last, it would not be forgotten by this country that did so much 'by the book'. And the Allies would win this war . . . of that, now, he was certain. Hitler was a fool, and fools do not prevail. And Churchill was obviously not a fool. The war would be won. Somehow.

Driving away from Dorothy, he felt more alone with each rotation of the wheels. She was so warm. And he had felt so light and fluid, lucid, in her arms, with her legs wrapped around him, and he longed to be back in her bed. It had cost him so much to get up that morning, to stumble out into the freezing dark morning air, to wash and dress, eat her breakfast. Watching her as she so carefully sewed the buttons back on to his shirt, such a patient woman, how his love had risen for her then, her honey-brown hair shining in the candlelight. He realised she was certainly damaging her eyes while sewing in such dim light in the dark morning. But that was who she was, this most selfless of women.

Would she write to him? A proper letter at last? This time, he thought – he knew – she would write to him freely, with love and abandon. He could not wait.

23

We did Whernside today, Ingleborough tomorrow. Went to Bolton Abbey on Monday. So far weather is sunny and warm, aren't we lucky? We hope to do Penyghent if weather lasts, on Friday. Everything is comfortingly the same up here, just what we all love about it.

(A postcard of Hawes in Wensleydale. Sent to 'Mum and Dad' and signed by their daughter Abigail. This was found inside a 1946 copy of *Jane Eyre* published by the Zodiac Press, and a very good copy, priced at £12 and placed on the hardback fiction shelves in the back room. I was tempted to keep the book, as I had kept the postcard, but it sold quickly.)

It's a scourging late October day, that day in autumn where you finally understand that summer really is over. The wind is blowing hard, a cold rain is drifting across the churchyard. It's the sort of rain that seeks to slap your face and blind you.

I am standing at my father's grave. It's at the bottom of the churchyard, by the wall, where there had once been stinging nettles and a compost heap. I tiptoe through the graves, some of them familiar from childhood. Mary Sarah Wight, beloved daughter, sister, niece, wife, aunt, mother, grandmother, great-grandmother and friend, 1868 to 1967.

That was always my favourite. I always thought, what an amazing life Mary Sarah Wight must have led. To be all those things, to all those people, for all that time.

I stand now, alone in this bleak churchyard, and I feel so small. It frightens me. I had not spoken to my dad about . . . certain things . . . and now we can never speak again. He died a fortnight ago. The decline was sudden and swift. The breathing problem returned, only much worse. He was rushed to hospital. And there he stayed for four days, begging all the while to be allowed home to die. I backed him up, and finally I took him home. A kindly nurse called Lisa came to Dad's house and brought oxygen, showing me how to help him use it. She administered morphine and other drugs. They, all of them – Dr Moore, Lisa, a couple of Dad's friends – wanted him in the hospice, it was 'the best place for him'. But when I discussed it with Dad, while he could still reason and say what he wanted, he refused. So I refused too. And between us, somehow, Lisa the nurse and I looked after Dad. And how strange it was. I became familiar with my father's body, his bodily functions. I washed him, brushed his teeth, combed his hair, washed the bedlinen when it was soiled, dressed him, undressed him. I had to be like a wife to him. Lisa and I were with him when he died. It was swift, in the end, and merciful. Lisa said she had witnessed far worse deaths.

I felt no shock, at first not even any sadness. Then, that night after his death, trying to sleep, I realised I had not phoned anybody to tell them the news. There were a few friends, a few former work colleagues, from his days at Pietrykowski and Wallace, but I would gather myself and ring them in the morning. In fact, I would email most people, which was so much easier and safer. My voice would not hold out, I feared, over the telephone. They were all the sort of people who would not mind my crying, they would come to the funeral and say nice things about my father, and it would be truthfully meant, and it would even be comforting.

There is one other person to tell, of course. I think, I wonder if . . . I know I should . . . tell Babunia that her only son has died. We have never told her about his illness. Dad and I discussed it after he first told me he had it, years ago. We would not worry her; the chances were that she would die before he did. But she is still alive, and Dad is not. And it will take some thought, and sensitivity, and I seriously doubt I am up to the job. I have put it off so far. The time needs to be right. I need to feel strong first. And right now I feel as weak as a soaked tissue.

I've been going through my father's things and I have found his birth certificate, neatly folded and stored in a Manila envelope along with his decree absolute. And my Polish grandfather was alive, according to the birth certificate, on the day that my grandmother registered my father's birth, which was 13th January 1941. I can only assume my father knew this, as he must have read his own birth certificate. And she was already calling herself Dorothea Pietrykowski, which I think must have been an outright lie – the deed that Suzanne showed me wasn't drawn up until March 1941. Were my father and grandmother in cahoots? Did Dad know the full story? I wish I had pushed him, and got some answers. Because, of course, now, as I feared, it is too late, another piece of the jigsaw is missing and I may never build up the whole picture. Do I want to, though? I don't really know what I want any more. I seem to have become bereft of all my energy, as well as bereft of my father.

I miss him. I loved him so much. He was my friend as well as my father.

And if I expect anybody, anyone at all, to pull up in his car and find me standing alone at my father's grave in this whipping-whispering rain, to stroll over in a nonchalant yet purposeful way, to put his arm around me in friendship, as a colleague might do, and tell me how sorry he is, and offer to buy cakes, and make a sweet, hearty mug of tea, and make me laugh with a pithy and sardonic comment about the inexplicable nature of death, or grief, or of life, I am to be disappointed.

Why do I feel this need to be rescued? I have lived alone, essentially alone, for sixteen years. By alone I suppose I mean without a long-term partner. By alone I suppose I mean without children. For most of my life, I have been without my mother. Now I feel tears blooming, I cannot stop them, and I know I am feeling sorry for myself, that most despicable of emotions. And I need a friend, I know this, I want a friend so badly. And by friend I mean lover, confidant, trusted individual, significant other. Maybe I even mean husband. Maybe all this distils down to that. I have denied myself all of this. I stand still, looking at the sky, the church, feeling the rain mingle with the tears on my face, and I cannot look into my future. I stand alone – for hours, it seems – and finally I recall myself, and I walk back to my car. I climb in, and I am so cold I cannot get the key into the ignition for several pained minutes.

24

O h, but Nina was so cold. Dorothy put the shivering girl and her baby boy in the girls' double bed, and banished Aggie to the spare room. Initially, Aggie baulked at this – knowing what had only recently occurred in the room, and in particular the bed – but Dorothy told her briskly to help herself to fresh bedding from the linen cupboard and to stop being silly, for heaven's sake. Aggie found the forgotten dough set to rise in the cupboard that morning, and Dorothy told her to throw it away. It was a hell of a waste, but it couldn't be helped. Dorothy delved into the bottom of her wardrobe and retrieved the stack of nappies and pins she had bought two winters ago. They were huge on the tiny newborn, but they would do. She hauled armfuls of logs and a scuttle of coal upstairs and lit the fire in the double bedroom, then she dressed Nina in a flannel nightgown and bed jacket and put fresh warm socks on her poor cold feet. She piled an extra eiderdown over Nina, tore a bed sheet in half and swaddled the baby in it, and instructed Nina to keep him in bed with her that night, but to be careful. Dorothy helped her to arrange pillows and showed her how to wriggle down the bed so her head was level with the baby's head, meaning she would not pull up the covers and suffocate him.

Dorothy took to her own bed, but kept her door open so she could hear each time the baby woke up. And each time he did, she got up, poked the fire and added more coal.

Nina did not want to feed the baby. So Dorothy explained, with patience, that there was no suitable milk available and Nina would have to feed him if she didn't want him to die – at least, until they could get milk for him.

'Might be best if he did die,' said the bewildered girl, holding her baby awkwardly, but trying to feed him.

'Do not talk like that,' said Dorothy as she helped Nina to position him comfortably.

He latched on, squeezing shut his tiny eyes, his little body rigid with the richness of suckling his mother. Dorothy was wakeful, watchful, fearful, all night. She didn't mind the little boy's cries and whimpers. She thought these sounds had been taken from her forever. Nina was clearly exhausted, as all new mothers are, but she rocked him and fed him with Dorothy's help.

By the first light of dawn, as the cockerel announced its arrival, Dorothy was both delighted and dismayed to wake from a fitful doze to find Nina fast asleep, cuddling her little boy, also fast asleep, mother and child breathing in unison, pink-faced and contented. It was a vision Dorothy couldn't tear herself away from, and a rage ballooned inside her, a blind and fierce feeling of hatred and nausea. She was still rational enough to recognise jealousy, although she had never truly felt it until now.

She put on her pinny and made breakfast, and Aggie went off to work with a concocted tale of her friend's illness, her vomiting, her incapacity. The need for recuperation. Poor overworked Nina, it had finally brought her crashing down. If anybody questioned her story, Aggie was to ignore the questions. On no account was she to tie herself up in knots. Nina wanted this baby kept secret, and Nina's wish must be respected. So. There it was.

Dorothy pulled her suitcase from under her bed, blew off

the wisps of dust, and with trembling hands unlocked and opened it. Sidney's clothes were pristine and fresh, and the evermore aroma of dried lavender swamped Dorothy with the welcome surprise of a spring heatwave. She took out the bundle of Jan's letters and threw them on to her bed along with her notebook and pen. With care she carried the case across the landing to Nina's room, and showed her all the things she had once made. Nina must use them, of course. There was nothing else. Dorothy gave the baby his first wash – just a lick and a promise, as Dorothy's mother had always called it – with Nina looking on as she gently wiped the baby's face and neck and hands with a flannel. And as she and Nina dressed the baby boy, it seemed to Dorothy that this baby was a charmed imposter, animating the ghost-clothes meant for a different baby. A baby who no longer existed, and who might never have existed, he was so distant from Dorothy now. The clothes were a large fit, but Nina's baby looked well, Dorothy thought, his little legs kicking, his arms quaking up and down as if in joy at the lovely new clothes he was so privileged to be wearing.

Nina was clumsy and still in shock. She was feverish and trembling. Dorothy hoped she would not need to call in the doctor, even though she knew, yes, this should be done, really, both for Nina and for her little boy. It was common sense, it was the responsible thing to do.

She brought the tin bath into the kitchen, boiled water and helped Nina to bathe. 'Let me look after you,' she murmured.

The girl was cold, hot, shivering. But she pronounced herself warmer after the bath, and Dorothy helped her back upstairs and tucked her back into bed.

'You're a good woman, Dot,' said Nina. 'I don't know what the bloody hell I'd do without you.'

'Nonsense. I'll bring you some tea.'

Dorothy threw out Nina's bright red bathwater, rinsed the bath and refilled it for herself. She hadn't washed since the morning of Christmas Day, and part of her didn't want to, but she knew she ought to. She luxuriated in the water, taking time to soap herself and to slowly rinse it off with her flannel. Her towel was stiff and warm, and she allowed herself to stand in it for some time, wrapping it tightly around her body. In time she dressed, threw out the bathwater and replaced the bath on its hook in the wash house. There were chores to attend to, a baby and his weary mother to look after.

Dorothy remained confident. She was vigilant. Nina was hardy. She would pull through. She stoked up the fire in the bedroom. Babies need to be kept very warm, she advised Nina. And you need to be warm too, so stay in bed and look after the baby.

'He was Polish,' said Nina as she watched Dorothy put coal on the fire.

Dorothy smiled a slow, rueful smile of understanding. It might have been compassion. She hoped it was compassion.

'He was funny,' added Nina. 'I liked him. It's wartime, ain't it? I think he's the one that died. In the crash out the back. The one you tried to rescue.'

'Oh.'

'It couldn't have been . . . I don't think it was nobody else. Not at that time anyway. Do you see?'

'Yes, I see.'

'But that's no help to me. My mum and dad . . . I can't tell them. They can't ever know about this baby. Shirley. My brothers. I can't tell none of them.'

'What on earth will you do?'

'Have you spoken to the nuns yet?'

'No, of course not, you ridiculous girl! Oh, I'm sorry, Nina. Forgive me. You gave birth only yesterday. I haven't had time . . . it's . . . I don't actually know of any nuns. Nina. Please understand.'

'You can find out. You're clever, Dot. People listen to you.'

The baby, who Nina had named David, suckled in unknowing peace at the young woman's swollen and cloud-like breast. His hair was dark and sticking to his head, and he was blessed with the tangy, musky, minty, yeasty, orangey, earthy, other-worldly smell of the newborn baby. The smell was a drug to Dorothy, but Nina appeared unmoved.

'Nina, there is no real shame in having a baby, you know. Whatever the circumstances may be. A baby is a gift.'

'I don't care about that,' replied Nina. 'I don't want it. I never even knew I was carrying it. You believe me, don't you?'

Dorothy patted her free hand. 'I do. I truly do. I didn't know you were carrying him either, and I'm much older than you and I should have realised. There were signs that I should have noticed. You've been so hungry! You even fainted, do you remember?'

'I do. Rotten feeling, that was. Like falling off the edge of the world.'

'Just try to get some sleep, will you? If you want to get back to work this week, you must rest.'

'I am going back to work this week.' Nina's jaw was set stubbornly. 'But what about David? How can we hide him?'

'What do you mean, "hide him"?'

'I don't want anybody knowing about him. Please, Dot. Not anybody.'

'Mrs Compton? She could look at him, make sure he's all right?'

Nina shook her head. 'No. After what happened with your little . . . oh, sorry.'

'That's all right,' said Dorothy. 'We'll keep her out of it, shall we? Dr Soames? But on second thoughts, he's terribly officious. I'm not sure he'd keep your baby a secret.'

'Not him, then. Nuns it is. Nuns know what to do with babies, don't they?'

'There are no nuns!' said Dorothy.

Nina wilted a little. 'Then what the bloody hell am I going to do? I'm not a mother. I don't want a baby. I'll be disowned by my mum. She always said to me and Shirley, if either of us gets into trouble, she'll never see us or the baby. She'll have nothing to do with us. She meant it too, I know my mum. I ain't going into one of those homes for unmarried mothers either. I've heard about them.'

'But you're nineteen, Nina. You're a grown-up young lady. You can do with your life as you choose. Think ahead, think about five, ten, twenty years from now. You'll be your own woman and nobody will necessarily know or care that your son was born illegitimately. People get over things like that. And besides, perhaps your mother will actually love her little grandson. Her first special grandchild.'

'Love him? She don't even love any of us, so why would she love a child born out of wedlock?'

Dorothy frowned. 'Nonsense. Of course she loves you.'

Nina snorted. 'No. She does her duty by us. There ain't much love to spare in our house. She hates Dad, and he hates her. She's always said, if she had her time again, she wouldn't get married and she wouldn't have kids.'

It didn't look good for Nina, Dorothy had to admit to herself. Her mother had not written to her since she had been at the farm – could she even write? Dorothy wondered – nor had her elder brothers. Her father, Dorothy gathered, was often drunk. How would the baby fare in such a family? The thought hung heavy over Dorothy like the snow-laden sky she glimpsed through the lace curtains, the large golden-black clouds once again threatening to disgorge themselves.

It was impossible. What were Nina's options, truly?

'I'll take care of him for you.' Dorothy wasn't sure at first if she had uttered the words aloud. But they resounded around the room, portentous, like a roll of thunder in the mountains.

'You?' said Nina, astonished. 'What, you'll be his mum?'

'If you want.'

The women locked eyes, both desperate, searching. Dorothy felt as if she were finely and perilously balanced on a mountain ledge, and if she were to let go, or stumble, she would fall into a dark and endless oblivion. She breathed hard.

Finally, Nina shook her head.

Dorothy looked at her, trying in vain to silence her heaving heart.

Nina opened her mouth as though to speak, and closed it again. But finally, she spoke. 'You'd be good to him? You'd look after him, properly? And you wouldn't care what people said about you, would you?'

'No.' Dorothy could barely speak, her throat tight with fear and anticipation.

'That's because you ain't afraid to tell people where to get off. Not really. You've got brains. You can work people out. But I'm scared, I am, underneath it all.' Then, 'You'd really look after him?'

'Yes,' said Dorothy fervently.

'What, as if he was your own? How would you do it? Everyone knows you ain't been carrying. You're thin as a bloody rake. People will know.'

'People around here will, yes.'

'You mean, you'd take him away?'

'I have family in . . . well, miles from here.'

'I see,' said Nina. For the first time since Dorothy had known her, she looked as though she were deep in thought.

'What do you think?' said Dorothy, after a while.

'It sounds all right. Better than nuns. But I can't ask you to do it for me.'

'In that case, ask me to do it for your baby,' said Dorothy, taking Nina's hand now. 'I can't bear the thought of . . . David in a home, with no real mother. It's not what the dear little chap deserves.'

Do it for me too, Nina, damn it. Don't go all doubtful now, you oafish girl, not now it's within my grasp. I wrap my life around this longing.

'And nobody would know?' said Nina. 'That I was his real mum, I mean? You'd not tell?'

'I'd not tell a soul.'

'You'd say he was yours?'

'Yes.'

'You'd love him?'

'Oh yes.'

'You love babies, don't you? You miss yours.'

Dorothy could tell Nina wanted to convince herself. 'I do. Very much.'

'So David would be the son you didn't have?'

What to say? What was she looking for? What to say now, not to destroy everything, not to ruin this chance, with the wrong words, the wrong tone, the wrong look. The words came to Dorothy, one by one, as if in translation.

'No, Nina, he wouldn't be that. I believe . . . I know that I can give David all the things you can't or won't be allowed to give. I'm fortunate to be able to give him a life you can't even imagine. I mean that in a kind way, Nina. I will have property one day. Money, I hope. There is a nice home for him, a bedroom all of his own. I shall fill it with toys and books. He'll go to a good school. He'll make friends. He'll want for very little. Of course, you can send him to the nuns if you feel that would be better for him . . .'

Nina looked at her baby, fast asleep at her breast, milk glistening on his chin, his breathing soft and calm. Dorothy watched the girl, then looked at the baby – who she knew she would not call David – and she prayed, as hard as she ever had, with all her heart, so hard she almost believed that somebody was actually listening and could help. And when Nina handed her the baby, dressed in Sidney's clothes, Dorothy took him in trembling arms, and held him close to her heart, and kissed his head.

Nina turned away to sleep, and stated that she would not feed him once Dorothy had sorted something else out, because milk leaked on to her clothes and she couldn't have people seeing that. It was embarrassing, and it would give her away, wouldn't it? Dorothy said she understood, and then she carried the baby downstairs and laid him in the big black pram that had been languishing and mouldering out in the shed for two years. She had brought it in, late the night before, scrubbed it clean and aired it by the fire overnight. She covered the baby boy in the blanket she had knitted once in such hope and gladness.

Unaware, the baby slept.

Practicalities took over. Dorothy would need to procure milk. She had bottles, bought for Sidney – Dorothy had planned to feed him herself, but Mrs Compton had recommended the purchase 'just in case'. She dug out the four bottles, still in their boxes, and washed them, enjoying the sensation of the smooth glass in her hand as she traced the odd banana-like shapes. She inserted the teats into the bottles, in readiness. She had never fed a baby before.

Bottles were easy, milk less so. Dorothy did not want to use the powdered milk she had heard about. It was unnatural. No, real milk it would have to be. But cow's milk was too much for a tiny baby, she knew. It would make him sick, give him stomach ache, or worse. Goat's milk? She knew it was nourishing, good for poorly babies. A wet nurse, even if there were any left these days, was out of the question.

Nina's milk would dry up. In a few days she could return to work, and Dorothy could make arrangements. In a delirium of joy and fear, she stood, alert, gently rocking the pram. She felt – she knew, intuitively – that from this point on her life would be governed by falsehood. It would be so, and her life, with this baby, no matter what, would prevail above all else. There was no other future for her. It was laid out before her like a map, and she could trace every turn she would have to make.

She rocked the pram, and waited for the baby to wake up. Unbearable hope bloomed again in Dorothy Sinclair's heart. And she knew if her hopes were to come to nothing, yet again, the disappointment would crush her, finally and forever.

And Jan. She almost did not want to think about him. He had been but the briefest of interludes. Sweet, welcome and glorious. Just yesterday – *yesterday!* – he had been her great opportunity. Today, he was gone. It was inconceivable, but already she had another, a greater, opportunity.

And Sidney, her precious little boy, what of him? She allowed herself to worry that he might not like this new baby, this other little boy taking his place. But Dorothy knew such thoughts were illogical, irrelevant. Her secret was safe from Sidney.

The baby shuddered, and sighed, and slept.

25

Marshall
 I hate you Rachel hates you we all hate YOU so the best thing you can do is never get in touch with us again do you hear me you ugly little man? My sister and me, we're going to be okay after all but not until you are history so please leave us in peace to sort things out we no longer require you do you get that?
 Jacqueline

(Letter found inside John Gray's *Men Are from Mars, Women Are from Venus*, quite a well-read copy, so priced at a reasonable 80p and placed on the self-help shelf in the back room.)

Portia fails to understand the grief that follows my father's death.

I weep, I rage.

She stares at me, cold and uncomprehending. 'Histrionics!' she seems to say.

I don't think I like cats very much. Why is she even here? Her mission in life, apart from irritating me, seems to be to wilfully destroy delicate life, birds and mice and shrews, such dear little trembling creatures. I make a note to contact the Blue Cross. Let them take her. I don't want her here any more.

I am alone in the world. My father is actually dead, my

mother may as well be dead, and I don't even have Charles Dearhead any more to make sterile love to. I miss him, all of a sudden – because, I believe, even sterile love is better than no love at all.

And I no longer remember to eat. My clothes are becoming loose, my hair lank. I can't be bothered to hoover or dust, wash up or shop.

I fret, I sleep.

I dream that I am a little girl again, being bounced on my father's knees, squealing with delight, waving my hands around, too vigorously, scratching his cheek, but I didn't mean to – 'I'm sorry, Daddy' – and he's dabbing at his cheek with his handkerchief, annoyed, but telling me not to worry, little Robbie Roberta, and he tells my mother my nails need cutting, and my mother, sitting in her chair by the fire, her long hair shining in the firelight, ignores us. And now I can no longer decide what is real. She was still with us. Maybe it was the following day that she left? She didn't collect me from school. I waited and waited in Miss Romney's class, and she let me cut paper and card in the guillotine. Miss Romney remained bright and cheerful, but I knew she was worried. Eventually, Dad came into the classroom and picked me up and hugged me. He was crying, which I didn't like. He shook his head at Miss Romney, thanked her and carried me home.

I must be unwell, I have a temperature, I think. I feel aglow. A day in bed. That's what I need.

Day one: sleep. Sweat, a lot. The logical part of me that appears still to function underneath the raging tells me I have flu, a fever.

Day two: more fever, more sweating, Portia's endless complaining, my mother's sleek and shiny hair in the firelight. Nothing happens, but I think I feed Portia. I ought to feed Portia. My father has a gravestone, but it's written in a strange script that I cannot read, and it is high summer. The bees are buzzing around the honeysuckle that grows under my kitchen window. The bees are buzzing around me, swarming, hideous and loud. I think my phone is ringing, I think I hear a girlish and familiar voice saying she'll try my mobile. My mobile, plugged into its charger on the bedside table, rings. I can't move. It rings, it stops. I think I sleep.

Day three? Feeling hot and thirsty and weak, and hating Portia. She looks thin too, I think. And then I understand, she would look thin, I'm not feeding her. I ran out of her food, possibly yesterday, possibly the day before. I'm surprised she is still here and has not absconded to the neighbour who, I am fairly certain, feeds her regularly, just as she fed Tara. This could be day three, or day six, or seven. I can't count any more. And the awful truth is that there's nobody to help. I am alone in this world and living now among the fevered and garish rubble that once was strong and good, my life that I had once built for myself.

Day four, I think, or eight? The doorbell ringing, and my not truly hearing it or connecting with it, and it ringing again.

My mobile rings. I grapple for it as it falls on to the floor. I pick it up, I can't read the name. Was it my father? Surely not my mother?

'Hello?' I think the voice is mine. Or maybe it's Portia's? She has been speaking to me recently. At least she is still here. I am not alone. Oh, she looks hungry.

'Roberta? It's me. Philip. Are you all right? I'm at your flat. But I guess you're not in?'

Philip? He's never been to my flat.

'I am here,' I manage to say. My voice sounds like a squeak. 'Hang on. Please.'

I stumble into the hall and, sure enough, there is the shadow of a real person through the frosted glass of the door. I eventually unlock it, and I stare at a man who looks exactly like my former boss, Philip Old, only more handsome. He stares back at me. The first person I have seen in four days. Or five. Or eight? Is it Friday? Somehow, I think, it must be a Saturday. The sun is shining like it does on Saturdays. It's bright, and shining frostily, like it does in autumn. Is it still autumn? I have been floating through the poetry of summertime. My Dad has a gravestone, but I can't read what it says. The language is foreign, it is gobbledegook. The honeysuckle is in full bloom. The bees torture my head, they crawl inside my ears and into my mind, colouring my world – ugly, visceral colours. My mother is so beautiful.

'Roberta, you—'

I think he gets no further. The world is folding in on itself, I can't breathe, my throat is tight, I can't think or compute, but I know I'm slumping, and I know there is someone there to catch me, so I must let it happen, I must slip down into the unconsciousness which I know is waiting for me.

I can feel arms, I hear heavy breathing. 'Oh fucking hell!' somebody says. But whether it's Philip or Portia or myself, I don't know.

And I am gone. Into the darkness. And it is heaven.

I wake up in my bed. It's been hours, I think, since I faded out. I am in clean pyjamas. It is dark outside. I can smell coffee, cat food, toasting bread. I am not alone. I sit up, fragility keeping my movements slow and pained.

'Hello?' I call. I can hear Radio Four murmuring from my kitchen.

Philip appears in my bedroom doorway. 'Hello,' he says, his head on one side, smiling. He is eating toast.

'I don't really know what's going on,' I say.

'You're ill. You've been ill for days, I suspect. Sophie was worried when she couldn't get a reply on either of your phones. She rang me at home this morning. I came to see if I could help. You fainted on me in your hallway. Nutshell.'

'What day is this?'

'Sunday.'

'What time?'

Philip examines his watch. 'It's twenty-six minutes past seven.'

'At night?'

'Yes.'

'What time did you get here?'

'Around two this afternoon.'

'I passed out for five and a half hours?'

'No, you were out for a minute or so. Don't you remember? I carried you in here, we changed you into your pyjamas. I tucked you into bed.'

'I don't remember.'

Was I wearing knickers? Unwashed for days? Had Philip removed them? Did Philip see me naked?

I blush.

'Don't worry, Roberta,' he says. 'Your dignity is more than intact. Besides, we've known each other for quite a while now, haven't we? So if I happened upon your under-wear while helping you into bed, it's of no great consequence. Is it?'

'No.'

There is a strange silence in the room. Philip stands in the doorway, looking at me. I have not seen this expression before. He looks like he feels sorry for me. I don't like it much. I am relieved when Portia glides into the room and jumps up on to my bed. She purrs as I stroke her and hold her to my face, feeling her soft fur, reacquainting myself with her familiar cat smell.

'Thank you,' I say to Philip, burying my face in Portia.

'For what?' he says.

'For everything. Thank you. For being such a good friend,' and here I am now, crying, tears rolling down my cheeks, the cat leaping away because she has never liked crying. I notice she is no longer speaking to me.

Philip sits on my bed, puts down his toast and takes my hand in both of his. His hands are warm and buttery.

'I'm sorry about your father,' he says.

'I didn't tell you about him.'

'No. But everyone else did. It's a small town, Roberta. You should have told me. Why on earth didn't you ring? I could have helped. And I would have liked to have gone to the funeral. As it was . . . it was difficult. You and I parted on bad terms, I felt.'

'I couldn't . . . I don't expect anything from you.'

'I'd do anything for you, Roberta. Any time you ask. You may have worked that out by now.' He smiles kindly at me.

'No, I haven't worked that out.'

'Then you must be extremely dim.'

I have no reply to this. Philip is sitting on my bed, holding my hand, making what sounds like a declaration of loyalty, if not devotion. And I am scared and sad and feeling rotten and I can't imagine how I must look and smell. I wonder if he has emptied Portia's litter tray. I rather think I was sick in the bathroom at some point in recent days. I don't recall cleaning it up.

'Roberta. Look. We've been beating around the bush for so long now. It's all becoming such a bore. We've already wasted too many years in the sense that we have not been honest with each other. Whether from simple shyness or fear or even compunction, I don't know. What I mean is, I love you like a sister. But that doesn't make me your brother, does it?'

I think Philip just uttered the words 'I love you'. Ambiguously, of course. Typically. But he's right, too many years have been wasted, too much time has passed, and if I were to die now – and, believe me, I feel close to that state – I know what my one overwhelming regret would be. I know this, I have admitted it to myself. I just need to find the guts to admit it to him, and now.

'I don't have a brother,' I say. It's not, of course, quite what I meant to say or wanted to say, but it will have to do. At least it's true.

'Would you have liked one?'

'Yes. Oh yes.'

'Me too. I have a sister. But she doesn't approve of me.'

'Philip?'

'Yes?'

'I love you too,' I mean to say. I am breathing hard and fast, and my heart is thumping like it has to be free of my body. And I'm sweating – but that doesn't matter, because I've been sweating for days. I have to say these words to this man, who is still sitting on my bed holding my hand. I have been quiet for too long, quiet and stupid. I deserve this chance. I'm going to take it.

But all I can manage is, 'Can I come back to work?' It's pathetic.

'I thought you'd never ask,' says Philip. 'Of course. But only when you're up to it.'

'Thank you,' I say. Nothing more.

'No, thank you.'

'Philip, does she make you happy? Jenna?' I feel breathless and charmed. Slowly, slowly I'm building up to it.

'Sometimes. It's . . . difficult.'

'I'm sorry.'

'I'm awfully stupid, Roberta. I'm a man, after all.'

'You're not stupid in the least,' I say.

'I don't find relationships easy.'

'Does anybody?'

'My parents did. I never heard a cross word between them all through my childhood. Mind you, I was away at school much of the time.'

'Boarding school?'

This is the first time he's told me anything about his childhood.

'Boarding school, indeed.'

'I see. You were . . . quite well off, then?'

'I still am, my dear, I still am.' Philip winks at me. He's not done that to me before. 'When one is fortunate enough to go through life with sufficient money . . . it should make life so easy, shouldn't it?'

'Yes, I . . . I suppose so,' I stammer, blushing.

He seems amused. 'Yes, well. Enough of this bullshit. I'm going to get you some toast, you can't have eaten properly for days. Then I'm going to leave you to get more sleep, but I'll bed down on the sofa tonight, if that's okay?'

I nod weakly.

And he carries on. 'I phoned Jenna earlier to fill her in. She's being very understanding, actually, and hopes you feel better soon. And don't worry about anything, I've fed the cat and cleaned up. I'll be here in the morning, and we'll talk properly. You're still feverish, but I need to know you mean what you say about coming back, and I want you to understand that I mean what I say. All you have to do is eat, then sleep. Do you mind if I open that bottle of Pinot Grigio in your fridge?'

I eat two slices of hot buttery toast, then two more. Then I sleep. I dream, drifting in and out of sleep. He loves me, he loves me not. Finally, I lie still, I close my eyes, I go over all that Philip and I have spoken about.

And he's here all night, watching over me, my friend.

26

Dorothy and her boy. He was dark-haired, skinny, alive, and together they were sitting on a riverbank at nearly twilight. The river moved softly, a water vole scurried from the water into his hole in the bank. She heard a noise like a thousand angel wings beating, but it was starlings, a huge flock of them, a murmuration swarming over the treetops, black, moving as one, this way, that, evening sunlight reflecting from a myriad of wings like shimmers of pure gold. Dorothy reached for her son's hand and he smiled as, together, they watched the birds, the mother and her son, hand in hand, contented and joyous. But there were no more starlings. Instead, there were crows, and they were angry. And in front of them, fleeing for its life, was an owl, its wings beating furiously, a fear in its eyes that Dorothy and her son could clearly see. Dorothy clutched her boy to her, cradled his head in her arms and rocked him until the terrible spectacle was over. And like all dreams it was soon over, half remembered.

But that day in 1939, the day of Sidney's birth, was never just half remembered, although she tried hard to forget. The pains did not abate.

She couldn't finish her laundry, and had to leave Albert's Sunday trousers in the mangle, her undies floating in the copper, the soapsuds forming a scum on top. She sent Albert on his bicycle for Mrs Compton, who followed him back on her own bicycle, both arriving red-faced and tired. It was three o'clock in the afternoon, a warm, fresh day in May with a softening breeze. Mrs Compton bustled into the kitchen with a heavy-looking carpet bag, black and worn, which she placed on the table. Dorothy, sitting by the range, looked up at Mrs Compton.

'What do we have here, then?' Mrs Compton asked, hands on hips, looking down on Dorothy malevolently, or so it seemed to the labouring woman.

For surely this *was* labour, the pains coming and fading rhythmically, each one harder and longer than the last? It had been going on for six hours now, more or less, by Dorothy's reckoning. But she couldn't say exactly when they started, those first faint tremors, gradually turning to pain.

'You're quiet enough,' said Mrs Compton. 'The baby isn't on his way just yet. Get a nice cup of tea.' She looked at Albert, indicating the kettle on the range.

Surprised, he shook it to make sure there was water inside. There was.

'And then relax, eat, get to bed early, both of you. I'll come back in the morning. I'll leave my things here.' She indicated her bag with a tap.

Dorothy did, and did not, want Mrs Compton to leave. Fear of what was to come, the task before her, and dismay that the baby wouldn't be born in the next hour or two fuelled her anxiety. 'What if the baby comes in the night and you're not here?' she said.

'He won't, love, trust me, I've seen hundreds of women like you. And it's your first, he'll be a while yet. I'll come back nice and early, I'll come at six. How's that? Try to sleep.'

She left. Albert and Dorothy sipped tea, Dorothy catching

her breath with each pain as it surged through her body, stinging the tops of her legs, crashing through her belly like a newly sharpened knife. After a while, they ate and talked a little, Albert eyeing her anxiously. They went to bed at nine o'clock, and he tentatively rubbed her belly until he slept. Dorothy stayed awake and wished forth her baby. The idea of the pains getting any worse was becoming inconceivable.

Dorothy listened to Albert snore for a while, until she got out of bed and walked around the house. She decided to be useful, so she returned to her wash house. In between pains, she finished off the laundry and hung everything out on the line to dry overnight. The night was warm, the breeze still present, it was a perfect night for drying. That task completed, she returned to the house, quietly retrieved the suitcase from under the bed and carried it down to the parlour. She took out all the things she had made for this baby, for Sidney. She was convinced the baby was a boy, so much so that she had not even considered any girls' names this time. She smelled Sidney's clothes, shook them, smoothed them and laid them out on the settee, trying to decide which outfit she would dress her baby in first. Then she packed them all away again and napped on the settee.

Around three o'clock in the morning, she awoke with a strong wave of pain, suddenly stronger, harder, and she doubled over, crying out. She feared something was wrong, some indescribable tragedy was surely unfolding inside her. The pain was unnatural. She woke Albert, sending him for Mrs Compton. Yes, she knew she'd said she would come back early, but she was needed now. It was only just gone three, yes, she knew that, but please, Albert. I'm scared. Albert thought her melodramatic, but Dorothy didn't care. It was happening only to her and so only she knew.

When she was alone again, the pains grew stronger, harder, more frequent and urgent. It seemed that Mrs Compton and Albert would never return, she would have to give birth on her own, it would be bloody, the baby would wail and she wouldn't know what to do. She struggled upstairs between pains, got on to the bed, and rocked on all fours, trying to keep up her breathing. She tried to focus on something else, the day ahead, whether it would be warm and dry. It seemed likely. She got off the bed, as the rocking motion and squeak of the castors were making her feel sick and reminded her of this baby's conception. She knelt on the floor, trying to concentrate, trying to remain alive and sane.

They arrived. Dorothy could hear Mrs Compton heaving up the narrow stairs, calling over her shoulder for Albert to boil the kettle.

'Hush now, Dorothy, all's well!' said Mrs Compton as she entered the room.

Dorothy did not realise she had been making any noise. 'It hurts. I'm scared.'

'I know, it will hurt, you're giving birth. It's all normal, and you will survive.'

'There's something wrong. Wrong here.' Dorothy pointed between her legs and gasped, she grappled for air, a pain sweeping over and through her. Was she being squeezed through her own mangle?

'Nonsense! There's nothing wrong here, nothing at all,' said Mrs Compton. She whisked open the curtains and lit candles, and she told Albert to light the fire.

And he did, glancing anxiously at his labouring wife, worried for her but also wanting to escape the confines of the birthing room as soon as he decently could. It was no place for a man.

Mrs Compton bustled and busied and prepared Dorothy, removing her knickers and making her lie down so she could examine her. Her hand felt huge and rough, without finesse. It wouldn't be long, she announced, washing her hands at the washstand. It was nearly time to push.

'I can't.'

'You can and you will. You want this baby born soon, don't you? Don't you want to hold him?'

Dorothy did. Of course. So when the time finally came, an hour or so later, Dorothy pushed.

She strained she sweated and screamed and cried out that she couldn't go on that it was impossible that something was wrong very badly wrong she knew it the pain was too much she couldn't bear it any more when was this going to end why was she in pain and deep in her mind Dorothy thought of her mother probably asleep now but she would be up later and dressed prim and proper sipping tea from what was left of the rosebud teacups that Dorothy smashed when she fainted and fell on them as a young girl in her stiff starched frock she would never forget that day she thought of Albert downstairs in the kitchen was he pacing was he listening she didn't want him to hear these animal noises she knew now she was making these screams and cries and grunts these desperate noises of a woman who is struggling to enter motherhood while outside her window the swifts were swooping and screeching who knows that despite what she is being told by the woman before her something is wrong very badly wrong and she wanted to kiss Albert suddenly kiss him hard on his mouth on his strong hard stomach because she hadn't done this nearly enough even though it pleased him beyond measure she wanted the pain to stop stop stop please stop stop then burning tearing ripping bursting burning burning the worst

pain yet everything inside her was being propelled out of
her she was on fire burning burning to death and then a
gush an outpouring a slither and a small strangled cry that
was not the baby and Mrs Compton in her haste knocked
her bag and a candle on to the floor and she swore and
grabbed the baby who was in fact born and purple and wet
and she grabbed him and smacked him hard and a voice
screeching No! and the baby blue blue not purple after all
but blue and small so small and black hair and slippery skin
and Dorothy reached out for him and blood spurted from
somewhere Dorothy thought the cord which was coiled
around the darling boy's neck a serpent and Mrs Compton
white-faced clutching at the cord, pulling it over the baby's
head but it was tight too tight too constricted blowing into
his mouth and gasping panicked crying for Albert to fetch
Dr Soames immediately now hurry Albert something is
wrong with the baby hurry Albert and not a noise from
downstairs save the banging of a door and Dorothy lying
back exhausted on her pillows all sense of pain all sense
gone all hope gone because she knew yes she knew that this
would happen it was written in her blood her guts she would
not be a mother for long if at all and darling Sidney destined
not to live in this world it was in his colour and his stillness
the quietness of the baby unnatural and horrible and dead
he was dead Dorothy cried out loud she thought and Mrs
Compton sitting on the end of the bed holding the bundle
blood-soaked and empty of life.

'I told you something was wrong,' said Dorothy.

Mrs Compton stared back at her, formulating a response,
Dorothy thought.

'Nobody could know. It's nobody's fault. It happens sometimes like this, and I tried to free him. I did. It was too late.
It happened before he . . . he was deprived. I'm sorry.'

The doctor came and examined the baby, then Dorothy. Albert did not enter the room. The doctor turned to Mrs Compton and instructed her to take 'the body' away, to wait outside, and on no account to show it to either of its parents. He would certify the death and take 'the body' to the hospital. He put his hand on Dorothy's shoulder and said he was sorry, my dear, and he instructed her to rest for a few days, and to let the milk dry up and let the blood dry up, let her wounds heal, she had torn a little. He left the room to speak to Albert, and a single anguished cry rang from the kitchen.

Dorothy stared out of the tightly shut window at the May blossom, creamy and curling this morning in the lush hedges, the blue sky looking so cheerful and knowing, but not caring that this happens sometimes, and it was a beautiful warm May morning as all the May mornings had been this year. And Mrs Compton, still clinging to her bundle with one arm, packed away her paraphernalia with the other. She blew out the remaining candles, they weren't needed any more, and she made for the door, bearing the bloodied bundle, not looking at Dorothy, not saying a word. She crept from the room with the bundle that was now hers, stealing away Dorothy's baby.

'Let me see him,' said Dorothy, her voice low and defeated.

Mrs Compton took one step back into the bedroom. 'No, love, it's best if you don't. You heard what Dr Soames said. You have to forget. They do say it's bad luck.'

And Mrs Compton left, cradling her bundle, pulling up the door behind her, dropping the latch with the sound of finality.

27

The baby was hungry. Dorothy arranged with Mrs Twoomey for a large jug of fresh milk from her goats to be brought up to the cottage each morning by her lad. Dorothy would pay a shilling a time, which she felt was a fair price. Could her lad please leave it by the gate? Dorothy was trying to keep the house silent, you see, so as not to disturb Nina. The poor girl needed her sleep, until she was strong again. Oh yes, she was exhausted, she had a terrible cold, headaches, vomiting. Dorothy thought it might be influenza. It was the season. And her nerves! The poor girl. And the coughing. No, no need to see a doctor, a few more days of rest and she would be fine. Thank you. Nina wasn't one for doctors.

Mrs Twoomey thought it odd, at first. But yes, she had heard that one of them girls had fallen ill and was recuperating. Hope she goes on all right. Strapping girl, that one, you wouldn't expect her to go down with any sort of illness. Mrs Twoomey's goats were fine goats, as she always boasted, and their milk was quality. Fed it to her eldest lad, she did, when he was a tiny baby, when he was barely alive. Got him through when she thought he was going to die. And look at him now. Oh! But she forgot. She was sorry.

'That's quite all right, Mrs Twoomey. I'm just grateful you can spare me some milk,' said Dorothy.

Mrs Twoomey told Mrs Sanderson that Dorothy Sinclair

had turned up at her house that morning, begging for milk, looking peculiar. Mrs Twoomey had handed some over, and accepted a shilling for it, so where's the harm? But the look in that woman's eyes. She looks right through you. She was desperate for that milk. Always a strange woman, that one. And a little easy (which you wouldn't expect of a woman like her), so they say, especially where the Poles are concerned. All over the village, that story. For a woman of her years! She's still a good-looking woman, of course, to be fair to her. Not pretty, but pleasing on the eye. On men's eyes, at least. She has a sort of nobility. Rumour is she's head over heels, and poor Bert still alive, as far as anyone knows, and him coming back in November to patch things up. He got short shrift, they say. Well. We all know why, don't we? A red sports car was spotted speeding through the village on Christmas Day. Oh yes, Mrs Pritchard saw it, and her husband, he thought it was an MG, and very nice too, and it wasn't seen going back *until the following morning*. Mrs Pritchard doesn't see so well these days, of course, but she swears the Polish squadron leader was driving the car. They say Mrs Sinclair has taken it hard, him being posted down south, and he writes her love letters. And is *he* married? Not a very young man. Funny goings-on up at that cottage over Christmas. Those girls are tight-lipped, though. Worship her, they do. And now one of them is ill. That's why she wanted milk, she said. The big lass. Not the little pretty one. You'd think it would be the other way round, but there you are.

Mrs Compton listened to this gossip, and more, as breathless Mrs Sanderson rattled away, barely drawing breath in her eagerness to pass on any 'news'. And next, Mrs Pritchard, who confirmed the sightings of the red sports car.

Mrs Compton thought it none of her business. Dorothy Sinclair was a law unto herself. But she should pop in, perhaps? It was such a pity she was always made to feel so damned unwelcome. She knew by now that Mrs Sinclair did not want her there, probably because she still blamed her for the loss of her baby the May before last. But the poor thing was dead before it was born. Perhaps it had been dead for several hours, a whole day even. It had happened before, it would happen again. Mrs Compton recalled her own first-born. A girl. Born dead. And Mrs Compton remembered that feeling of emptiness afterwards. For years afterwards, even with the safe arrival of five consecutive babies, Mrs Compton felt there was a hole in her life that only her first dead child could fill. And, of course, it could never be filled. It was a woman's tragedy. The years had gone by, and Mrs Compton rarely thought of it now. You just had to get on with your life and soldier on with what the good Lord saw fit to grant you. It wasn't your place to question Him. But still, Mrs Compton felt a strong sympathy for the Sinclair woman. It was compassion, she was pleased to realise. Poor Mrs Sinclair had a head on her shoulders. She didn't gossip. There was no malice.

She would go, just this one last time, to see if there was anything she could do. Losing a baby, and such a longed-for baby, that was hard on a woman. It could bring about such low feelings, low thoughts, for years afterwards. Mrs Compton understood this.

Yes. She would go. One last time.

28

Baby John, eight days old, was already chubby and rounded. His dark hair lay flat around his head, his cheeks glowed pink and his big blue eyes seemed to look at everyone and everything in a state of perpetual astonishment. Mostly they locked on to Dorothy, the woman who fed him, clothed him and rocked him. His little fingers splayed out as he waved his arms around in between his swaddlings. She found she was swaddling him less; the poor little boy seemed to prefer being able to move freely. She would not upset him. He slept now in her bedroom, in the crib Albert had made for Sidney. Finally, now, on the eighth day, she was bathing him. His cord stump had shrivelled and dropped off, and the time seemed right now to wash him properly. Dorothy buried her nose in his hair to breathe in his glorious baby smell. A smell that, she had to admit, was beginning to wane. He no longer had the intoxicating scent of the newborn.

She was nervous in case she dropped him, his body was so slippery. But he was still and calm in the crook of her arm as she washed him in the kitchen sink, so she stopped worrying and enjoyed the look of wonder on his face as she trickled water on his belly and head. He squinted as drops of water splashed into his eyes. Afterwards, Dorothy wrapped him tightly in his towel and sat with him in front of the range, cuddling him and humming to him. While he slept,

Dorothy began to mentally compose the letter she would later write and post.

Nina was back at work on the farm. Her breasts were drying up, after swelling for a day or two and then subsiding like balloons with a slow puncture. Dorothy made pads for them, just in case, which Nina was careful to place inside her bra each morning. The baby had mercifully taken quickly to the bottles of goat's milk, suckling noisily and frequently, but in such tiny amounts that Dorothy was shocked he was still alive, let alone gaining weight. And so much of the milk was secreted, loudly and triumphantly transformed, into his nappies.

Dorothy made her plans. She would tell nobody. She knew where she would have to go, and what she would have to do. Nina, although exhausted, was relieved to be back at work and had relinquished all responsibility for her baby to Dorothy. The young mother barely glanced at her son.

Dorothy had overheard, the evening before, Aggie and Nina talking. She hadn't meant to listen. Their bedroom door was ajar, hers wide open. The girls were whispering but, in the silence of the cottage at night, their voices carried.

'Did you really not know you were pregnant?' Aggie could not, it seemed, let sleeping babies lie.

'I said so, didn't I?'

'I know what you said.'

'Why are you asking, then?' said Nina.

'I just don't think I would go through the whole nine months without knowing. I don't see how any woman can.'

'I don't think it was nine months. Thinking back on it. More like eight. That's all I can say.'

'I'm your best chum, Nina Mullens, and I know things about you.'

'You don't, though.'

'You can tell me the truth. Didn't you have even an inkling?'

'No.'

'But you were in labour for bloody hours. Didn't it occur to you?'

'Nope. I just felt poorly. I was scared, I thought I was going to bloody cop it. I was as shocked as Dot when he came out. Honest.'

'Oh, Nina!'

'What?'

'I wish you were keeping him. Can't you think about it?'

'No.'

'You will regret this,' said Aggie, 'one day.'

At this Dorothy sat up in bed, clutching her knees, listening intently. Baby John slumbered in his crib.

'No, I won't.'

'He's your baby. Not hers! It's not right.'

Dorothy winced. But she could not stop listening.

'Why ain't it right?' asked Nina.

'It's not . . . I don't know. Official. She's going to keep your baby and nobody will even . . . what if she treats him badly? You won't know.'

'Do you really believe that Dot is going to treat John badly?'

'David,' corrected Aggie.

'John. David. Don't matter to me.'

'What if her husband comes back? He'll know it isn't his, even if he doesn't know it's not hers.'

'Eh?'

'You know what I mean!'

'None of his business, is it? Besides, he ain't coming back. They fell out, didn't they?'

'But have you thought it through, Nina? I mean, properly?'

'I can't keep the baby. I don't want the baby. We've been over it a dozen times. She does want a baby. She can have mine. It's perfect for everyone, ain't it? Apart from you, it seems.'

'He's not a bloody doll!'

'Ssh! Keep your voice down,' hissed Nina.

'And where's she going? And when? She can't stay here. People will put two and two together. I'm surprised nobody's got wind of this baby already. I don't know. Perhaps they have.'

'Have you said anything to anyone?' said Nina sharply.

Dorothy's heart was jumping and thudding, and she wondered if the girls would hear her breathing, would know they were being spied on. She tried to breathe slowly.

'Of course not. I'm true to my word.'

'I haven't told either. And Dot definitely hasn't. There's nobody else. Nobody knows, do they?'

'I don't see how they can. But one snooping person calling round and it will be all over the village.'

'That's the beauty of it. Nobody comes to her house. Keeps herself to herself, don't she?'

'But what if the postman hears him crying? What then?'

Yes. What if the postman heard him crying? But it was taken care of. Wasn't it? It was seen to. She'd thought of it all. Hadn't she?

'He won't hear. You know she keeps all the windows shut now, and the back door locked. Stop mithering me, Aggie. She keeps him upstairs most of the day, you know she does. Nobody's going to hear. Stop your worrying.'

'What if somebody sees all the nappies and clothes on the washing lines?'

'Don't you notice anything? She puts all that stuff on the horse around the fire overnight. She's not bloody stupid!'

'Ssh!'

'Have a bit of faith. Like I have.'

'She's going to just leave, you know. I know she is. We'll come back one day and . . . she and that little baby, they'll be gone. You'll never see David again.'

'John. I'll never see John again.'

They said no more.

Eventually, Dorothy slept.

3rd January 1941

Dear Mother,

Forgive me for not writing to you for such a long time. Much has happened in my life. Albert is missing. I am a widow, or so I must believe, and I have a child. Mother, the child is not Albert's, and in a way I think you will feel relieved to hear that. I now believe you were right about him. He was not good enough for me. The father of my child is a special man indeed. Cultured, intelligent, courageous. But he is in danger, as so many are in these times. I hope that after the war, if all is well, we shall marry. He is a Polish man, the sweetest, kindest man I have ever met.

Mother, I would like to come home. With John, my baby. He is eight days old today. Please can I ask you to consider taking us in? The estate wants the cottage for others now that Albert is presumed dead. Your grandson is a beautiful baby and I know you will love him as much as I do.

I shall wait for your reply.

Your daughter,

Dorothy

★

John had wetted her lap after his bath, too long had she sat with him by the glowing fire, singing to him. She put him in a clean nappy and dressed him, then she put on a clean skirt and stockings. In a moment or two, John would be asleep. But until then, she was holding him tight, rocking him and singing to him some more. They were sitting in her chair by the window, in the parlour, and his gaze seemed drawn to the bright snow-light streaming in from outside.

These days in January, the coldest and bleakest in the year, the month itself grey and white and interminable, always filled Dorothy with gloom. But not this year. This January, her days were filled with the utmost joy. Blissful in her new life, revelling in the motherhood that had at last revealed itself to her, its glorious sacrificial abundance, she was the happiest she had ever been. She was getting on top of her chores now, catching up with the estate laundry as well as her own. John still slept for much of the day, so she worked quickly while she could. Regretfully, her work was not as thorough as once it had been. But nobody had noticed, she hoped.

She rocked John and sang 'Summertime' to him – badly, she knew, but John seemed to enjoy it. And suddenly he had fallen asleep, as only babies can do. She placed him in the black perambulator and covered him with his soft blanket, positioning him closer to the fire, but not too close.

She knew that soon she would have to leave Lincolnshire, she would have to abscond with this baby. Aggie's overheard warnings from the night before filled Dorothy with apprehension. It was time to take action, to stop revelling in the beauty of the moment. She would not be able to take much with her. She made a mental list. And her biggest worry: How on earth was she to get to Lincoln station unseen? Or, failing that, at least arousing no suspicion?

She needed to get the letter to her mother posted, but

what should she do with John? She did not want to carry him, in case she was spotted, and pushing him in the perambulator was out of the question for the same reason. He was so very fast asleep, breathing quietly and evenly, sighing occasionally. Quickly, she put on her coat and her gumboots. She could get to the postbox and back in perhaps five minutes. She carefully locked the kitchen door behind her and ran, as best she could, through the crisp, cold air, the frozen snow slippery beneath her feet.

The ice sleeked itself across the path leading to Mrs Sinclair's kitchen door. Mrs Compton picked her way along it, slowly, slowly. She felt unsteady on ice these days; she wasn't getting any younger and she had a morbid fear of falling and breaking her hip. It happened to older women. Mrs Compton had cycled out to the cottage; it was only a two-mile trip, but it had taken her over an hour. Once or twice, where the roads were particularly slippery, she had pushed her bicycle. It was a relief to reach Mrs Sinclair's cottage and leave the bicycle propped against the hedge.

She reached the kitchen door and pushed it gently, just to see. She tried the handle. Locked. That was unusual. Of course, out of politeness, Mrs Compton always knocked when she visited, but she knew that Mrs Sinclair's door was usually unlocked – or, in the warmer months, ajar. But then Mrs Sinclair was alone all day, with no immediate neighbours. In her position Mrs Compton might have locked her door too.

She knocked again, and waited.

Was nobody home?

She had noticed that the lace curtains were missing from the window in the parlour, so she retraced her steps back round to the front. Gingerly stepping across the frozen grass, she shielded her eyes and peered through the window.

29

A photograph: a little girl in white socks and T-bar shoes, her hair in bunches, wearing with apparent pride a frilly dress whose colour must remain a mystery. A huge smile, with her two front teeth missing. Holding the hand of a woman, but a woman with no face, no head, just legs, a dark skirt, an arm and a hand, holding the little girl's. Nothing written on the reverse.

(Found inside Hilda Boswell's *Treasury of Nursery Rhymes*, very good condition, priced at £15 and placed on the children's collectables shelf. It sold the same day.)

Philip visited me each day while I regained my strength, staying for many hours, during which he cleaned my floors, cupboards, windows and fridge freezer. I hadn't been aware that my flat was so grubby. He fed me and encouraged me to shower and dress. On the third day, he finally left, telling me his work was done, and he said I could turn up at the bookshop whenever I felt like it, whenever I was ready. I wasn't ready for a while. I still felt feeble. I had weight to gain, skin to bring back to life. I was determined to look like myself before I returned to my old job and faced everybody. I took my time.

But now I am ready. Sophie hugs me, Jenna hugs me and Patricia, our new recruit, shakes my hand. Philip emerges from his office, smiling. I offer to make coffee. After I've handed round the mugs, Philip sets me to work. Today I am to go through the hardback fiction, remove all books that have been on the shelves for a year or more, and make a bargain shelf of them, all at half price. It's the sort of job I adore.

Book dust is a comforting smell, but it's bad for you. And I feel precarious, a little vulnerable. If I look around too much, if I move too much, these walls, these shelves, like living entities, will they turn in on me, will they sneer and jeer, will they see me run home in tears, laughing at how clumsily and slowly I run? Are these books actually alive, whispering about me, hating me?

Get a grip, I tell myself. For God's sake, Roberta. They're just books, and you're better now.

I saw Babunia yesterday. I thought it made sense to go to her before returning to work, before December really gets going. I went along with the intention of telling her about Dad, and took her flowers for the birthday I'd missed in November. She liked the flowers, but hadn't realised it was her birthday. Was she 108 now? she asked. Or 107? I said, something like that. And she'd had another telegram from the Queen. But she didn't think the Queen had really signed it.

'You look peaky,' she observed, looking at me closely. This I liked. This awareness, always so comforting.

'I'm fine, Babunia.'

'Have you been ill?'

'No! Just a cold. Nothing to worry about.'

'Even so. You must take care of yourself. You young things don't wear enough.'

'Look at me!' I gave her a twirl.

She eyed my thick polo-neck jumper, cardigan, jeans and boots, and harrumphed.

Aha, defeated!

'How's that son of mine?' she asked.

And I hesitated. What to say? She was so happy and sparkly and bright, like the decorations I was putting up in her room.

'He's fine,' I said eventually. 'A little busy with work.'

'I thought he retired,' she said, pulling a long piece of golden tinsel from the box of decorations, many of which were as old as me, if not older.

I took the tinsel from her and shook it out. 'Oh, he did, but you know Dad. He likes to keep his eye in.'

'I'm proud of him. My son.'

'I know you are. I am too.' To stop my voice from breaking, my face from crumpling and giving it all away, I wrapped the tinsel gently around her shoulders and kissed her forehead.

She laughed.

So I dust, I am happy, I am home again. And each book I examine becomes warmer in my hands, softer somehow, and I am pleased to be hidden away in this back room, with the French windows firmly shut against the gathering gloom of winter, and Sophie on the till, and Jenna and Patricia decorating the foyer with a Christmas tree and holly and ivy, and only the occasional customer finding me as I sit on the squeaky footstool cleaning books, repricing books, repositioning books.

An envelope falls out of a reprint of a 1949 edition of Elizabeth Bowen's *The Death of the Heart*, a novel Philip and I both love. I recall discussing it at length during the early days of my employment here. I pick up the envelope. It looks and smells new; the ivory-coloured paper is thick and watermarked, linen, a high-quality envelope. It is sealed. I turn it over in my hands. It is addressed to 'Roberta'. And, of course, it takes me a few seconds to digest that this letter is for me.

30

Dorothy, running back to the cottage, stopped in her tracks as she reached her front gate. She let out a small involuntary scream, at which Mrs Compton, standing at the parlour window, turned towards her.

John cried out too, short and sharp and clear as the day's crisp air, despite the glass separating him from the two aghast women.

Dorothy stared at Mrs Compton. Mrs Compton stared at Dorothy. Neither woman spoke, nor blinked. Whose move it was, neither knew.

Oh God, no, this could not be, not now. So close now, to John. So close to her plans coming to fruition, so close to fulfilling her long-held dream, so close to the happiness she had stopped believing could ever be hers. And this woman, this awful woman, her own living *nemesis*, staring through the parlour window, the clear window stripped of its smoky-yellow lace early that morning, the curtains drying now on the horse in the kitchen, this odious woman staring at the huge black perambulator in which the baby was now awake and screaming, in innocence and without guile.

What could Dorothy do? Did she have the gumption to tell this woman what she truly wanted to tell her? But what was the use? It was too late. She could see. The woman had eyes – oh, how she had eyes – and Dorothy closed the gate behind her, marched to the kitchen door and unlocked it.

She sensed Mrs Compton following her, and felt as tethered as a dog on a lead.

She slammed the kitchen door behind her and locked it.

'Dorothy?' called Mrs Compton, her voice only slightly muffled by the door. 'Dorothy? Let me in. Please? I'm not going to . . . it's cold out here. I've ridden on my bicycle to see you today. I've been hearing things. Worrying things. I promise I am here to help. Nothing more and nothing less.'

Dorothy ignored Mrs Compton and stumbled into the parlour. She picked John up, and he calmed quickly. She held him tight. Tears rolled down her cheeks as she cursed her own stupid forgetfulness, her carelessness. She stumbled and shuffled back to the kitchen door, slow, slow, trying to put off the inevitable confrontation. She held baby John even more tightly to her.

'Cold!' pronounced Mrs Compton briskly when Dorothy finally opened the door. Dorothy stood back, trembling and clinging to the slumbering baby, pulling his knitted blanket closer to him.

What was cold? Dorothy wondered. The weather? Dorothy's reception? The house? No, not the house. Fires were glowing in all the grates.

Dorothy laid the baby, now sound asleep again, back in his perambulator, and wheeled it into the kitchen where it loomed large and black in the corner. She made tea, hastily, barely giving it time to steep, and poured a cup for each of them with hands still shaking. Mrs Compton affected not to notice, and sipped. The clock ticked. Small talk was made, more observations on the weather. Enquiries after Nina's health. Neither mentioned the sleeping baby, his blissful sighs, his sweet-whispered rumours erupting into the room.

When John cried again, Mrs Compton rose from the table,

but Dorothy jumped ahead of her and stood in front of the perambulator, barring the other woman's way.

'No!' cried Dorothy.

'But it's crying.'

'I'll pick him up. You don't touch.'

She picked John up and rocked him, soothing his cries. She took him to the kitchen window and stared out into the whiteness of the day, and again she cried, soft and low. How strange, she thought, how strange that this baby was no longer a secret. His presence was known about – by the last person Dorothy thought entitled to know about him – and John himself was so unaware of the battles ahead. He wanted comfort, and he didn't care who knew about it or who comforted him. The awful truth: anybody would do.

Dorothy whirled round from the window to face Mrs Compton, whose face was a picture of confusion and concern.

'Please leave,' she said.

'Whose is this baby?' replied the older woman.

'It's a baby. Just a baby. I asked you to lea— No. I'm telling you to fuck off. I want you to fuck off out of this house and never come back. Do you understand?' Dorothy could feel her cheeks blazing, both in shame at her language and fury at the thought of losing John.

'There's no such thing as just a baby, Dorothy.'

'He's mine,' she blurted.

'Yours?'

'Yes.'

Mrs Compton looked utterly baffled. 'But you're not . . . you weren't pregnant, were you? I saw you before Christmas. You were thinner than ever.'

'This is my baby,' insisted Dorothy.

'Impossible,' replied Mrs Compton crisply.

If they were stags – or rhinoceroses or even elephants

– Dorothy thought they would have locked horns by now, they would have been grappling, fighting to the death. She was breathing hard and fast, and her heart was thumping in her chest like never before, harder even than when Albert had raped her.

Clutching John to her breast, she stroked and kissed his head, and couldn't prevent her tears landing in his soft dark hair. 'You are not taking this one!' she hissed, glaring at the older woman.

'All right, then,' said Mrs Compton. She seemed oddly calm, almost friendly.

'Is that all you have to say?'

'What else can I say?'

'Nothing, I suppose.'

'Please tell me about this little chap. Please. It is a boy?'

'A little boy. Yes,' replied Dorothy, warily.

'And how did you . . . come by him, Dorothy? Did you . . .? Oh, God forbid. You didn't steal him?'

'Of course not.'

'I know how hard you took the loss of Sidney. It wouldn't be the first time a baby was stolen by a grieving mother. And I would understand, if that is the case. Really, I would. But,' and Dorothy noticed a new authoritarian tone in her voice, 'this baby would need reuniting with his mother. Have you thought of how she must be feeling?'

'Don't presume to talk to me about my Sidney,' snarled Dorothy.

'All right. But I do want to talk about *this* baby.'

'Have you heard of any babies missing?'

'No. I admit, I haven't. But that doesn't mean—'

'This baby is not stolen,' said Dorothy. 'You have my word.'

'So whose is he?'

'He's mine. I told you already.'

'We both know that cannot be. Is he a nephew, then? A friend's baby?' Mrs Compton's brow was furrowed with the effort of trying to understand.

'No.'

'Dorothy. Please tell me.'

'He's Nina's baby!' yelled Dorothy. 'All right? Nina gave birth to him. But she doesn't want him. Nobody is to know. I look after him. She says I can have him, if I want him.'

'Oh my!'

'Indeed.' Dorothy shushed John, who had woken at her shout and was fretting.

'Nina's?' repeated Mrs Compton.

'We didn't know she was expecting. She claims not to have realised herself.'

'I can scarcely believe it. When was he born?'

'On Boxing Day. I helped deliver him, up at the North Barn.'

'Born in a barn? Like the good Lord himself.'

'If you like,' she replied, wearily.

'Well, I must say, you gave me quite a fright. I feared the worst, I really did. I'll get on to Dr Soames. He'll know what to do. Has Nina seen him?'

'No, of course not!' Dorothy was gripped by a new panic. 'Nobody is to know. Don't you understand?'

'You did say. But is Nina well?'

'I believe so. She's still bleeding, but she has no pains. She tore a little, but she tells me it feels like it's healing. And there's no fever. She's not particularly weak, just rather tired.'

'Why don't I have a look at her?' Mrs Compton spoke softly, a tremor in her voice Dorothy had not heard before. 'I've sewn up many a new mother. It's too late now, really. But I could have a look and make sure all is well?'

'And then what?'

The clock ticked and John began to mewl for milk.

Dorothy waited, her heart thumping and her breath coming in shallow pants.

'That will be between you and Nina,' said the other woman, eventually. 'You have your own arrangements in place, I am sure.'

Dorothy was unsure that she had heard Mrs Compton correctly, but the woman's face was kindly and placid.

'She wanted me to send him to the nuns,' Dorothy told her, stroking John's hair, gently jigging him up and down against her chest. He was becoming more agitated, the hunger of the newborn baby unbearable, edging him towards the point of no return.

'God forbid,' said Mrs Compton with feeling. 'Why don't you warm his milk? And I'll look at him properly. He looks well, I must say, but you never know. Is he drinking goat's milk by any chance?'

Mrs Compton pronounced the baby to be bonny and in no danger.

The goat's milk was agreeing with him, she could see, and yes, the more she thought about it, the more sense it made to keep all of this quiet. Nina, God bless her, was not the cleverest of girls, not even knowing she was expecting, and she didn't even want the little chap. She was not maternal enough. Some girls weren't. How old was she? Nineteen? Well, quite young still. And fond as she was of the good times . . . and Dorothy, you are, well, you are mature, and capable, and you have had such rotten luck . . . and any fool can see you love him already, with that love only true mothers have, love for a newborn. The ancient desire to protect. Nina could not be relied upon to have the sense . . . she might, in time, find a husband willing to accept her illegitimate child, settle down to motherhood, do all right by her son.

But the little darling needs that now, as well as in ten years' time. And Dorothy, you are such an excellent mother. You deserve this stroke of luck, this gift, whatever you want to call it. Just let me know how I can help. I can help.

And the morning gave way to afternoon, and the afternoon wore on, and the fires glowed in the grates and more tea was made; sandwiches were cut. The baby was cuddled, and fed again, and changed. And at three o'clock, Mrs Compton left, to return to the village on her bicycle through the sullen January twilight.

A pact had been made, secrecy assured, an unlikely alliance formed.

Days passed, in which nothing much happened. Each day seemed to remove Nina further from her child, and pull Dorothy closer to him. It was cold, day and night. The winter would last forever, Dorothy felt.

Each day she waited for a letter. They were anxious, long days.

Eventually, the postman came, and a small letter fluttered on to the doormat in the kitchen.

8th January 1941

Dear Dorothy,

I received your letter with surprise and delight. Dearest, of course you and your baby must come home, regardless of all that has passed between us. I find that this war has softened me rather. 'Life is short' is a much-used adage but, nevertheless, it is true. I am alone often these days and I must confess the idea of company, and a grandchild, is appealing. I shall expect you in your own time.

Mother

★

The office was large and austere, with oak-panelled walls and a ceiling like a moonless night. Dorothy hated the feel of the slippery leather seat, fearing it would prove treacherous and precipitate her on to the floor. She was sweating, though the room was by no means warm. The woman opposite her, huddled inside a thick cardigan, smiled at Dorothy.

'Well, I'm ready now. I need a few details.'

Dorothy gave John's name, her own name, her maiden name, her address, the father's name, his address, his occupation. She had written out the night before all that she was going to say this morning. They were newly-weds, she and Jan, she explained. They had rushed to marry before the baby came. It was wartime. People do rash things. Dorothy shrugged.

The registrar – a world-weary woman, by the look of her – did not react. She just wrote everything down, not looking up – except to query the spelling of Pietrykowski, of course. Dorothy had to ask her to spell Jan with a 'J', not a 'Y'. Her jumping bowels were more than ready to propel their contents from her body. She thought, for one awful moment, that she was going to vomit. She breathed deeply, and told the registrar that she had been a little unwell, very tired, since the baby arrived.

'And when was John born?'

'On the twenty-sixth of December.'

'And where was he born?'

'In a barn.'

'Good Lord.' The woman glanced up again at this, sharply, as if suspecting a joke.

'At Lodderston Hall Farm.'

'In that case, I'll put the farm's address as his place of birth. Heavens above, the poor little thing.'

'He caught us . . . he caught me unawares. It was very sudden.'

'I should think it was. But isn't that the best way? My poor sister laboured for hours with her children. I know which I would prefer.'

No further comments were made, and Dorothy left the office clutching John's birth certificate. She ran for her bus, catching it just in time, found a seat at the back, and opened up the certificate. It was there, in front of her, on pink paper, in blue ink. John's mother. John's father.

She had broken the law; the certificate was a work of pure fiction. Yet it was unequivocal. It was surprisingly easy.

And Dorothy felt strangely, truly *alive* for only the second time in her life. She sat on the bus, looking out of the window, knowing she would never make this particular journey again. A new excitement reeled through her, a fear, a huge shudder. She recalled the owl in her dream, fleeing the mobbing crows.

And if thoughts of Jan crept in, she ignored them. She did not want to hear his voice – his wise words, his common sense and, above all, his disapproval. She was going to take this chance, the chance of a lifetime, and nothing anybody could say or do would sway her from the path she alone had chosen.

She would sacrifice anything; she would sacrifice everything. She knew that now. That too was unequivocal.

Back at the cottage, John was asleep in Mrs Compton's arms. He'd had milk and two nappy changes, and in between he'd slept like a lamb nearly the whole time. He was no trouble, the little dear. Now. It was done?

Dorothy nodded.

'And tomorrow, you must leave, as we've planned. I'll be here at half past six sharp. Don't worry how I'll manage it, just trust me. You be ready to go. All will be well, Dorothy. You must not look back.'

31

Earlier than usual, Dorothy made sandwiches for Aggie and Nina and filled a Thermos flask. Not one each today, unfortunately, she explained. She had broken one of them; it was smashed to smithereens, what a nuisance. She would have to replace it as soon as she could. She said goodbye to the girls as normal, casually, bidding them to keep warm, checking they had their scarves and gloves. Wiping her hands on her pinny, brushing a strand of hair from her face. It was another day, just another day in this, the new realm of ordinary since Boxing Day.

Mrs Compton and Dorothy had decided it was best to say nothing. What if Nina had a change of heart?

Be careful. Tell a white lie. Tell as many white lies as you need to. Young girls can be so fickle. It would be inconvenient, to say the least. It would break your heart, Dorothy. Say nothing. Act normally.

Dorothy stood at her kitchen window and watched the girls pick their way across the Long Acre, two forlorn figures becoming smaller and smaller, finally disappearing. She cried, just a tear or two, feeling she would never see either of the girls again. They had been through so much together, these difficult months of war, such hard work, losses and death all around them, bombs and crashes and heartbreak. Dorothy hoped, sincerely, that both girls would fare well.

Somehow, in that part of her where sure and secret knowledge lodged, she knew they would be all right.

Dorothy made sandwiches for herself, wrapping them in brown paper, and hurriedly cleaned up the kitchen. She gathered up her essential items. In the suitcase she packed John's birth certificate, his clothes and blankets, and Jan's shirt. (She had sewn the final button on, but as yet she had not laundered or pressed it, wanting to preserve the scent of the man she loved. She could not bring herself to forget him, reject him, swap him completely for the baby who had taken her now for his own. She never would send the shirt to Jan.) She added the bundle of his letters, along with minimal toiletries and a change of outfit for herself. She packed her sandwiches in her shopping basket, along with John's Thermos of warm milk, the one glass bottle she had room for, some bibs, nappies, pins and powder, and his washcloths, wrapped up in a knitted nappy cover. Her purse was in her handbag, and she could at least sling that over her shoulder. She had two pounds, loaned to her by Mrs Compton. Once she was settled, she would repay the older woman. They had discussed money at length, of course.

At least she had no cumbersome gas mask, because she had not gone along to any of the fittings. Regrettably, she could not take the perambulator, impossible on such a journey; it would have to stay where it was. She wondered if she would be able to free up her hands enough to buy, hold and drink a cup of tea at the stations on her journey. It seemed unlikely.

Other worries assailed her: What if her mother had changed her mind? What if she were to turn her away? Dorothy hoped her mother would remain softened, upon seeing her little grandson, and allow her 'widowed' daughter to take up residence once again in the Oxford home Dorothy had been so relieved to escape from seven years before. The whole plan was pinned on this. This was the heart of the matter. Going home. Returning to her mother. A simple plan, an obvious plan. She could but hope that her mother had not reflected too much and had a change of heart. Dorothy knew she would have to tell her mother everything, in all probability, in the end. But she would think about that when the time came.

Mrs Compton, true to her word, arrived at Dorothy's cottage early, carefully timing her arrival to ensure the girls had left for work. She was driving Dr Soames's car. How she had procured it, Dorothy had no idea, and she didn't ask. Mrs Compton and the doctor were pretty thick. Perhaps she had concocted a story about needing to go further afield in all the ice and snow – complaining, perhaps, of the relentless cold of January, and a woman labouring and in need of help.

Before leaving the cottage, Dorothy wandered from room to room for the last time, looking at all the things she would be leaving behind, which was almost everything. She imagined that Aggie and Nina would continue to live in the cottage, at least for a while, perhaps with another couple of land girls, and wondered how they would find time to cook and clean and launder. She lingered over the music box, wiping off a thin layer of dust, lifting and lowering the lid. It was a borrowing, always that, not a gift. She should find a way to return it. But she could not. She would have to leave it for the girls to take care of. And continue to enjoy, she hoped. Until it could be collected by its true owner.

In the feverish days since John's birth, Dorothy had tried hard to give no thought to Jan. Yet he was there, in her mind, her body, trying to get her to notice him. He was impossible to forget. She could not conjure up for herself his face, his voice, the feel of his firm brown arms, she could not recall clearly the blueness of his eyes or the blackness of his hair. Already he was a memory from some long-gone era. She was sad for him, this dear man who had given her so much in the brief months of their acquaintance. He was her first and only lover in the true sense of the word. And if the baby had not entered her life in his haphazard, squalling fashion, she would have taken her future with Jan, probably marriage, a life together. There would have been no babies, certainly. She felt her body was now done with trying to bear children. This terrible atrophy would have panicked her just a few days ago. But now she had John, and nothing else mattered.

Jan and John. Jan *or* John.

The choice, if it had to be a choice, had been made.

Mrs Compton said little in the car on the way to Lincoln, concentrating on her driving. She did volunteer that she had taught herself to drive, many years ago, against her late husband's advice. She thought she was a good driver, she told Dorothy, but she didn't like it, especially in the winter. Still, it was proving useful now. And Mrs Compton smiled sidelong at her, a slow smile of conspiracy.

Dorothy was trying to resist the urge to cry. Leaving her cottage, her home of six years, was not easy. It had been the scene of the major events in her life – in this cottage she had lost her virginity, conceived several babies, given birth to one. She had lost her Sidney, fallen in love with Jan and taught herself to sew and to cook. Above all, it was the house in which John had been given to her. She knew she would never see the house again; she would never even set foot in the county again.

At the station, both women looked around nervously before emerging from the car into the freezing morning fog.

Mrs Compton insisted on carrying the basket and the suit-case to the ticket office and holding John while Dorothy bought her ticket. Then Mrs Compton bought her a cup of tea from the station cafe.

'You may not get another chance,' she said. 'Have one now, for heaven's sake.'

Dorothy thanked her and drank the tea hastily, and soon they were making their way to platform three in silence, the click of Dorothy's heels the only sound. It was early, she was catching the first train out, and there were no other passengers about, mercifully. Yet Dorothy was uneasy, looking around, licking her dry lips, clearing her throat. On the platform, Mrs Compton insisted on waiting with her and stood close to her, too close, like a guard.

'What's going on?'

Dorothy and Mrs Compton started as a slight figure in long coat, hat and gumboots stepped out from the waiting room.

'Aggie,' said Mrs Compton, moving to stand in front of Dorothy and the baby. 'What are you doing here?'

'Getting wise to your game, that's what. What are *you* doing here, anyway? She can't bloody stand you.'

There was silence on the platform for a moment, then Dorothy gently eased round Mrs Compton and said, 'Aggie, can we talk?'

'That's what I'm here for. That, and to stop you stealing Nina's baby.'

'I'm not stealing him,' cried Dorothy, indignant.

'What *are* you doing, then?' Aggie's expression was fierce.

'Giving him an opportunity. Giving him a life.'

'Rubbish. You might be able to fool Nina, but you're not fooling me. This isn't right, and it's probably against the law. I'm going to find out. If you get on this train,' and indeed it was now entering the station, steam and smoke and grit billowing around it, a low whistle announcing its arrival, 'I'm straight off to the police. They'll most probably hook you off at the next stop. Fancy getting arrested, eh, Mrs Sinclair?'

'I'm getting on this train,' said Dorothy stiffly, clutching John tightly.

'Go ahead. But you leave David with me, or just you wait and see what happens. I thought you were a proper person. I really did. But you're not. You're selfish and rotten and I hate you.'

Mrs Compton, who had maintained a fretful silence since the two women began arguing, now hurried to open a carriage door as the train halted in a cloud of steam and a spray of black salty grit. Dorothy shielded baby John, from the steam, from the grit, from Aggie, as Mrs Compton picked up the suitcase and basket and climbed up into the train. Aggie stood in front of the carriage door.

'Come on, Dorothy!' called Mrs Compton. 'Get on the train.'

With surprising speed and strength, Aggie reached out and grabbed the baby from Dorothy's arms.

'No!' cried Dorothy.

Mrs Compton leapt from the train, light on her feet for a woman of her age, and rounded on Aggie. 'You give that baby back.'

'No. I won't. She has no right to do this! It's terrible.' Aggie's jaw was set in defiance, her eyes blazing.

'You stupid girl,' said Mrs Compton. 'What do you know about "rights"? What about John's rights?'

'His name is David, and he should be with his mum,' retorted Aggie. 'She's not thinking, she's still in shock. At first, I thought she must have known. But now I reckon she didn't, and it surprised her even more than it did us. But she'll get used to it, being a mum. I'll help her, and so will others. She'll get by. But you, and *you*, both of you, you're taking it all away from her.'

'Please understand,' said Dorothy passionately, 'no harm will ever come to this little boy. I love him as my own child. He *is* my own child, and I will love him to my dying day. I beg you, please, Agatha, please do not go to the police. Think about the consequences. Nina will not bring up this child, you know that. He'll be sent to a home, an institution, at best he will be adopted by strangers. I'm giving him security, and love, a comfortable home. I'll give him an education. Everything.'

Aggie shook her head, looking down at the baby.

He gazed up at them all, eyes wide and unknowing.

The girl's shoulders sagged in defeat. 'What can I do?' she said, tears beginning to trickle down her cheeks. 'Go on, then! Take him. But shame on you, Dorothy Sinclair,' and slowly, sobbing, she handed John back.

Dorothy stepped up on to the train, followed by Mrs Compton. Aggie sank on to a bench, rooting in her pockets for her handkerchief.

'Good luck,' said Dorothy's unlikely ally, gently stroking John's cheek. 'And good luck to this little man too. I'll take care of her,' she added, indicating Aggie with a wave of her hand. 'Perhaps you could send more money once you're settled?'

'Yes. Of course,' said Dorothy. She felt she ought to sound grateful. She *was* grateful, damn it. 'You've been very kind.'

'Nonsense.'

'Will it be all right, do you think?' cried Dorothy, suddenly gripped by anguish. 'What if Aggie's right?'

'It's going to be fine,' soothed the older woman. 'Think of the future, forget that silly girl out there. She'll not tell a soul. She's not going to the police, I'll see to it. Nobody will ever know.' Mrs Compton leaned in, and lowered her voice even further. 'I will never tell. You have my word. Think ahead, that is what you must do. Don't look back, ever. You have a glorious life as a mother ahead of you. Good luck, Dorothy.'

The whistle blew, so Mrs Compton hopped off the train and slammed the door shut behind her. Dorothy placed the remarkably unruffled baby on the seat, opened the window and leaned out. The two figures receded rapidly as the train pulled away, and she thought how small Mrs Compton was, how small Aggie was. Nobody waved. Then they were gone, swallowed in the steam and the smoke and the January gloom.

Soon Lincoln was gone too, and the train was in the countryside, passing between flat fields. Then came the first small station, with soldiers, aircrew, sailors. But there were no policemen. She looked around anxiously, sweating, heart thumping. But the train eventually pulled away and on into Nottinghamshire. At each station they passed through, Dorothy braced herself for policemen, but none appeared, just more servicemen. The waits were agonisingly protracted, and she tried to remain patient. Her last train journey, as she had travelled up to Lincolnshire towards Albert and marriage, had been relaxed and easy, and the memory of that long-ago November calmed her, a little. But perhaps the police were waiting at Nottingham, where she would need to change trains.

But no. The change was harried, jostling, chaotic. There were more soldiers, sailors, airmen, an inexhaustible flow of young men, loud and raucous, and some of these young men – young women too – were heading for oblivion and some would still be alive in fifty years, she thought, and it was a horrible, horrible fact but somehow triumphant too, the triumph of life, its rampant arbitrariness. And now there *was* a lone policeman. As she walked past, carrying her baby, her basket, her suitcase, her handbag, he smiled at her, but that was all, a small sympathetic smile. So Mrs Compton must have 'taken care' of Aggie, as Dorothy would be 'taking care' of Mrs Compton. But she put such bitter thoughts to one side. She needed her mental and physical fortitude to carry her and John through this trial, to endure this long and momentous day. She knew that this was the most significant journey of her life.

But would she always be glancing over her shoulder, expecting to be caught? Would she be afraid forever? Or would it heal over, this crack, this fear, this irrefutable knowledge that John was not truly her child and the whole world would know it?

John slept, milky and contented. The swaying of the train had lulled him to sleep, and she cradled him on her lap. She was glad, because after a while the earlier train had seemed to unsettle him – or perhaps he had just sensed her own discomfiture – and he had cried so much that Dorothy resorted to walking up and down the corridors with him. She had to push her way past servicemen, who were ever swelling into a large homogeneous group, lounging in corridors, leaning out of windows, sitting on kitbags, smoking, making jokes, nudging each other, one or two of them leering at Dorothy. Some were obviously perturbed by the crying baby. She recognised none of the faces on the train. She was anonymous, a freedom she knew she would seek for the rest of her life.

The last train of the journey, boarded at Birmingham New Street, was just as crowded with servicemen, just as smoky and dark and noisy. In the carriages it was stifling, in the corridors icy. Leaving Birmingham, Dorothy was offered a window seat, and a brash but polite soldier placed her suitcase on the rack above. She settled into the corner as best she could, and fed John his third bottle of goat's milk; the Thermos had enough milk left for one more feed. Dorothy hoped it would be enough to pacify him for the rest of the journey, and prayed he would not need another change of nappy – having already changed three of them on dirty, rocking, cold corridor floors, she did not relish the thought of changing any more. She would not use the filthy toilets.

But what to do with the soiled nappies? They were in her basket, and they reeked. She wished now she had had the forethought to dispose of them in a rubbish bin on a plat-form when changing trains. She would have to do something about them now, so she smiled at the servicemen who looked her up and down as she pushed past them into the corridor, carrying John and the basket of dirty nappies. She put down the basket and forced open a window with her free hand. The blackening air whistled past her like a sudden wish for death, and one by one she threw the wet, filthy nappies from the window as the train rattled and swayed through the darkening afternoon.

At three minutes to five, the train at last pulled into Oxford station and Dorothy was able to disembark for the final time, carrying her suitcase, her basket, her handbag and her baby. She felt that now the journey was almost over, now that she and John had reached Oxford and were a long way from Lincolnshire, from Aggie and Nina and Mrs Compton – the people who knew her secret – he *was* finally hers. Trembling with fatigue and anxiety, Dorothy found a seat in the ticket hall, where she sat for a few moments, composing herself. John was asleep, and she held him gently.

A minute or two later, she left the station and entered her home city for the first time in seven years, marvelling at its old familiar grandeur, its air of insistent superiority. It was dark, cold, and the dastardly blackout had settled over the early evening. Dorothy knew she would have to walk home. She estimated it would take an hour or more to get to her mother's house in the north of the city, carrying everything. She was so tired, but she would avoid the buses. She could not bear the thought of another smoky and overcrowded journey. There was less snow here, she noticed with some relief, and the evening was milder than she had been used to in recent days. She walked past the Ritz cinema on George Street, with its queue of cold and war-weary people waiting to get inside its warmth and be transported to an altogether lighter, more sparkling world. She walked past shops, some of them familiar to her, all of them closed now. The shop workers were making their way home, as she was.

She walked. One foot in front of the other, one step at a time.

Be in the moment, she told herself. Be here, and now, and be thankful for it.

The house just off the Woodstock Road still looked the same, as far as Dorothy could tell in the dark. The front door, she thought, was still blue. She stood a minute or two, breathing deeply, preparing herself for this final hurdle, then rang the bell. John began to whimper. Her arms burned with the burden of holding him for so long, one-handed, with the suitcase in the other, and the basket and her handbag hooked over her elbows. It might be nice, Dorothy thought, to lay John down. It would be a relief to have that weight lifted from her, just briefly, to hand him to somebody else. She felt that, any moment now, everything – including John – would tumble from her.

Her mother answered the door. She peered through the gloom at her only daughter, seemingly without recognition. Had Dorothy changed so much? Then, suspicion clouded her mother's face. Yet the bitterness around the mouth was gone, although the lines were deeper. Her mother looked tired. Perhaps lonely. Definitely old.

'Hello, Mother.'

'You came?' gasped Dorothy's mother, a wrinkled hand held to her chest. She stared at the baby, who was mewling like a kitten, his little restless movements becoming stiffer, angrier.

Dorothy knew the mewling would soon become screeching. He needed milk, quickly. They had come so far. And he had been so good.

'This is your grandson, John. Mother, we've come home. Like I said we would.'

Dorothy's mother held out her arms and took John, and Dorothy slowly lowered the suitcase, bag and basket on to the doorstep. The shock of suddenly empty arms made her feel light and insubstantial, as if her arms were floating, and she found herself in the queerly painful state of emptiness, after hours of burden.

'I'm in the soup, rather,' she began. 'But John's father is a good man. Make no mistake. He flies a Hurricane. He's a squadron leader, like Douglas Bader. Only he's Polish. He had an injury and he carried on flying. He's a brave man and he's very honourable. I was asked to leave the cottage. Like I said in my letter.' She stopped abruptly, aware that she was babbling.

Her mother had been ignoring her, cooing and shushing

at the baby. Now she looked up at Dorothy quizzically. 'The house is not, perhaps, as you remember it,' she said slowly. 'Have you really come home? There are no more servants. There is not a great deal of money any more. Your room is as you left it, though possibly a little dusty. But nothing you can't manage.' Then she seemed to realise where they were. 'But what on earth am I doing!' she cried. 'Come in out of this cold, child! Whatever next!'

'Mother—'

'You're exhausted, my dear. The fire is lit and tea is on the hob. Perhaps I was expecting you? That's it, in, in, let's close this door . . . it still sticks, do you see? Oh, Dorothy, let's not mind what has passed between us. Mothers and daughters should never talk over the threshold.'

Dorothy stepped into her mother's house, and her mother shut the door firmly behind her.

32

'Happy Mother's Day to Mummy I love you soo much, love from Bobby': A home-made card with a child's drawing of a mother and a little girl, with a tree, grass and flowers and a huge sun in the corner. The writing inside is wobbly, up and down. It is sweet. I think the creator of this card could be another Roberta and I wonder if her mother regrets losing, or even knows she has lost, this precious card. I keep it safe.

(Found inside a mint 1950 Penguin edition of *Black Narcissus* by Rumer Godden, priced at £5.00 and bought by myself.)

I put the letter addressed to me in my handbag. I haven't opened it. It's from Philip – his writing is always recognisable – but I have no idea what the letter says, and I am too scared to find out. Stupid. But I fear I was too honest with him when he came to my rescue and I know, I fully expect, this letter is his way of letting me down gently. I can't bear the embarrassment of reading his rebuke, his explanations, however elegantly put. So, I'm ignoring it and carrying on as normal. As is Philip, it seems. You would almost think there was no letter.

Today is bright and cold. I make coffee for everybody once we have all arrived. Philip has decided he needs me to help him sort out his 'disastrous' office. It hasn't been cleaned 'properly' since 2001, he claims. He may be right.

We work together for an hour or so, diligently and quietly, as usual. There's a good deal of dust and clutter and piles of books, and we uncover many forgotten treasures, books that ought to be out on the shelves.

'Roberta?'

'Hmm?'

I'm dusting books. He's sorting through paperwork.

'Your mother.'

I stiffen. I stop dusting. 'What about her?'

'Did you, I mean, of course, I'm trying to ask, it's not my business but . . . does she know about your father passing away?'

Silence.

Eventually, 'I haven't told her.'

'Do you not think she should be told?' he says quietly, eyeing me over his spectacles. 'Would it not be the right thing to do?'

I look away from him. I do not speak about my mother. Philip has never mentioned her before, and I don't like it. 'I don't have anything to do with my mother,' I say, stiffly, continuing with my dusting. 'I haven't done for years.'

'Why not? Your parents were divorced from each other, you know. Not from you.'

'Is that so?' I say.

Philip looks at me sharply. 'Is it not?' he says.

'No. It's not.'

'So?'

'So what?'

'Would you tell me the truth? About your mother?'

The truth about my mother? What is that? My truth would

certainly not be her truth. My truth is actually the frantic
ravings of a confused six-year-old. But I'm going to tell him
this secret, this thing of which I have always felt ashamed,
even though I was, am and always will be entirely innocent
of blame. This thing that has cut me in two all my life.

'It's all a bore, as you would say,' I begin.

Philip nods patiently.

'My mother left us when I was six years old, just walked
out one day while I was at school. Dad didn't know if she
was alive or dead for three days. She rang us after the police
tracked her down, and she told Dad she couldn't cope any
more with married life or with motherhood . . . with him, she
meant, and me. I haven't seen her since then, and from that
day my father and my grandmother brought me up. Nutshell.'

Philip is stunned. I can see realisation flood through him.
But he has no idea what to say, and now I am crying, though
I hate myself for it. So he gets up from his desk, walks round
it, stands beside me and puts his arms around me. He whispers my name. He kisses me on my head, I think, I can't be
sure. He rubs my back. And at that moment, of all moments,
that most innocent of moments – far more innocent than
secret (and unread) letters planted in books – Jenna bursts
into the office to ask if we would like coffee or tea?

Later, I show Philip the letter written by my grandfather.
Embarrassed, stammering a little at first, I tell him about
the parts of it that don't make sense, and about Suzanne's
revelation. We are coming to the end of our big clean-up in
his office. It's been a long day. I ought to talk to Jenna to
explain. My mind is racing.

Philip scrutinises the letter, then hands it back to me. 'Why
don't you just discuss it with your grandmother?' he says.

'It would upset her,' I reply.

'Wouldn't it be worth it to discover the truth?'

'Possibly. But I don't want to upset her. Obviously.'

'Did you ever ask your father about it?'

'I tried to once, but I didn't get anywhere. I got the feeling he knew things but didn't want to talk about them.'

'Well, so what if your grandparents weren't married? It's not the end of the world, is it?'

'No, I suppose not. I just hate the idea that her life has been a lie.'

'That's up to her, Roberta. Did she draw a war pension, do you know?'

'I don't think so. I'm not sure. I never heard her talk about one. But then if he was Polish, she perhaps wasn't entitled to one.'

'She wouldn't be entitled if she wasn't married either. It all adds up, rather. But she was married to this other chap, you say? Hmm. It's all quite a mystery, isn't it? Of course, that would appeal to you. But don't eat yourself up over it.' He sips his coffee. 'I'm sure this Suzanne woman is telling you the truth. And you've seen the deed poll, you say? There's your answer.'

'Oh, I don't know what to think any more. It's driving me crazy.'

'It's been a hard few weeks for you,' says Philip, softly.

'You have helped me so much. I'm ever so grateful. Really.'

I wonder if I should bring up the subject of the letter I found and say I don't intend reading it. That actually I understand. And I don't need a letter to let me down gently.

But Philip waves his hand, and moves the moment on. 'Will you tell her about your father?'

'I couldn't bring myself to last week. She's lost her only son.'

'Hmm. Perhaps it would be kinder to say nothing.'

'I think so, but she asks about him every time I visit. I'm running out of excuses for his absence, you know?'

'Poor you. What about your mother?'

'What about her?' I snap, angry that he's brought her up again.

'Couldn't she throw any light on this letter?'

'Oh. I see. Actually, I don't know. I've not considered that.'

'Well, it might be worth trying to make contact with her over this, if nothing else. This business seems to be consuming you, rather,' and a strange look clouds Philip's face.

I'm not sure if it's something he said, or something I said. But he looks pink and flustered. Jenna enters the office and strolls over to Philip, snaking an arm around his waist and declaring herself very, very bored. Can't they call it a day? She'll cook. The office looks immaculate! She beams at me, with a smile that I'm not certain is really a smile.

I must talk to her.

From:	Roberta Pietrykowski
Sent:	08 December 2010 20:25
To:	Anna Mills
Subject:	John Pietrykowski

Anna,

I hope you don't mind my contacting you out of the blue like this. If you are the right Anna Mills, I am your daughter. I thought I should let you know that your former husband, John Pietrykowski, died in October. He had been unwell for many years. He was brave and strong until the very end, avoiding hospital as much as he could. Maybe you can recall how much he hated hospitals? He died at home, and I was with him. I thought it only right to let you know.

Regards,

Roberta Pietrykowski

From: Anna Mills
Sent: 09 December 2010 18.19
To: Roberta Pietrykowski
Subject: RE: John Pietrykowski

Dear Roberta
Thank you for your email. I wonder how you tracked
me down. But, of course, nobody is invisible these
days. I have also wondered if I would ever hear from
you. I am sorry to hear about your loss, and I am not
surprised to hear that your father was stoic in his
illness and death. You have not asked me about my
life, and that is understandable, so I will not volunteer
any information. The people in my life know nothing
of you.
Anna

From: Roberta Pietrykowski
Sent: 09 December 2010 19:52
To: Anna Mills
Subject: RE: John Pietrykowski

I have no intention of giving away my existence to
the people in your life. Sorry I am such a shameful
secret.
Roberta

From: Anna Mills
Sent: 09 December 2010 21.40
To: Roberta Pietrykowski
Subject: RE: John Pietrykowski

You are not shameful, Roberta. I have just moved on
with my life in more ways than I ever thought possible

and I bear no resemblance, on any level, to the woman
that was Mrs Anna Pietrykowski.

From: Roberta Pietrykowski
Sent: 09 December 2010 21:58
To: Anna Mills
Subject: RE: John Pietrykowski

I understand.

From: Roberta Pietrykowski
Sent: 10 December 2010 19.03
To: Anna Mills
Subject: My grandmother

Anna,
Sorry to trouble you again. I still don't want anything
from you, apart from some information. I wonder if
you know anything about my grandmother, Dorothea,
who I am sure you can remember. I have discovered
that she was not married to my grandfather. Did she
ever speak to you about this? And also, do you have
any idea when my grandfather died?
Thank you,
Roberta

From: Anna Mills
Sent: 11 December 2010 09.34
To: Roberta Pietrykowski
Subject: RE: My grandmother

Roberta,
I guessed I had not heard the last from you. Dorothea
and I were never on close terms, sadly, but I do

remember her quite clearly. She was a noble woman, which may sound odd, but I can't think of a better word to describe her. She did tell me, while I was expecting you, that your father was a 'miracle' in her life. And that she lost a baby boy before John came along. I have no idea if your grandparents were married or not, but I wouldn't be surprised if they hadn't been. Dorothea didn't discuss him with me, but I always got the sense that John's father was her lover. There was never any husband talk, if that makes sense in this day and age. To be quaint, I suspect your father was a 'love child'. I don't know when your grandfather died. During the war, wasn't it? John never knew him.

If you would like to meet up, somewhere neutral, I am happy to do this. I live in London. I won't blame you if that is not on your agenda, I will understand perfectly. The offer is on the table, that's all.
Anna

From: Roberta Pietrykowski
Sent: 11 December 2010 20.17
To: Anna Mills
Subject: RE: My grandmother

Thank you, Anna. I am researching the family tree so that is why I asked. Ancestry is fascinating, at least to me. I didn't know that my grandmother had an earlier baby. Isn't it odd how we all keep secrets from those we love, or are supposed to love? She is still alive, by the way. She turned 110 in November. Tomorrow I am going to visit her. I will think about meeting up with you and I'll let you know.
Roberta

From: Anna Mills
Sent: 12 December 2010 12:11
To: Roberta Pietrykowski
Subject: Secrets

Roberta,
Your grandmother was – is – a deep woman.
Sometimes secrets are necessary. You will find this out
in life, if you haven't already.
Anna

33

Dear Mrs Compton,

I enclose an order for thirteen guineas. It includes the two pounds you kindly lent to me and some extra for A, if you think it will help. I do hope she will see sense over this. At any rate, I was not apprehended on the journey as I feared I would be. J and I arrived safely at my mother's house. The journey was long and arduous, as I expected. My mother is delighted with her grandson. She is less so with me, I think, but I am happy to say we get along well, much better than we ever did before I left. J has broken the ice between us and we are set to make a happy household, I hope.

I have registered for war work and Mother will take care of J while I am out of the house. I hope to be useful. The money I earn will certainly help Mother too, as her own source of income has practically disappeared. I wonder she had enough to lend me to send to you. Of course, I did not tell her what I needed the money for, and I shall work hard to repay her. My father left her money, but she has been using it for living expenses for many years now. I had no idea. I have suggested to Mother that we sell the house and buy something smaller, in which case we may leave Oxford. This would also mean my whereabouts will be less detectable, just in case. I know I shall live in fear of discovery all my *life, but all mothers live in daily fear anyway, I have realised, even my own.*

Thank you for all your help with J. I do appreciate it. Perhaps it might be prudent if you were to destroy this letter? I think it best if my exact location was to remain unknown. For that reason I am not including my address. I trust you will keep your side of our agreement, as I have kept mine.

Thank you again, and kind regards,
D

26th January 1941

Dear Jan,

Forgive me for not writing to you before now. I hope you received my last letter. It was written in a mad haste after your departure on Boxing Day. Was that really a mere month ago? Four short weeks that seem to me a lifetime – and in a sense, that's exactly what they are.

I expect I made a complete fool of myself writing such silly sentimental things in my last letter, things I can't even recall now. Perhaps you have replied? But I will not get your letter, because I no longer live at the cottage. I have left no forwarding address.

Darling, events took such a turn after you left on Boxing Day. I hardly know where to begin. So I'll just plunge in, as it were, and tell you everything. Nina, poor silly Nina, she had a baby. A darling little boy, on Boxing Day, after you had left. Do you recall she was complaining of feeling unwell that morning? None of us had any idea she was expecting. She claims she didn't know either. Somehow, against my better judgement, I believe her. I thought at first she was fibbing. How could any woman not know she had a baby nestling inside her? But she's not bright, I must be honest. And a large girl, as you know. And, if I can mention such a thing, she was irregular in her monthly cycle. So you can see how she may not have realised.

The little chap was born in the North Barn, among the straw and the hay and the sacks and the cows. It was positively biblical. He is a beautiful boy, born a little small, but in these few short weeks he has become plump and pink and healthy. I helped to deliver him – I was alone with her – and, Jan, it was incredible, and it has changed my life.

So, now to the crux of the matter. Nina doesn't want him. She seems to have no maternal instincts and, Jan, I have. I have them in abundance. You know that about me. I have taken the baby as my own. I have told a lie here and there, I confess. No doubt I shall continue to do so for the rest of my life. But Nina is happy. She would have had him sent to the nuns! I had to step in, don't you see? Her parents would have disowned her, she says, with the baby being born out of wedlock, of course. It doesn't do, as you know. Just think of the poverty this poor boy would have been brought up in. And think of me. I smile now, all the time, I am bursting with joy. Living with my mother again is hard, granted. But she has welcomed her grandson into her home and I believe she has welcomed me.

I have started work, making torpedoes. The day is long and it's hard to leave John, but my mother does a grand job of caring for him. She is a far better grandmother than she was a mother. I am not sure why that should be, but there you are. So you see, we get on all right. And, Jan, do you know, people will never again look upon me with pity in their eyes. I despised those looks people gave me, people who knew about my losing Sidney.

Darling, I know you will react strongly to this news. You will disapprove of what I have done, I know. But please try *to understand how I feel. I have a child at last, to love and care for, and motherhood has eluded me for so long, I thought forever. And once upon a time I thought death preferable to life because losing my child was so unbearable to me. Now my life is almost complete.*

But I dearly want you to be part of my life too. Dare I hope you had marriage on your mind, as much as I did? I'm sorry for being so forward but, Jan, I can be myself with you, and marriage is something I considered and even hoped for after our very first meeting. I didn't realise at the time, of course, but yes, it felt like you were my husband even then. Can I ask you to please think about it? You must know, and it is only fair that I tell you, that I will not turn back. I cannot. I have named the baby John, for you. I love him as I did my Sidney. He has become my son and you must understand it is impossible for me to give up this child whom I now hold so dear. I have to be honest with you, even though I shall be dishonest with everybody else.

Your music box waits for you at the cottage. I trust the girls will look after it until you are able to collect it one day. Will you? I wonder. It was a marvellous gift, thank you. I shall always love the songs of Billie Holiday, and whenever I hear her sing, for the rest of my life, it will remind me of you, and the time we spent together. It was a marvellous time, my dear.

Yours always and forever in hope,
Dorothea

Jan posted his reply to Dorothea. As he heard it flutter down into the pillar box, so his heart and his hope sank ever further. His life settled back down into its pre-Dorothea state, a state he could only think of now as oblivion.

This woman had soared so high in his imagination. Leaning his head on the cold, hard pillar box, he closed his eyes, for a second . . . two . . . three . . . four . . . five.

But no. He could do this. He began a slow walk back to the squadron car. It was time to get back.

Everything ached, everything was cold.

34

Dear Helen, How's it going at uni? I kind of wish I'd gone too now, things are a bit boring around here since you left. I went to the wedding of the year, and I have a report for you, as promised.

It went well, I suppose. Arlene looked a fright in her frock, of course. And Craig looked, well, like Craig, the big-headed arse. Arlene's mother was totally blotto and cried loudly all through the ceremony, and she got even more pissed up in the evening. Darren looked daggers at Craig the whole time, I thought there would be a scrap once the booze started to flow, but he managed to control himself. Don't know what he ever saw in Arlene anyway. I think he had a narrow escape, don't you? She picked the wrong brother to marry, that's for sure. But hey, they deserve each other, I reckon. The disco was shitty, as you'd expect, and the first dance an embarrassment, I thought. But hey, that's weddings for you!

How's it going with you?

See you in the holidays, I suppose. Missing you,
Vanessa

(Letter found inside a book club edition of Maeve Binchy's *Circle of Friends*. A fair copy, priced at £2.50 and placed on the hardback fiction shelves.)

I disembark from the train at Marylebone station and bustle through the ticket barriers with everyone else, caught up immediately in the hustle and haste of the city. I pop to the loo, and afterwards I stand and look around me, trying to spot my mother. I have a strong image of her in my head, though I know she must now look quite unlike the slender young woman she had been when I last saw her.

I sweat, a little. My heart beats faster than it normally does. But why? She is the one who should feel nervous, not me.

And then I see a woman, petite, wearing high heels to compensate and wearing them very well, moving serenely through the crowds, smiling at me. She stands before me.

'Roberta.'

'Anna?'

'Yes. I could see you straight away. I knew it was you, I mean.'

We look at each other; I don't know what to say next. I have her eyes. But she is elegant, and I am not. I am tall, a little clumsy, a little bumbling. She is compact, graceful, contained. And I, thankfully, am my father's daughter.

'Would you like to get a drink?' she says.

I nod.

We find a table in the corner of the pub on the station, and she glides to the bar and returns with two glasses of wine. All the while, I can't keep my eyes from her. She is hypnotic. She looks no more than ten years older than me. She is sensual in her movements, attractive and confident. Is this woman really my mother? I imagined her bitter and cruel, wizened, old. Not this. I am having problems recognising her, even though I know, I can tell, I can remember her. Her hair is glossy, an expensive shade of pale caramel brown – not at all mousy, like mine.

'I feel I owe you an explanation, Roberta.'

'Yes, please. I'd . . . like that.'

'But first I want to know how you are, what your life is like.'

'My life is good, usually.'

'I'm sorry your father died. He was a good man.'

'He can't have been that great, surely, if you felt the need to walk out on him,' I say, thrilled to have scored the first hit. She makes me feel like a child, which is not good.

'We'll come to that. I promise. But first, tell me about you. I have often wondered, so much.'

And I tell her, bit by bit, and she asks questions, and I answer them, and we have another glass of wine.

'So,' she says eventually, leaning back in her chair, fiddling with her wine glass. 'Your boss, Philip. He sounds very nice.'

'Yes, he's great.'

'Mm-hmm.'

'Jenna's nice too – his girlfriend I told you about. They make a good couple, I think.'

'Mm-hmm.'

I want to change the subject. My . . . Anna is looking at me with some sort of glint in her eye, and I don't like it. What does she know about my life? About my friendship with Philip? Only what I've told her and, well, it's nothing, really. And it's not what I came here today to discuss, anyway. And how can she be so composed? I'm your fucking daughter, I want to shout. Or feel that I should want to shout. But I don't really feel that. I know I'm a bit of a pushover at times, a bit naive, as Jenna said, but my mother is *likeable*. She is confident and poised, and I like having people like that around me. People like Philip.

'Can I have that explanation now, please?' I say, fiddling with my own wine glass. I feel slightly drunk.

She suggests lunch first, and yes, I am hungry, all of a sudden. She orders, pays and returns to our table. 'I'll begin at the beginning, shall I?' she asks.

It sounds light-hearted, but really it isn't. And perhaps, just perhaps, this is harder for her than it is for me.

'All right, then. I was young when I met your dad. Just twenty, and already married, can you believe that? My husband was a brute. A rough man, a bully, he left me scarred in many ways. Your dad was the opposite, so kind and gentle, much older than me. He was already an architect then, getting his career off the ground, and quite lonely, I always felt. I had an affair with him and he encouraged me to leave my husband. It caused something of a scandal in my family. They seemed to think that Simon – my first husband – was this great guy, a good catch for me. Nobody could see, or they refused to see, what he truly was. I fell out with my family, and moved in with your father, and fell pregnant with you. I divorced my first husband, and John and I were married just before you were born. And you know, your grandmother, Dorothea, was never anything but kind and accepting of me, the situation, all of it. I'll always remember that.'

'So what went wrong?' I ask, so quietly I'm surprised she hears me.

'I went wrong, Roberta.'

'What does that mean?

'I shouldn't have married your father. I shouldn't have had a child. I'm not a natural mother, Roberta.'

'Again, what does that mean?' My voice is angrier than I intended.

We sit in silence for a few moments. I eat my salad, finish my wine and look around the pub, which is louder now, busier. I notice it is gaudy with tinsel and fairy lights. Everybody looks inordinately happy.

'What I mean is, I'm not mother material. I couldn't stand it. I loved you. But that was all. I couldn't bear looking after you all day . . . the boredom . . . no stimulation . . . being at home all day. I know it sounds horribly, horribly selfish.'

'If you hated it so much, why did you have me? You could have got rid of me.'

'I'm so very glad I didn't.'

We talk on.

She thinks I did the right thing to terminate my pregnancy at university. But she thinks I'll be a good mother one day. She says to have one child, maybe two, but not to subsume myself. Be me. Do things I want to do. Get babysitters. Get help. Be an interesting woman for my children to live with. I must inspire them.

'I let you down,' she says. 'As your mother.'

'Actually, the letting down part was when you left. I didn't want you to go. I don't know how you did it. You must be very . . . hard.'

'I am hard.'

'Well, it's not a good way to be. Dad was a nice man, you said so yourself. What did he do wrong?' My voice is wobbling and warbling, and the pain in my throat is proving too much as I fight tears.

'Shall we get coffee?' she says, putting her hand on my arm.

It's good to see there is still a spark of wisdom in my mother.

And later, after the tears, after a second coffee, I show Anna the letter from Jan to Dorothea. She reads it once, then a second time, frowning a little.

'What do you know about them?' I ask. 'If anything?'

'A little. I think I told you that Dorothea confided in me once, many years ago, when I was expecting you. We had a little talk. I remember she lent me a dear little old suitcase full of beautiful baby clothes.'

'Really? Did you know Babunia changed her name to Dorothea Pietrykowski?' I say. 'She was really Dorothy Sinclair. The woman at her care home is adamant that my grandparents weren't married.'

'I think she's right. I think your babunia – God, I'd forgotten that name! – I think she had a love affair. I always assumed John was the result of that. Sinclair, you say? That rings a bell for some reason.'

'It's written on a label inside the suitcase, I think it must be the same one. I have it now.'

'Yes! You're right! I thought nothing of it at the time.'

I carefully fold up Jan's letter and put it back in my handbag alongside the unopened letter from Philip that I carry with me too. I should – I must – open it. Soon. I must face the music.

'I have to go now,' I say. 'My train . . . Do you know when he died? My grandfather? Did she ever . . .?'

Anna shakes her head. She glances at her watch. 'No, I don't know. I think during the war but, well, perhaps not when she liked to claim. When did you last see Dorothea?' Anna stands and puts on her pretty coat.

'Last week. I try to talk to her but she's pretty confused most of the time. She keeps calling me Nina.'

'Nina?'

'Yes.'

'Is there a Nina in the family?'

'No, I don't think so. There is no family other than Babunia and me. You should know that.'

'Of course. She must have been a friend, then. Maybe

you look like her. We all have that confusion to look forward to.' She grimaces.

Anna leaves the pub with me. She's going home on the Tube. I realise I know nothing about her life now, the 'people in my life' she referred to.

'Perhaps we could meet again, another time?' I ask.

'Yes. I would like that. In the New Year? Merry Christmas, Roberta. It's been wonderful to meet you.'

I stand and watch her disappear down into the Tube, before heading for my own train home.

35

Mrs D. Sinclair

(Inscription inside my suitcase)

When I get home from my trip to London, I retrieve the suitcase from the top of the wardrobe. I use it now to house out-of-season clothing, so it's stuffed with summer tops, shirts, shorts, sunglasses, a floppy floral sunhat, a swimming costume I stubbornly hang on to even though I wore it only once and it's at least one size too small. I take out the summer gear and toss it all on to the bed. Suzanne was right, I think. Babunia must have been married, and my grandfather must have been her lover. I have never seen any marriage certificates, any decrees for divorce or any death certificates. Only the deed poll showing her change of name. No wonder she was so sympathetic towards beautiful, twenty-year-old Anna. I look closely now at the label and, yes, it does look like my grandmother's handwriting – a younger, larger, bolder, firmer version of it. I wonder that I didn't notice on the day Dad gave me the suitcase.

I have so many questions and I cannot articulate them all. Why did she call herself Pietrykowski? To hide her shame? I do know that many a woman has done that – women not actually married to the man they call 'husband' – to save embarrassment, to throw nosy neighbours, colleagues, friends, perhaps even family, off the scent. Did she marry my grandfather at a later date? If she did, why didn't Dad remember him? Did this Sinclair, her actual husband, die in the war? Was *he* really my grandfather? And, finally then, it's an unavoidable question . . . who am I? I am called Pietrykowski, but am I really a Pietrykowski?

I notice the name label is peeling off, so I carefully press it back into place, smoothing it down, holding it firmly until the glue takes. I trace over the letters, lingering over them with my index finger, letter by letter.

A week before Christmas, and we're throwing a party for our customers. Philip's idea – uncharacteristic, but something he seems excited about. Jenna's gregarious nature must be rubbing off on him, I suggest to Sophie. She shrugs. Upstairs in Philip's flat, Jenna and Patricia are preparing trays of mince pies, bottles of champagne, orange juice, mulled wine, coffee. Nibbles and cheeses. The till will remain open until late into the evening, of course, and I think Philip hopes the whole soirée will generate sales. We could do with them, he says. But he says this every year, and we're still here.

The shop fills with guests, and Jenna looks so pretty in a pink silk frock and heeled shoes, her blonde hair softly curled, and Sophie is laughing, chatting easily with the guests, recommending books. Patricia is mingling, confident, loud-voiced but not jarring, her severely short hairstyle belying her warm nature. I think, yes, Philip must be pleased with the team he has built up here. The team works.

I am standing at the top of the wide stairs that lead to the upper floors. I've just closed the heavy shutters at the large window, and I'm surveying the foyer below, watching the guests circulating and chatting and buying, hearing the cash register ring. Christmas carols are playing softly on the shop sound system. The door behind me marked 'Private' opens, and Philip comes to stand beside me.

He hands me a glass of champagne. 'Cheers!' he says. 'Merry Christmas, Roberta. It's going well, don't you think?'

'Yes. Very well. Everybody seems to be having a good time.'

'And you?'

'Yes. I'm fine. It's a lovely idea of yours, Philip.'

'Actually, I can't take credit for this. It was Jenna's idea.'

We both sip champagne, surveying the scene below. A strange silence descends on us, and I know we are both aware of it.

Philip tuts, sighs and turns to me. 'Thank you,' he says.

There is a look of panic about him.

'What for?' I ask, quietly, scared that my voice will come out too loud and people in the foyer will look up, meaning Philip and I will be required to descend the stairs and be swallowed up in the festive throng.

'For putting up with me,' I think he whispers.

'For what?'

He leans in, I feel the brush of his face on mine.

'For putting up with me.'

And I see Jenna in the foyer, chatting to dear sweet Mrs Lucas. She looks up and meets my eyes as Philip leans in to me and whispers, his cheek brushing against mine.

A little later, Philip disappears discreetly into his office, and not long afterwards his girlfriend follows him. Minutes pass, during which I chat and laugh and recommend books, but secretly, truly, all I can think about is Philip. The touch of his face on mine when he whispered to me. How it made me feel. The smell of his freshly shaved skin, his hair, his breathy scent of champagne, and something else. Something new to me, yet unfathomably familiar. Something I know, perhaps from my dreams.

Jenna emerges from the office, flushed, sad-looking. I wonder what—

'Roberta?' she says, stalking past me. 'Would you come upstairs with me, please? Just for a minute.'

I follow her up the stairs, all the way into the hallowed space of Philip's flat. She flicks on a light switch, goes into the bedroom she and Philip share, takes a suitcase from the top of the wardrobe and starts to throw clothes into it.

I stand in the doorway, watching her. 'What are you doing?' I ask.

'What does it look like?'

'You're packing.'

'I'm leaving.'

'Have you had a row with Philip?' I say.

'No. I've finished with him.'

'Oh, Jenna. Are you sure? I'm so sorry. Can I help?' I step towards her, instinctively.

'Help to get me out from under your feet, you mean? Out of the way?'

I step back again, stung. 'What on earth do you mean?'

'Oh, don't come the innocent with me,' she spits.

'I meant . . . can I help you to patch it up with Philip?'

'I'm not going to be second best. I'm worth more than that.'

'Yes, you are, of course you are. But I don't understand.'

'I have eyes and ears – and, despite appearances, I'm pretty smart.'

'And . . .?'

I watch her nervously, as she opens and shuts drawers

and cupboards, takes off her high-heeled shoes and flings them across the room.

'Maybe I'm not making much sense, Roberta. Let me help you out here. Philip is not in love with me. We don't have a future. I've just had it from the horse's mouth. As if I didn't already know.'

'But it's all rather sudden, isn't it?'

'So what? It's true, that's all that matters. He means it. He's in love with somebody else.'

'Did he say that?' I am aghast. I am full of wretched hope.

'He might as well have. I accused him of it, and he didn't deny it. I didn't need to ask who the lucky lady is.' Her voice is high and brittle, full of pain.

I look at the floor, my face burning in shame and anguish, disbelief and dawning hope. Jenna pushes past me and clatters around in the living room before returning to the bedroom and resuming her packing. She opens up a second suitcase.

'It's all right. I saw it coming. I . . . I haven't always behaved well towards you. I was the one who told Francesca Dearhead about you and Charles.'

My mouth drops open. She stops packing for a moment and has the grace to look embarrassed, but when she speaks again there is a defensive, defiant edge to her voice.

'I'm sorry, okay? I'll admit I wanted you out of the way, but I felt guilty as soon as I'd done it, and wished I hadn't. And you were so good to come to the clinic with me.' Her voice wavers on the edge of tears now. 'It's a shame we can never be friends.'

She's right, of course she is, but it's an awful, awkward way to end a friendship.

Her packing completed, she puts on a coat and a pair of boots. 'I'll get Philip to bag up everything else and I'll come back for it another time. After Christmas. Don't look so surprised,' she says, half kindly, half furiously, and she even rubs my arm. 'You'd better go and see him. I think he's waiting for you.'

She leaves the flat, descends the staircases, and – no doubt with a dramatic flourish – she leaves the Old and New behind.

Later – minutes, an hour, I'm not sure how long – I go back downstairs to the shop. Most people have gone. Patricia and Sophie are in a huddle at the till, talking earnestly, and they look up at me as I descend the stairs. I shake my head at them. I go to my handbag, which is hanging on a peg in the corridor where I left it, and take out my two letters.

I put one back, unread on this occasion, and finally open the other.

36

Dearest Roberta,

You have found this letter, obviously. This is something I feel must be left to chance. Of course, I'd probably end up simply writing you another one; better still, I'd be a man about it and ask you in person. But I know how much you like letters, I know you love to stumble across them, read them and keep them. I know how those glimpses into other people's lives fascinate you. So I am writing to you in the hope that you find this. And if this is all too much – or I've made a horrible mistake and you don't, in fact, love me as I love you – well, I'll just tell myself you haven't found the letter. Oh, the games we play.

Jenna and I don't have a future. It's sad, because she is not a bad person, and I haven't been entirely fair to her. But I don't love her, and somehow I need to get up the courage to tell her that. I will do so, in my own time. I hope it will be soon, because I don't want to keep up any pretence for longer than I have to.

Roberta, at some point in the future, when I'm free and you're free, I'd like to take you to dinner. I'd like to take you to several dinners. I'd like us to take a chance and see if we might not just be right for each other. I'm in love with *you, but I don't know how you feel about me. You probably think I'm a middle-aged fool.*

I don't know when you will read this. But when you do, come and find me. I'm here.

Philip

I breathe deeply as I knock on the office door. I clear my throat.

'Come in.'

I enter the office, close the door behind me.

Philip stands behind his desk. He looks at the letter in my hand. 'Has she gone?' he says.

'Yes.'

'Is that . . . my letter?'

'Yes.'

'I knew you'd found it. It wasn't where I left it. I thought—'

'I found it on my first day back,' I interrupt. His face falls, so I hastily add, 'But I've only just opened it.'

'Oh. I see.'

'Jenna was rather upset.'

'I know,' he says, sadly. 'I tried to be kind. She wasn't totally surprised, so my conscience is soothed a little. And she was sick of me and the bookshop, she said. I'm dreary, apparently.'

'Do you mean it?' I blurt.

He strides round his desk, stands before me and places his hands on my shoulders. 'Of course I mean it. Jenna, she . . .'

'She was nice about it, really. She told me—'

'Listen to me,' he says, cutting me off. 'Jenna was an opportunist. She probably wouldn't see herself in such terms, but she was a gold-digger, I think, to be blunt.'

'God.' I don't know what to say.

He fills the silence. 'I can tell you something Jenna didn't know, though she clearly had some inkling.' He looks rather pained as he says, 'I'm extremely well-off. A millionaire. Several times over, in fact.'

'Oh,' I say. 'Well, thank goodness for that.'

Philip laughs. 'I'm actually the seventh Marquess of Monmouthshire,' he says, grimacing again. 'If I want to be. Which I don't.'

'I see. That makes sense.'

Somehow, none of this is surprising me. It's as though I'd known all along, or half known, half guessed. I have an image of Babunia, sitting alone in her room in the care home, her secrets folded and wrapped deep inside her like layers of sedimentary rock.

'Will nothing impress you, Miss Pietrykowski?' says Philip in mock exasperation. 'And you're quite wrong, it does not "make sense". It's bollocks. I don't believe in titles.'

'None of this is really my world, Philip.'

'And you couldn't give a toss, could you?' he asks hopefully.

'Not really.'

'That's what I wanted to hear.'

'Jenna—' I venture.

'She had the good grace to stand down, as it were. And she had absolutely no idea about me, not truly. Very few people do. So here we are.'

I feel weightless, like I am floating an inch or two above the floor. I don't want to land. 'Indeed. Here we are. What happens next?'

'Let me buy you dinner and let's see how it goes. It's hardly a blind date, so I'm confident it will go swimmingly, but I don't want to stuff it up. Our friendship's a delicate thing.'

'Yes,' I say. 'Dinner would be nice.'

'Tomorrow night? Or whenever you can make it. I don't want to rush you. The new bistro? Candlelight and all that? If it's too much, just say so, and we'll go to the cinema or whatever. I really don't mind.'

'It sounds lovely, Philip. Tomorrow. It's a date.'

37

She is listening to the radio again.

I bought it for her as a Christmas present after Suzanne told me she no longer showed any interest in the television. It's a DAB, but she asks anybody who enters her room to tune in her 'wireless' for her. She has not yet learned to trust herself to use it. She probably never will, Suzanne says. It's asking a lot when you are one hundred and ten years of age.

Suzanne is still spending a lot of time with my grandmother, she tells me, painting her nails, brushing her hair. Talking. In fact, Suzanne has some information for me. Something rather odd that Dorothea told her.

'I think it might be important,' she says to me breathlessly, on my arrival. She has intercepted me in the entrance hall, eager to share her news.

'Really?' I say. 'Can I catch up with you after I've seen Babunia?'

She looks a little crestfallen, but I know she understands. I want to glean information myself, if it's possible, if my grandmother is in the right frame of mind. It wouldn't be right for Suzanne to snoop for me. She will be my last resort. I owe Babunia that.

I close the door of her room quietly behind me and smile at Babunia. She turned when she heard the door opening; she is remarkably alert today, which is lovely to see. A warm spring breeze wafts through her room from the open window. In the garden, children scream and run around. It's another resident's birthday, and her family are all visiting.

I pull up the footstool and sit before my grandmother. 'Good morning,' I say.

'Shh. Please.' She gestures at the radio.

'Shall I brush your hair? No? Shall I paint your nails, then? I've brought you some red polish.'

'If you like. Quietly, though. Please.'

Suzanne has started a vanity box, filled with nail polishes, lipsticks, eye shadows, Olay, cotton wool, cleansing lotion, hand cream . . . no matter her age, she maintains, a woman likes to be pampered. So I thought I'd start 'doing' Babunia's nails too. I set to work. The skin of her large hands is red and wrinkled, the nails yellow and brittle. Years of doing laundry, she always tells me.

'Is your father here?' she says now.

'No, not today. He's busy.'

'Oh, what a pity. He hasn't visited me in such a long time.'

'I know, Babunia. But he sends his love.'

'How's that wife of his?'

'Anna? Oh, you know. Gone. She left years ago, remember? When I was six?'

'That doesn't surprise me. I don't trust her one bit. She's a nice enough young woman, but . . .'

It's a strange kind of lucidity. But I'm getting used to it. As a matter of fact, I know that Anna is well; we met for lunch in London again last week. But I don't tell Babunia that, mainly because I think it will confuse her.

I have completed the nails of one hand. I adjust the stool and take up her other hand. Red suits her, despite her advanced years. The radio programme is about Billie Holiday. I half listen to the story of her infamous life. Insistent jazz music seeps from the radio and dances around the room on the breeze.

'I know this one!' I say. 'Are you still a fan of Bill— Babunia? Oh, what is it?'

Tears roll down her thin, colourless cheeks, and her lips are trembling. I continue to paint her nails, knowing that when you are crying the last thing you want is to be looked at.

'I always think of him,' she says eventually, in a whisper. 'When I hear her sing.'

'Think of who?'

'Him. When I hear her songs.'

'Do you mean John?' I ask.

'John?'

'John. My dad. Your son?'

'No. Not him. Not today. Not even Sidney, today. I do wish my sons would visit me!' she cries, suddenly animated.

Who was Sidney? Was he the lost baby Anna mentioned to me? Anna. The woman who is slowly becoming my mother again. Despite everything, I like her. She's funny and sharp and unconventional. There's a freedom in forgiveness. And she's thrilled for me and Philip.

'You don't have to tell me anything you don't want to, Babunia,' I say, taking a chance, opening the door, inviting her to confide in me. 'But I'm here to listen, if you do want to.'

There is a long, dreamy pause during which she seems to drift off from me, arguing with herself, in silence.

She frowns. 'My husband,' she says at last.

'He died in the war, didn't he? A long time ago, wasn't it?' Silence.

I decide to jump in and say it. 'Jan *wasn't* your husband, Babunia, was he? It's okay, you know. Nobody minds.'

She ignores me. 'I don't think he died at all. Not then.'

'Oh.' I slowly paint the nail on her wedding finger. She wears no ring, and I can't remember there ever being one. Why didn't I notice this before? Widows wear their rings, don't they? 'When do you think he died, then?'

'I don't know, you see. It's not for me to know. But I always felt he was alive, breathing air just like me. It was a comforting thought. I miss him so much. Do you know, I thought I saw him once. But he didn't see me. And goodness knows, it probably wasn't him. He was with a woman with blonde hair. She was much prettier than I ever was.'

Babunia's hand shakes, but I squeeze it gently in reassurance, careful not to smudge the polish. I wonder if she notices. I sense she is somewhere else, a long way from here, and a long way from now.

'He was a good man, Roberta,' says Babunia finally, and she looks out into the garden where the children are frolicking in the sunshine, playing tag. But she does not see them.

'Of course he was,' I tell her.

'But proud. Like all men.'

'That's their undoing sometimes, isn't it?' I say, glad to have some common ground at last. 'Pride?'

'Often it is,' she says sadly.

'Do you miss him still?'

'Of course I miss him.'

'You didn't live over the brush, did you?' Sometimes it helps to keep things light, to make little jokes. Despite the endless confusion, she still has her sense of humour, subtle and quiet.

'No. We never lived together. He didn't want me to keep the baby. Was it so wrong of me? I never saw him again . . . but I don't think it was wrong. Do you?'

I feel drained, exhausted. Her words are off-kilter, like

discordant music. *He didn't want me to keep the baby*. So she *did* have an abortion. I wonder. Oh, that pivotal, tantalising line in my grandfather's letter! What you do, to this child, to this child's mother, it is wrong.

'Oh. I . . . I'm not sure what to say,' I whisper.

'He wasn't my husband's child. But he wasn't even my child, you see. It was all rather . . . confusing. He was Aggie's. No. Not Aggie's. What am I talking about? Oh dear. Oh. What was her name? Nina! Yes, that was her. Tall girl, fat. Stupid girl, really, and I . . . oh, the poor thing. She was hopeless and helpless. I tried. I did. I told her. I expect she's dead by now. I'll never know if I'm truly wicked or not. I had an accomplice, but she was a witch. But he thought I was. I had to go home. I had to go back to Mother's house. Do you know what I found under my bed?'

Mute, unsure of what to say, I shake my head. Did she help somebody else to have an abortion? This Nina she keeps talking about, this Nina she has mistaken me for on several occasions?

'*The Infant's Progress*. Of all the things. I'll never forget that wretched book. I put his last letter inside it. He told me off, you see, in his letter. I kept that book for years. I think it's gone now, and the letter with it. And I lost my temper with him and I burned all the other ones. I burned the blue ribbon. I even burned his shirt, Roberta, can you imagine? I had never washed it. All those buttons . . . what a fool I was. I should have kept that, I should have kept everything. I have nothing of his, nothing else at all. I lost him, you see. I was so angry he wasn't going to marry me after all. I was furious with him for years and years. I asked him to be my husband. Can you imagine? I thought he wanted to be my husband. But he wouldn't forgive me. I can't tell you how terrible it made me feel. He broke my heart into so many pieces. So small I couldn't find them and put them back together again. Just as well they're all gone, isn't it, really? But I don't regret what I did. John was worth it. It was right. We don't get everything in life, do we?'

Well, at least that makes sense. My mind is racing as I try to piece together all that she has said.

'Who was Nina?' I ask.

'Nina? I don't know any Ninas! Don't ask questions. I can't remember everything . . . I'm not going to tell you!' and now the sad, wise old lady is a stroppy child again.

I know I have pushed her too far. So we sit in silence, listening to the radio, and I make tea. She sips hers with a shaking hand. I look at her and wonder if we shall ever talk again. She is barely present now, grey and thin as rainfall on a winter afternoon.

Possibilities present themselves to me. I don't like any of them, so I turn them away, one by one, like tiresome beggars. She was a marvellous mother, both to my father and to me. Nothing else matters. As Philip would say, the rest is all bollocks.

Philip. My fiancé. How grand that sounds, and how strange. I decide to tell her my news.

'Did I tell you? Philip and I are engaged.'

'Philip? I don't think I know a Philip.'

'He's a nice man, the very best, and we are going to be very happy,' I tell her.

She nods, seeming satisfied with that.

'We're getting married in August, and I want you to come.'

She raises her eyebrows and smiles. 'We'll see,' she says, with a flash of that wry humour I have always loved.

The programme about Billie Holiday has finished. I turn the volume down to a soft background murmur, half-hearted waves breaking on a distant shore, but Babunia doesn't seem to notice. Carefully, because I don't want to disturb her, I reach for my handbag. I find Jan's letter, now much creased and crumpled, open out the two fragile pages, smooth them flat and place them on the side table next to Babunia's chair. She has fallen into a childlike doze and, after undoing her chignon, I gently brush her long grey hair, over and over, until it shines.

38

And now that it was over, he had only vague ideas of what to do, or where to go. He was done with flying, and that was his only certainty, apart from knowing he would not return to Poland. Perhaps America? One day, yes, perhaps. But there were things to do first, here in England. There was unfinished business to attend to.

He drove to the cottage in Lincolnshire, and from the road it all seemed much the same. He fancied the same curtains were still hanging at the windows. Yet, on closer inspection, he saw that the garden was not nearly as well kept as it once had been. There were no hens. There was no laundry on the lines, although it was a warm day in May.

He opened the gate and shuffled along the path, and suddenly it was five years ago, and he imagined he could hear the woman's mournful humming. But he could not. He knocked on the kitchen door. It was opened by a young man, who regarded him with suspicion and impatience.

'Yes?'

'I am Squadron Leader Jan Pietrykowski.'

'Do I know you?'

'No, but I knew this cottage. I stayed here. I was a friend to the lady who lived here then. Do you know her, I wonder?'

'Sal might. Sal!'

A young woman, a land girl, came to the door. She was neither Aggie nor Nina.

Jan bowed. 'I am looking for a Mrs Dorothy Sinclair.'

'Oh. I didn't know her. I think Aggie did, though.'

'Is Aggie still here?'

'No. She left in 1942, I think it was. She got moved to a farm in Yorkshire. I heard she's going to marry a GI when he gets demobbed. They're going to Alabama, I think. Or is it Arkansas?'

'And Nina? Do you know the girl named Nina?' Jan tried to suppress his impatience.

'No, but I heard talk of a girl called Nina having a baby.'

'You did?'

'A little girl. She got married, I think. I don't know what became of her, though.'

'Ah.'

'Aggie used to talk about a woman named Dorothy. But I didn't know her.'

'Is there a music box here? A gramophone?'

She looked startled. 'Yes.'

'May I have it, please? I lent it to Dorothy at the start of the war. I have come to reclaim it.'

'It makes no odds to me,' said the girl. 'Bill, what do you think?'

The young man shrugged. 'We're leaving soon to go home, only going to leave it here. Do what you like with it.'

They stood aside to let Jan enter the kitchen, which was no longer Dorothy's kitchen. It was dirty and dark. The parlour beyond was dusty and tatty, with packing boxes jostling for space. The young woman indicated the gramophone on the sideboard, and Jan, thanking her, lifted it, wincing. The younger man offered to help, and Jan was forced to accept. While Bill took the music box to Jan's car, Jan gathered up the remaining records; some were missing, he thought. He thanked the girl.

She smiled. 'So where you from, then?' she asked.

'Poland.'

'Oh.'

'You going back?' asked Bill, who had come back inside.

'Sadly, no.'

'Don't bloody blame you.'

He thanked them again, and returned slowly to the car.

And a few weeks later, Oxford. He was feeling better, stronger. The drive to Lincolnshire he should perhaps not have undertaken. Then, he had been weak. But now, all was on the mend. It was summer, and Oxford was a nice city, he thought, grand. And he wandered, marvelling at the colleges, the ivy-clad buildings, unscathed. And he asked people, those he met by chance, in shops, in libraries, in the street. He made himself a nuisance, but a charming one.

'Honour? I am looking for a Mrs Honour?' (For hadn't Dorothy once told him her maiden name was Honour?) 'With a grown-up daughter, Dorothy?'

He was on the point of giving up, tired, unconvinced, his initial energies and hopes waning, wishing he had kept Dorothy's letter or at least memorised her address before his stupid pride had made him throw it away, when a woman, eager to help a handsome foreigner, brightened and did not shake her head.

'Ruth? Ruth Honour?'

And thus he found himself, tired and shaking, outside a house with a blue door in the north of the city. He breathed hard and knocked. Nobody answered. He peered through a window. The house seemed to be empty, forsaken. He spoke to a neighbour, who was peeping at him over a neatly cut box hedge.

Yes, he'd known the people who had lived there. An old

lady and her daughter, both widowed, and the daughter's little boy. Nice family. But they'd gone, oh, three or four years ago? No, he had no forwarding address. The daughter, he thought, had married a Polish man who had died early in the war.

'Do you recall her married name?' Jan asked him.

'Pilkowski? Pentrykowski? Something like that.'

'Thank you,' said Jan, his chest swelling with a feeling he could not put a name to. 'And did she marry again, do you know?'

'I don't think so, no. But as I say, it's been a good while since they moved away. The house has an owner, but nobody lives here. They do collect post periodically, so they may have a forwarding address. Are you Russian?'

'Ah. Of course. Thank you for your time. No, I am not Russian.'

14th August 1945

My dear Dorothea,

I have been trying to find you, with no success. I have got as far as your mother's house in Oxford, and there your trail seems to run cold. I write to you there, in the hope my letter can be passed on to you. A vain hope, but all I have. I think, if I try hard enough, I will find you. I suspect you go by my name, and you are most welcome to. In fact, it is my privilege. There can't be too many Pietrykowskis living in England! But at the same time, I do not want to bother you. You may be married again, with new name, and happy, and you no longer think of me. So if this letter reaches you, that is good. If not, so be it. I have a plan for my future, and if I do not hear from you, I will carry it out.

As you can see, I have survived the war, as I told you I would. I fought long and hard, and I became exhausted. As you say here, I ran out of steam. Last few months of war, I am in hospital. My old injury gives me gyp, I tire greatly, in my mind and body, and in the end I suffer a collapse of it all. Terrible. Thoughts of dying, feeling so weak and feeble and sick. But I am better now and all in my life is dancing and singing and light again. Almost all, because you are missing. I let you go and I should not have. It is the worst mistake of my life. I love you more than ever, and I was wrong to judge you so badly about your baby. I want you to forgive me and marry me, as we expected, if you are free to do so, of course, and if you want to. No doubt you are angry with me, disappointed by the letter I sent to you. I regret each and every word of it. I was wrong.

That is all. No more to be said, for now. I am not returning to Polska, to live under Communists, no, and I am bitter about that. But my life will be mine. I have a plan to go to Italy, be with the sun, swim, eat, find work. There will be work. I have a friend who says it is a good place to regain strength. Then, I think of the USA, land of opportunity. Perhaps you and your son could join with me there? This is my most cherished hope.

Jan

39

I'm still here, just. Still breathing and sleeping, waking, watching, thinking.

I remember now, that day we travelled down to London on the train. Just the three of us – me and John and Roberta. It was her tenth birthday, into double figures, so something to be celebrated. John was recovering from the break-up of his friendship with a woman called Kate. It hadn't been a very serious affair, and I had thought all along it had been ill advised. John could be intense when he was younger. And in those days he was, of course, still suffering from the shock of being abandoned by Anna. I'm not surprised Kate broke it off. She understood the heartache both of them laboured under, and she didn't fancy trying, and failing, to fill Anna's shoes. You really cannot blame her.

So, to London. Madame Tussauds first, which Roberta loved. Then, on the Tube to Trafalgar Square. We fed the pigeons, admired the lions – we got Roberta to sit on one for a photograph. She was wearing a striped sweater. It was a chilly day, so we decided to eat lunch indoors. We none of us knew London well enough to have a restaurant in mind, so we wondered what to do and where to go. I was tired.

About to suggest the cafe in the National Gallery, I turned towards the building and I saw her, a tall woman, somewhere in her sixties, staring at me. She may have been looking at me for some time, I'll never know. She was standing by one of the fountains. With her, a woman, fortyish, and two children, about Roberta's age, a little younger perhaps, both boys. I thought them twins. They were both tall, with mousy hair, and definitely, terrifyingly there was a look of Roberta about them. The younger woman was a feminine version of John. The older woman, Nina – for it was her, unmistakeably – stared at us. She looked at the two young boys, surely her grandsons, and back at John. She was plump, more so than before. She looked tired, grey and careworn. But, I dared to hope, she did not look unhappy. For a second, perhaps two, we looked straight at each other. And in her eyes, behind her eyes, I saw the brash nineteen-year-old, strong, loud, ignorant. All of this in a few seconds. By then my eyesight was failing, of course, but a person's essence never leaves them – especially, you cannot mistake the face of a woman who was once in pain, in need, begging you to help her.

And soon enough she was obscured by other people, with other lives, who had stories of their own, and I realised, with relief, that she was not going to advance upon me. I stopped looking. We found lunch, but I could not eat. My heart would not slow its beating, not for an hour, two hours. Finally, later, as we wandered around the galleries, I found myself thinking about Aggie. Had they kept in touch? And also, thank goodness it had not been Aggie. She might have stormed over, she might have caused a scene.

And soon after that, I found myself wondering about Jan, of course. Always, it was Jan. I don't believe a day of my life has passed since I last saw him when I haven't thought about him, and wondered what became of him. I harboured a hope for many years that I would hear from him, that he would track me down. But he did not. There has been one other man, but he was no more than a minor possibility, five decades ago, divorced, charming. Rich, I think, and rather lonely. We had a love affair that never really ignited. He wanted more from me than I could give. He faded away, or I did.

And now, all of them must be dead, as I should be. Even John is dead. She thinks I don't realise. Roberta, the dear, dear girl, and her with a fiancé now, a very nice man, she tells me. I think I can recall him, bookish and quite funny and charming. They must go on, have children, and build a good, strong life together. I know they will.

I am happy that I can frame these thoughts, happy that this core of me is intact; I can still think clearly in this innermost part, this kernel we all have, that remains undamaged throughout our lives. And I must sleep, of course. I'm so tired. I should have been asleep for years by now. Roberta is brushing my hair, she is so gentle and I am fading, I can feel myself, cell by cell, dropping away. I think it is time. Yes. I will keep my eyes closed now, and not open them again, and I shall go to Jan. If I think it, it will be so.

But — no! Roberta wants something. She wants to know the truth, just like John did. Yes, so simple, in two minutes I can tell all, pull myself together, and put an end to this fretting of hers, so—

'Roberta?'

'Yes?'

There. It is done. Confusing at first, but I got there in the end.

And she's shocked, a little, but not very shocked. I rather think she already knew more than she realised. And her hug, so strong, and she meant it, and I'm still her babunia and always will be. And it might have been nice to meet Jan, because he sounded like a wonderful person.

She was proud that I had tried to save the life of her 'real' grandfather. I had to keep that part in; everybody else believed it, so Roberta must too. Perhaps it will become a family legend. That's all right.

She tried to show me something . . . but I couldn't see what it was, I couldn't understand what she was telling me. It's a terrible thing to grow so old, to lose everything you once had, and to find life, the act of living, weaving your way through the day, so impossible.

And now, to Jan I must go. At last, it is his moment and mine. Such a roar, and that sun, my goodness it is hot, and my smooth, strong legs are bare and here comes the squadron, such a roar, and there is Jan's Hurricane, dipping from the sky like a pebble falling through stilled waters, and his face, his beautiful face, his smile, his wave, and I wave back ('Hush, Babunia,' I think I hear Roberta whisper), and stillness now, and heat, all around, and no sound, no sight, and there, it is perfect. And his words, those words at the last, cruel to me then, a comfort now: I knew you were for all time, even as there is no time.

ACKNOWLEDGEMENTS

I'd like to thank everybody at Hodder and Stoughton, especially my keen-eyed editor Suzie Dooré. Thank you to my agent Hannah Ferguson for taking a chance on me and my work. Also to Debi Alper, Ian Andrews, Victoria Bewley, Sonja Bruendl-Price, Emma Darwin, Katherine Hetzel, Sophie Jonas-Hill and Jody Klaire for the advice, opinions, 'WIP' cracking and all round helpfulness and encouragement. And thanks to Neil Evans and Mark Forster for the technical input. I'd also very much like to thank Susan Davis and all at Cornerstones Literary Consultancy, and Jo Dickinson.

My research led me to three books that were a particular pleasure to read: I forgot I was supposed to be researching! They were *Battle of Britain* by Patrick Bishop, *How We Lived Then: A History of Everyday Life during the Second World War* by Norman Longmate and *For Your Freedom and Ours: The Kościuszko Squadron – Forgotten Heroes of World War II* by Lynne Olsen and Stanley Cloud. Any mistakes are my responsibility.

Thank you to my friends Radosława Barnaś-Baniel, for her help with the Polish language, and Tessa Burton, for her delight and encouragement. My mum and dad provided me with the books and the time to read from a young age, thank you to them, and to Pete for being my brother and so much more. Thank you to my children Oliver, Emily, Jude, Finn and Stanley for all the inspiration and excitement; finally, thank you to my generous husband Ian, who makes everything possible.

Questions for Discussion

   Do you identify with any of the attitudes towards mothering in the novel?

   How important are Nina and Aggie to Dorothy? Does she 'mother them', as Jan claims?

   Does Dorothy 'adopt' or 'steal' Nina's baby?

   Does the 'adoption' have a positive outcome for Dorothy, for John and for Roberta?

   Why do you think Jan is so against the 'adoption' of baby John?

✑ Do you think Mrs Compton is a good or bad person? Is she neither? Or both?

✑ Do you like Roberta? She has been described as spiky, cold, distant and lonely. Do you agree with any of these?

✑ Do you think Anna's desertion of Roberta had a big impact on Roberta's life, her choices and attitudes?

✑ Why do you think Philip has renounced his title?

✑ In what ways is Dorothy still effected by her miscarriages, and in particular, Sidney's death?

✑ Should Roberta have been more honest with her grandmother about her son's death and with her family about their heritage?

✑ How important are the setting and time period in Dorothy's story? Could this have been the same story if set in a different era?

    What effect did the Land Army have on women's lives during WWII?

    What are your thoughts on letter writing as a form of communication – is it more powerful than modern methods such as text and email?

    Dorothy tells Roberta that she thought she once saw Jan many years after the war. Do you think she did see him?

    Do you think Roberta and Philip will find long term happiness? Do you envisage a future for them?

    How do you feel about the ending? Would you have preferred a different outcome for Dorothy and Jan? Do you find the ending sad or happy?

An Interview with Louise Walters

Hi Louise, Can you tell us a bit about the book?

Well, it's a dual-timeline novel set in 2010 and in the 1940s; it's about two women and their search for who they are and what they want in life. They also discover some secrets along the way.

Where did inspiration for the book come from?

Various places – I used to work in a bookshop and that was one of the inspirations because part of the novel is set in a bookshop. I also

have a suitcase at home – I have a lot of
old-fashioned suitcases – and one of them has
a label inside and it says 'Mrs D Sinclair' on
the label, and that gave me inspiration for
the title.

I had the initial idea about eight years ago; I
had a character in my mind from the name in
the suitcase and I kept thinking about her. I
didn't write anything for a while but then I
had a go at writing a radio play. It was
around six years ago and at that stage I only
had the Mrs Sinclair strand of the story. (The
modern day stuff came later.) I thought I'd
write a play because I didn't believe that I
would ever be able to write a full length novel.
However, writing a radio play was much
harder than I imagined. I actually knew
nothing about writing radio plays. So in the
end I shelved that idea. I thought a bit more
about it, I had another child or two and in
2010 I started to write it properly and it
turned into a novel.

Did you find the novel difficult to write because of your family life?

I did, it was quite difficult to find enough time so I used to write in the evenings and I used to write in the day when my baby was asleep. The book was written in small bursts really rather than long chunks, which is why I think it took so long to write. Some days I wouldn't write at all; some days I'd write for ten minutes and on other days I'd get a whole day in if my husband was around – he'd look after the children and I'd go out to my summer house with my laptop and write out there.

What was your career like before Mrs Sinclair's Suitcase – *have you always been a writer?*

No, not really. I've always been a big reader – when I was growing up I wanted to be a writer and I would write stories and things. I've had various jobs, one of which was working in a bookshop for six years and I really loved it, it was my best job. Mostly I've been a stay-at-home Mum since my eldest was born and I've had part time jobs in between. I've also written poetry.

ॐ

You studied at university and graduated in 2010 – how did that come about?

I studied Literature and it took me 12 years from the very first course for me to get my degree in 2010. I started when my eldest child was two or three years old and I did part time study with the Open University, mostly I did a year on and a year off with raising the children in between, but I got there in the end.

My Open University studies helped with my confidence as a writer I believe, because the last two courses I took to complete the degree were in creative writing.

ॐ

As a writer and mother, do you feel it's important to teach children about reading and storytelling?

Yes I do. We've (Louise and her husband Ian) always had books around for them since the day they were born – the children's bedrooms have got bookshelves with lots and lots of books. I've always read to them, shared books with them, and I think it's really important to do that. As a family we've always got a lot out of them; it's really helped the children to be confident with books.

છ

Have your children expressed any interest in becoming writers?

A little bit. They know I'm a writer and the younger ones understand that I have a book in the shops that people can buy. Every now and then they'll be colouring in and then they'll start to write and they'll say 'Mummy, I want to make a book' so I have to help them staple the pages together.

What are you currently working on?

I'm just starting what, I hope, will be the second novel. I won't say much about the plot, but it's different from *Mrs Sinclair's Suitcase* and it's more of a contemporary novel. I've only got 6,000 words at the moment so there's still a long way to go.

Interview by James Doherty, originally published on booktrust.org.uk

To find out more visit

Louisewalterswriter.blogspot.co.uk

On Twitter: @LouiseWalters12

☙

For another interview with Louise visit
Soundcloud.com/HodderBooks

HISTORY LIVES

at Hodder

From Anya Seton and Mary Stewart to Thomas Keneally and Robyn Young, Hodder & Stoughton has an illustrious tradition of publishing bestselling and prize-winning authors whose novels span the centuries, from ancient Rome to the Tudor Court, revolutionary Paris to the Second World War.

————

Want to learn how an author researches battle scenes?

Discover history from a female perspective?

Find out what it's like to walk Hadrian's Wall in full Roman dress?

Visit us today at **HISTORY LIVES** for exclusive author features, first chapter previews, book trailers, author videos, event listings and competitions.

🐦 @HistoryLives_

tumblr. historylivesathodder.tumblr.com

www.historylives.co.uk